The Beast and the Briar

ROBERT DREW

The Beast and the Briar by Robert Drew

CONTENTS

Chapter One

Faerie Stories

ong ago, England, Ireland, Scotland, Wales, and all the lands on the continent were ruled, not by men, but by the immortals. Some people called them the Fair Folk, others knew them as the People of Peace or the Good Folk, and still others thought of them as the Wee Folk, though they were not all of them small.

In truth, there were as many different types of faeries as there were races among mankind. There were tiny piskies and spritely spriggans, terrible sluagh and tricksy pucas, monstrous trolls, industrious dwarves, raving goblins, boggarts, brownies, and many, many more. Yet of all these many peoples only one ruled on high. They were called the sidhe and they were as cruel as they were beautiful..."

"Auntie Aisling," interrupted the young boy, "were they really cruel? Were they cruel as the king?"

"Hush up now, Thomas," scolded a voice from the room below, "let your aunt finish the story."

"Yeah, Thomas," added his twin sister, with the air of someone who was trying very hard to sound just like her mother.

"Aye, they were cruel; cruel as the king and crueler besides. They lorded over the other Fair Folk and over men. They used their beauty, their grace, and their influence to play people like fiddles. They could wind us round their little finger in an instant. Why, with a wink and a smile, a sidhe woman could make even the most virtuous knight forsake his vows."

The young girl who spoke was only thirteen years old, though she had the look of a girl several years older. She had sprouted like a weed at ten, towering over her playfellows and siblings both. Yet, it wasn't simply her height that made Aisling Mason appear older, it was the harried look that hid behind her pale green eyes, which were the color of grass in the heat of summer.

Or it might have been the premature lines in her youthful face, lines that disappeared entirely when she smiled, but that always crept back in when worry took her. Then there was the single streak of white that shone like a beacon amidst her sleek mane of flaming ginger hair. She was thin and rangy, having only just begun to show the signs of womanhood in her figure.

At thirteen, Aisling had already lived a troubled existence, one that many of her friends and remaining family members had also experienced. It was the year of our Lord 1530, the time of Henry Tudor, Henry the VIII they called him, and England had just finished suffering one of the most devastating plagues ever to befall her people.

They called it the Sweating Sickness, for that's what it was, a disease that came upon you of a sudden and bathed you in your own cold sweat. The pain and anguish that followed were but a few symptoms of the devastating malady. The most severe of them was sweat, which seemed to flow like a sieve out of every pore, draining the life from its victims. It had taken thousands of Aisling's countrymen and the disease had been so severe that even the king himself had fled London for fear of succumbing to it.

When it had finally abated, Aisling's mother and father, her aunts and uncles, her three older sisters, and two of her three older brothers had all been taken. All that remained of the Mason family were Aisling and Jonathon, her eldest brother.

In time, Jonathon met the young woman who would become his wife. Eleanor Smith had also lost most of her family to the sweat, all save her mother, who died soon after the wedding.

Jonathon and Ellie had two lovely children, twins in fact, a boy and a girl. They named them after their parents: Thomas for Jon's father and Mary for Ellie's mother.

Aisling, who was barely eight when their parents had died, came to live with Jon and Ellie. She was the best aunt the twins could hope for, and regaled them with tales of the Fair Folk, tales she had heard from her old gran, stories her mother and sisters and brothers and aunts had told her a thousand times; tales she knew by heart.

The children loved those stories. They pestered her night and day to tell them, but Aisling didn't mind. The stories were as important to her as they were to the children, more so, because they were the only remaining connection she had to her childhood before it had been forever marred by fear and sickness and loss. They were a light in the dark for Aisling, a link to simpler, happier times that she wanted to convey to her niece and nephew.

Currently, Aisling was sitting cross-legged next to the small cot the twins shared in the loft above the family's small home. It was a simple, straw mattress sewn by the same loving hands that had made the twins' single blanket and shared pillow. Aisling may not have been her sister-in-law's equal when it came to cooking or housework, but she was a dab hand at sewing just about anything, from bed linens to tunics. It was a skill, like her storytelling, that she had inherited from her mother.

Aisling also slept in the loft, right next to the five-year-old twins on a much smaller, much less comfortable bedroll. It suited her though, at least there she could keep an eye on the little ones. It was her most important job around the house, after all.

As she finished her faerie tale, the twins found that despite themselves, they couldn't seem to stay awake. One after another they fell into dreamland, first Mary, then Thomas. When she was sure they were both sufficiently tucked in, she descended the ladder to the other main living area on the ground floor, and went over to join Ellie on the hearth rug.

"They do love your stories," said Ellie, with a thankful tone in her voice.

Eleanor Mason was darning a pair of her husband's socks, which had seen their fair share of use over the past few weeks and were in dire need of repair. Aisling looked over at the socks and at the dreadful job her sister-in-law was doing, and gently snatched them out of her hands.

"Here, Ellie. Let me," she said with a grin. "Bless you, dear," replied the other.

Aisling's sister-in-law was a plain but pretty girl, with dark brown hair and light hazel eyes that shone almost blue in the sunlight. Her nose was like a button and her cheeks, which were ample, positively filled the whole of her freckled face when she smiled. She was not as tall nor as lanky as Aisling. Childbirth, it seemed, had a plumping effect on her body, but it suited her. Her increased bust and slightly chubby arms made her appear even more motherly than her already motherly temperament conveyed.

"Where's Jonathon? He's not back from the village yet?" asked Aisling, placidly.

"I suspect he's gone for a night hunt on his way home. Harry Tanner saw a herd of deer in the wood yesterday and it would be good for us to have one or more of them salted for the winter so we don't have to dig into any of our own livestock. He should be back by morning."

Aisling was only half listening, but frowned as she began the laborious task of undoing Ellie's haphazard stitching. She began to sew the sock anew. It wasn't that she didn't enjoy talking to Ellie, but the moment she had uttered the words 'night hunt' her mind had wandered off. All at once she remembered the thousand stories she had heard about the dark and terrible things that lurked in the forest at night.

She always worried about her brother, but that worry had become much more persistent after the Sweat. Jonathon, his wife, and the twins were all that she had left in the world. If anything ever happened to them, she didn't know what she would do.

Eleanor noticed Aisling's expression and placed a hand on her shoulder saying, "Jon will be fine, Aisling. He's done this a hundred times before."

Her sister-in-law's words did little to comfort her, but she smiled up at her appreciatively.

She finished darning the first sock, turned it right-side out, and moved on to the second, rattier one.

"He needs new socks," she said, deftly changing the subject. "Perhaps I'll make him some, if we've any wool left after it goes to market next week."

Eleanor's motherly instincts seemed to take over and she smiled warmly at her sister-in- law. Though she wasn't more than a few years older than Aisling, Ellie could always tell when she was lying or deflecting, and most importantly, she could tell when something was bothering her.

"It's late, dear. Let's go to bed. You can sleep down here tonight if you like, in the bed with me. No need to squeeze up between those two for once," suggested Eleanor.

Aisling shook her head.

"That's all right, Ellie," she said. "I don't mind. Besides, it lets me keep an eye on them." Eleanor smiled again, hugged her tightly, and with that, the two went off to bed.

The next morning, Aisling was awakened by the sound of placid hoofbeats coming up the dirt road. She sat up in bed with a start, knocking her forehead against the rafters. The resounding THUD stirred the two children sleeping next to her and Eleanor below.

"Are you all right?" asked Ellie, groggily.

"I'm fine," replied Aisling, rubbing the soon-to-be goose egg on her forehead. "Your father's home, little ones."

The two children, still in their night shifts, leapt from their bed then carefully down the ladder and out the front door. Aisling put on a shawl and followed suit, walking barefoot into the cool Autumn grass outside the house. Her brother Jonathon had already dismounted his horse and was kneeling down, hugging his children tightly and giving them kisses on their tiny foreheads.

Jonathon Mason was a tall man, as were most of the Masons before their untimely demise. He was broad-chested and his arms were strong and muscled, toned by two decades of hard work. He had a scruffy, brown beard and his unkempt brown hair, ginger in his youth, had small flecks of red in it whenever the sun hit it just right. His dark, kind eyes were the color of evergreen trees and when he smiled, his face crinkled at the edges, much like Aisling's.

"Morning, string bean," he said warmly, looking over his children's heads at his younger sister.

Jonathon stood up slowly on weary legs to greet Aisling, and his children reluctantly released him. She padded over to him and gave him a hug, the top of her head coming almost past his chin.

"You all act as though I've been missing for weeks. I was only gone a day and a night," he said with a laugh.

"We just missed you is all..." began Aisling.

"We all did," added Eleanor as she made her way out in her nightdress to greet her husband, kissing him on the lips. "Did you get anything for the pelts? Catch any deer?"

"Indeed, I did. A few coins for the rabbit, pretty much what I expected, but a silver for the beaver and the otter both. Also caught an old buck as well, it's down by the barn, still draining. Should be enough to hold us off when the snows come. What have you all been up to?" "Auntie Aisling told us about the sidhe, papa!" shouted Mary.

"Yeah, and she told us about the elf king and the giant wars and how the elves play tricks on people!" added her brother.

"Did she now?" said Jon Mason, smiling down at his children.

"Uh huh! And she said we gotta make sure we stay outta the woods while we're on our own 'cause the sidhe still hide out there under faerie mounds or in faerie rings sometimes," Mary proudly explained.

"That's very good advice. You should definitely heed your auntie's words," he said. "I'm afraid Papa needs to sleep now, loves."

Aisling could tell he was exhausted, beyond exhausted even. It was a wonder he hadn't fallen from his horse. Still, despite his weariness, he managed to pick Mary up and put her on his shoulders as he made his way towards the house.

Once inside, he put his daughter down and trudged over to the bed where he plopped, face first and still clothed, down onto the straw mattress.

"Breakfast first, Jon," scolded Eleanor.

"I'm not hungry," he mumbled, with his eyes still closed.

"You are. I know you haven't eaten since you left the market yesterday evening. Get up, take your boots and those filthy clothes off, and have something to eat before you rest," she instructed.

Too tired even to argue, Jonathon pushed himself up and began to clumsily remove his filthy boots. Meanwhile, Aisling took the children up to the loft to get them out of their nightshirts and into their day clothes, after which she did the same. By the time they got back down the ladder, Ellie had eggs and porridge ready for them all. In no time at all, Jon had finished his breakfast, abandoned his dusty clothes, and was snoring loudly in the bed. Aisling, Ellie, and the children finished soon after.

"Aisling, could you grab Jon's clothes and add them to your washing today? I need to take care of these dishes and with him out...I'm afraid I'm going to have to go down and begin dressing the buck," whispered Eleanor.

"Sure, Ellie," replied Aisling. "Kids, come outside and help me with Papa's clothes."

Thomas and Mary both scooped up a few of pieces of Jon's soiled clothing each and tottered outside with them. Meanwhile, Aisling grabbed up his traveling cloak and boots, placed them atop a rather large basket of washing, and went outside to the wash bucket.

Unlike the other women of the village who usually headed down to the washhouse to do their laundry, Aisling preferred to wash the family's clothes at home near the well, which thankfully sat on the family's property. That way, she could keep an eye on the children if she needed to. The wash bucket was out in the back of the house, a stone's throw away from the well.

Aisling told the twins to go play and proceeded to fill the bucket with water from the well. Once it was full, she hauled the clothes over and began to scrub them thoroughly in the water before hanging them on a long cord which she had tied between two trees. As she stood there, laying the drenched garments out on the line, she took in everything around her. Life was simple in their little part of the world and Aisling liked it that way.

While many of her peers still had dreams of becoming wealthy merchants, fighting in a war, or marrying a rich man, Aisling only wanted to stay home. Maybe she would raise a family, or if she didn't, simply care for her niece and nephew. After everything she had suffered, the loved ones she had lost, and all the innocence that had been stolen from her, one could hardly blame her for enjoying the simple things.

She had just sat down on a stool and began the difficult task of scrubbing the hard, crusted mud off of Jonathon's boots when suddenly, Thomas and Mary came running over to her. Thomas was holding his hands together gently, cupping one over the other and looking extremely worried.

"Auntie Aisling, we found it over in the hedge. It's really hurt..." he said, his voice quaking.

Aisling bent over to look into Thomas' cupped hands, but couldn't seem to see far enough inside of them to discern what he might be holding. A moment later, she saw an almost imperceptible fluttering in between his fingers.

"What have you got there, Thomas?" she asked.

"It's a bird," said Mary, who was on the verge of tears already. "His wing's hurt. He can't fly," explained Thomas.

Aisling gently took his hands in hers and began to prise them open, while simultaneously dropping the fluttering creature into her own.

The bird that fell into her hands was small and brown. A swath of red streaked through its tail. Its right wing, and indeed most of its feathers, were disheveled and appeared as though they had been forced into many different directions. Aisling gently prodded at the injured wing, drawing a faint, pained *cheep* from the tiny bird.

"We'll need to set this if we're going to make it better," Aisling explained to the children, while holding out the bird's injured wing for all to see.

"We've got to help it, Auntie Aisling!" wailed Mary.

"Yeah, we got to make him strong!" agreed Thomas.

Aisling, still smiling, led the children inside the house. After a few minutes of rummaging through her sewing kit, she pulled out a small, weathered swatch of cloth, bunched it up slightly, and placed it atop the kitchen table. Then, she gently laid the bird down in the center of it. It twittered appreciatively, but weakly.

"Thomas, go outside and find me two teensy tiny sticks, ok?" she requested.

The young boy, all too happy to be of some use, ran outside quick as a shot to complete his task. Meanwhile, Aisling helped Mary up onto a chair so she could watch and then began gently smoothing out the little bird's ragged feathers as best she could.

When Thomas returned not five minutes later, his tiny arms held what looked like a bundle of sticks of every size. After she had picked the two absolute smallest, Aisling reached into her sewing kit and took out a spool of royal blue thread. Using skills honed by nearly a decade of sewing work, Aisling expertly assembled a tiny splint on the bird's broken wing.

When she was done, the minuscule bird flexed the splinted wing and let out a doleful but contented twitter. Thomas and Mary, unaware that their voices tended to carry in the small space of the house, let out twin cries of jubilation that simultaneously roused their sleeping father from his very deep slumber, and turned the bird's feathers back into an agitated ruffled mess.

"What in the...what's going on over there you three?" shouted Jonathon Mason, in a tone tinged with both exasperation and morbid curiosity.

"The children and I found an injured bird, Jonathon. They were just excited because I managed to splint its wing," explained Aisling.

"It looks so pretty," added Mary. "Yeah," said Thomas.

"Huzzah," replied Jonathon. "Why not take it outside for a bit, loves?"

With that, Aisling, the children, and the new passenger of her apron pocket, headed back outside to finish the laundry.

A few hours later, Eleanor made her way from the shed back up to the house. Her hair, which she hadn't bothered to brush prior to her dressing the stag, was untidy and flecked with blood as was her apron and much of her dress. In her hands she held a small basket of offal and a few cuts of good venison.

It was in moments like this, when Aisling beheld her sister-in-law's outright and unabashed tenacity, that she appreciated why her brother had sought to marry her. She remembered her own mother, plucking chickens and draining hogs, and for the briefest of moments, she felt sad again.

Yet no sooner had the feeling drifted into her heart than the bird in her pocket began to sing. It was a low song, a twitter and a tweet that started out meager and became melodious. The children, who had been playing at tag, stood stock-still in the midst of their game and listened intently to the song.

It was birdsong, but birdsong unlike anything she had heard before. It made Aisling feel both elated and melancholy all at once. It was as if the sadness and longing love she had felt for her mother a moment ago was no longer something to be upset about but something beautiful; something to be grateful for.

By now, Eleanor had reached the top of the hill and she too had stopped to listen to the music. The bird's soft song soon came to a close and the silence was broken by the sounds of little footsteps running towards Aisling and Eleanor.

"Was that the bird?" asked Thomas in amazement.

"It was…" replied Aisling.

"You have a bird in your pocket?" asked Ellie with a chuckle.

Aisling reached into her apron and gently pulled the quivering songbird into her closed hand.

"Ohh," said Ellie. "No wonder. It's a Nightingale. I haven't heard one of them in years.

They don't usually live around these parts. Where did you find it?"

"Thomas found it in the bushes, it had a broken wing so I tried to splint it," explained Aisling. "That song…it wasn't like any birdsong I've ever heard before. It was sort of, sad...but also happy. Does that make sense?"

Eleanor chuckled again and sauntered over to the well to wash her hands off.

"In a way, it does. Tell you what, let me start supper and then afterwards, it'll be my turn to tell you a story for once," she said as she finished.

Eleanor cooked grilled venison for supper that night and served it with freshly baked bread and roasted parsnips and potatoes. By the time supper was over, almost all of it was gone and all of the Masons were near-full to bursting. Afterwards, Aisling and the kids walked over to the hearth rug and sat down cross-legged to listen to Eleanor's tale.

"I heard this story when I was a little girl. My great nan wasn't from England, she was from the middle of the continent, the Holy Roman Empire, where they speak German mainly. Anyway, she used to tell me a story about a nightingale who was once a beautiful maiden," she began.

"Her name was Jorinde and she was in love with a man named Joringel. They were both very happy and were even engaged to be married until one day, whilst walking in the woods, they happened upon a strange castle deep in the heart of the forest."

Though Aisling's sister-in-law clearly lacked her flair for storytelling, she was enthusiastic and the children were always hungry for tales of any kind.

"Jorinde was frightened and bid her lover that they quit the place as quickly as they could, but brave Joringel was not to be deterred. He urged her forward and no sooner had they gotten to the gates of the castle, than an evil faerie appeared out of nowhere..."

"What kind of faerie, mummy?" asked Mary, anxiously.
"Yeah, what kind?" agreed her brother.

Eleanor looked over to Aisling for help, shrugging slightly. "Probably a gwillion or a bog hag," replied Aisling, knowingly.

"My nan called her the Waldhexe. In any case, the faerie appears and uses her evil magic to turn Joringel to stone. Then, she turns to Jorinde and tells her 'Now you'll join my collection, my pretty one,' and turns her into a bird- a nightingale."

At this, Eleanor pointed at the small bird snuggling up in Aisling's lap.

"She did this often you see, and her castle was full of other maidens like Jorinde whom she had hexed into songbirds. With that, she picked up the nightingale, walked back towards the castle and when she was safely locked inside, returned Joringel back to normal. Then she looked down at him laughing and shouting, 'You shall never see your beloved again! Begone from this place!' Joringel had no choice. He knew he couldn't break the Waldhexe's spell by himself. And so, he was forced to walk away, to go out into the world to find a cure for his lost love..."

Aisling listened with rapt attention, but when she looked down at the children, found them curled up together on the hearth rug. Their mother's voice had lulled them both to sleep.

"I guess we'll finish the story tomorrow," said Eleanor with a smile.

"I'll bring them up, Ellie," interjected her husband, while picking both his tiny children up and taking them to their bedroom in the rafters.

"I might as well head up, too," said Aisling as she got to her feet. "That was a good story, Eleanor. I can't wait to hear what happens next."

She hugged and kissed her brother and sister-in-law good night, climbed up into the rafters, put on her nightshirt, and took a bit of straw from her bed to make a nest for the nightingale. As she placed the tiny bird in the makeshift nest, it ruffled its feathers and settled itself down for a good sleep after a long day.

As she drifted off to sleep, Aisling thought of the two lovers in Eleanor's nan's story and wondered for the briefest of moments if her nightingale, too, was a cursed maiden. Little did she know, she would soon find out exactly how remarkable that tiny, wounded bird truly was.

Chapter Two

The Bogeymen

s autumn departed and made way for the cold winds of the north, the encroaching winter weather seemed to bring with it a dense and chilly fog. It drifted in during the wee hours of the night and lingered, more and more as the days got colder, until the sun rose high into the afternoon sky. The fog hung above the ground for miles around, a thick cloud of heavy air that broke the shining light of the Harvest Moon into bits and pieces.

Outside the safety of the Mason's cottage dark forces swirled about their property, as ineffable, as mysterious, and as eerie as the mist itself. Aisling Mason and the twins slept soundly in their beds, unaware that just outside, right near the tree line, foul things were creeping towards them.

They had come from the hedge, the same hedge where little Thomas Mason had found the nightingale earlier that day. Like the nightingale, they were not of this world, but from another place entirely; a place that Aisling seemed to know much about but couldn't possibly have understood at that moment. In time, soon enough in fact, she would learn.

The foul things crept ever closer, shielding themselves from the piercing rays of moonlight by keeping to the shadows whenever possible. It was not that the light hurt them. No, they could stand the light well enough, but creatures such as they were accustomed to being seen only when they wanted to be seen, and not before.

They moved through the shadows effortlessly, as agile and adept as a fish swimming downstream. It was almost as if they were borne on currents of shadow as they twisted over hills, around trees, and past buildings. The creatures waded through the lightless seams of wooden planks, and into the dark corners of the Mason home; almost as if they themselves were made of shadow. The shadow things crawled about the house now, slipping past the feeble light of the guttering candles and making their way up to the loft where Aisling and the children slept. There was a reason for this, of course, for those beings which lurk in the darkest places carry it with them, no matter the light they are shown in. When they had arrived at their destination, they pulled themselves away from the walls and stood above the little straw bed.

"Thees'll do," said one of the shadow things.

Its voice was a guttural croak tinged with a pleasant Irish lilt and coated in mucus. It sounded like the morning after a night at the tavern.

"Twins, are they?" asked the second one, whose voice sounded similar but more nasal, as if it had a head cold that was dripping into the back of its throat.

The third shadow thing tried to respond, but only managed a hacking, retching cough of assent and a furious nod as it fought back another pained outburst.

Its fellows looked over at it with their mismatched, bulging, bloodshot eyes, and puckered their puffy, cracked lips as if to shush it.

Unfortunately for them, the initial cough was enough to rouse Aisling from her sleep. She opened her eyes and turned to look over at the twins. At first, her eyes passed right over the shadow things, which stood rooted to the spot mid-movement in an attempt to remain hidden.

This sort of thing would have easily worked with a normal child, but Aisling Mason was no normal child.

She had only just seen a flash of them out of the corner of her eye, but it was enough for her mind to fill in the blanks. She did a double take and what could have been a mere trick of the light were immediately thrown into sharp relief upon a second glance. There they were: three squat, shadowy somethings, shaped almost like monkeys, standing in their loft, staring right at her and the children.

The first of the creatures, knowing the jig was up, moved his long, gnarled finger to his lips and motioned for her to shush. Aisling, noticing how close they were to the children, and unsure what she was even witnessing at this point, did as she was bid.

She sat up in bed slowly and was suddenly aware that whatever she was witnessing, was staring right back at her in her nightdress. She hastily pulled the covers up to her chest and whispered, with no small amount of indignation,

"Who are you and what are you doing here?"

The three creatures exchanged wary looks, which given their overlarge eyes, warty, misshapen faces, and crooked teeth, made them appear far less frightening than creatures made of shadow have any right to be.

One of them, the one whose cough had woken the girl, rushed to tuck something behind his back. He wasn't fast enough, however, and Aisling caught a glimpse of the ratty gray satchel as it caught briefly in the dwindling light from the candle downstairs.

"You're bogeymen!" Aisling exclaimed, though her voice was still barely a whisper. "You stay away from them!"

"We ain't...no..." croaked the second creature, in his nasally mumble.

The first creature flashed him an exasperated look that very plainly said, 'It's over, you idiot, she knows why we're here.'

The third creature, who was more astute than his fellow bogeyman, let his arm drop to the side. The ratty old sack now sat in more or less plain view.

"You'll not take them," said Aisling triumphantly, though with enough trepidation to belie the uncertainty she was feeling.

The nightingale, awoken by the tension beside it, opened its bleary eyes and stared nervously up at Aisling.

"We's must," explained the first of the bogeyman, matter-of-factly. "Ey've been naughty chill'ren and need ta be punished."

The second part of the bogeyman's statement was less sincere than the first and Aisling distinctly noticed the slight quaver in his voice. She had to think fast. Despite the fact that she was almost certainly dreaming, there was still the looming uncertainty that what she was experiencing might actually be real.

Her mother had taught her that bogeymen were not to be trusted and she could already see why. The slumped creatures looked shiftily at one another and at her. The bulging orbs of their eyes, so wide only a moment ago, were narrowed now in a suspicious glare. She could see that they, too, were working out their next move, albeit with a great deal more difficulty than she was.

"Now, now...don't dawdle," said the second bogeyman, in the tone of someone who most certainly wanted to dawdle, if only so he might think a bit longer.

"We's ," started the third bogeyman, before losing himself to a hastily swallowed and particularly phlegmy cough.

"What 'e means to say," interrupted the first bogeyman. "Is that we's 'ere to take them, an thas that. Ere ain't nothin' ya can say that'll make us change our minds."

He crossed his overlong, flabby arms then and as he did so, Aisling could see the folds of loose skin jiggle repulsively. Then, just as she was about to take up arms against them in a last- ditch effort, she remembered the rest of her mum's lessons on bogeymen.

"Boggarts aren't like the other Fair Folk, Aisling," her mother had said. "They're strong as anything and their long arms can hoist a satchel of children and carry it clear across to the faerie realm lickety-split. You won't be able to fight them off or even frighten them. They're just like all faeries, though, they love a bargain more than anything. Thing is, they aren't as clever as their kin. If you're ever unfortunate enough to see them, or speak to them, remember this: you can usually get away by offering a deal. Sometimes even a worse deal if you're lucky. Just so long as it's a bargain..."

"What about a bargain?" asked Aisling quickly, without truly knowing what she would offer if they accepted.

All at once, the eyes of the three bogeymen widened again. They looked at Aisling, then at one another, smirking sinisterly and showing their yellowed, mismatched teeth.

"What kin' a bargain, lass?" asked the first bogeyman.

"I'll trade you. I'll give you something else instead of my niece and nephew," she offered, feebly.

"Something valuable!" she added hastily.

The bogeymen seemed intrigued by this prospect, but wary.

"Whatcha got to trade?" probed the second of the bogeymen, with the tone of a faerie who had been fooled more than once.

Aisling thought quickly, then reached beneath her bedroll and took out a small pouch. Inside the pouch were three items. First, was a gold crown she had received from Jonathon on the day they had left home. He told her that it was her inheritance from their father and that she needed to keep it safe because it was only to be used under the gravest circumstances. The second was her trusty thimble, which had belonged to her mother before her untimely passing. The third was a lock of her eldest sister Abigail's hair, cut from her head before they had buried her. All three were of great significance to her and she dreaded parting with any of them, but she would do so gladly for Thomas and Mary's sake.

"How about this?" she said, pulling the gold crown from

the pouch and holding it up so that the light from the slowly dying candles glinted off of its golden surface.

The bogeymen looked at the coin for a moment and then frowned, shaking their collective heads so hard that their flabby, fleshy bodies shook in a most unwelcome manner.

"We've no need of gold, girl," sneered the first bogeyman. "Wut do we look like? Leprechauns?" replied the second. "Wut else ya got?" added the third, this time without a cough.

Aisling put the coin back in the pouch and pulled out the thimble. She placed it on her finger and held the finger out towards them.

The bogeymen didn't seem to know what to make of the small, metallic item at first. The third one slouched over towards her, dragging his knuckles on the ground as he did so. Yet, no sooner had he reached up to touch the thimble, than he recoiled in horror and slunk back to the safety of his fellows' shadows.

"'Tis' iron!" he shouted, quietly, before devolving into a self-contained coughing fit. "You tries to poison us?" accused the first bogeyman, incensed. "You takes us for fools?"

"No, no. I meant no offense. I have one more thing...if you'll permit me," pleaded Aisling, knowing you must always be polite when dealing with the Fair Folk; no matter how impolite they themselves were being.

The bogeymen, though obviously still feeling a trifle affronted, nodded in tandem at her to continue. Aisling pulled out the lock of hair. It was auburn, but dusty and somewhat faded, yet when the rays of candlelight hit it just right, still shone as if had been freshly washed.

At last, she saw the bloodshot eyes of the bogeymen light up with hungry interest. They stared intently for a moment, then remembered themselves and regained their composure. It was too late though, Aisling knew she had their attention.

"If you leave my niece and nephew be, I'll give you this lock of my sister's hair. Do we have a deal?" she proposed, confidently.

The three bogeymen leaned in to face one another, turning their backs towards Aisling, then began to mutter to one another. Minutes passed as though they were hours as Aisling stood there, heart in hand, waiting for their reply. The nightingale looked up at her and twittered gently, almost reassuringly, and Aisling felt the corners of her mouth twitch slightly.

The bogeymen turned around suddenly, knocking the kneeling Aisling onto her bottom in alarm.

"We'll take the hair," offered the first Bogeyman. "But we wants somefin' else, too." "'E's right, you gots two kids there. Ain't right to trade two kids for one measly lock of 'air," added the second, matter-of-factly.

The third bogeyman, obviously not willing to risk another coughing fit, nodded in agreement, then proceeded to cough.

Aisling was panicked. She hadn't counted on the creatures to come back at her with a counter offer. She swallowed hard and began to reach back into the satchel for the coin.

"We told you, lass, we don't wants no gold. You wants us to trade two kids, we wants at least one in return," cautioned the first bogeyman, and there was a note of apparent threat in his tone.

Aisling looked over at her niece and nephew, then down to the landing below, where her brother and sister-in-law lay sound asleep. The bogeymen wanted her and if she refused, they would take Thomas and Mary. She didn't have a choice now and she knew it. She sighed heavily and stood up, her lean and lanky form towering over the squat creatures before her.

"You can have me," she said, triumphantly. "Me and the lock of hair for the twins."

All three of the bogeymen smiled. It was a smile that spread across all three of their hideous faces almost simultaneously and it made them appear even more otherworldly than they already did. It was as if the only part of them that reflected light at all was their crooked, broken, yellowed teeth.

"We have a deal," said the first bogeyman, extending a long-fingered hand to Aisling.

Aisling walked over to the creature and took his hand. It was cold and clammy and it felt as if she had just stuck her hand into a half-frozen bog. She shivered, then drew her hand away.

"We've not much time, girl," said the second bogeyman with an air of impatience. "We needs to be goin' now."

"Can I at least gather some things, clothes, shoes?" she asked, while hastily putting her apron on over her head.

"You won't be needin' those," snickered the third bogeyman while sucking down another massive loogie.

Without thinking, Aisling quickly reached down and

picked up the nightingale and tucked it into her front pocket with her treasured satchel. She moved to kiss the twins goodbye, but no sooner had she done so, than two of the bogeymen had grabbed her and shoved her violently into the sack.

"No!" she screamed. "At least let me say goodbye! Please!"

But her pleas fell on deaf ears. In a moment she felt herself and the sack being hefted up over the broad shoulders of the third bogeyman. Then, something happened that she couldn't quite describe.

To Aisling, it felt as if she was moving through patches of deep water in an uneven river.

One moment she would feel warm and the next, it was as if all her skin was covered in goosebumps. It began at the tips of her toes and made its way up her legs, into her chest, down her arms, and up into the back of her head. Then, as quickly as it came, the cold, uneven feeling would dissipate.

She could see nothing inside the sack save the small patches of moonlight that shone through its thinning surface. The canvas inside smelled of a mix of babies and sick and it made her want to vomit. The sensation wasn't helped at all by the constant bouncing and temperature fluctuations around her.

Things went on this way for quite a while until suddenly, it all stopped, and so did the bogeymen. Before she could speak up or even get her bearings, she felt a rush of wind and a surge of pressure in her stomach as if someone had hooked her right behind her belly button. And then there was light.

Chapter Three

The Foundlings

isling felt as though she was being tugged out of her own body. Around her, sound as she had never heard rushed past her ears. The pressure behind her navel remained almost constant. It felt as if she was falling from a great height and also that she was being thrown up into the air.

Light flashed before her eyes and though it was obscured by the gray fabric of the sack she was in, it still danced around her. Then, as quickly and alarmingly as all those sensations had come, they ceased.

Aisling blinked frantically as spots of light and color danced before her eyes. They felt as though she had rubbed them too much. The scent of wet leaves, soil, and fresh flowers filled her nostrils. She recognized that she was in a forest of some kind, but the sounds of insects and nightbirds in the distance sounded unfamiliar to the ones that lived near the Mason farm.

The tight tugging she had felt in her stomach had ceased but a rumbling, quivering sensation still lingered. Her voice having finally returned to her, Aisling decided to find out what exactly she had just experienced.

"Where have you taken me?!" she shouted from the confines of the bag.

The bogeymen, who it seemed had forgotten about their prisoner, looked about quizzically for a moment. Then, upon realizing that he was carrying someone, the third bogeyman dropped the sack unceremoniously onto the ground and quickly untied it.

Aisling pushed herself out of the bag and breathed the fresh air. The three bogeymen were encircling her. She stepped out of the bag and trod barefoot into the muddy, leaf-strewn earth beneath her. The ground, still wet with nighttime dew, was so cold that it sent a chill up into her bones. She shivered and shook off the sensation, then, after taking in the small forest bclearing for a brief moment, looked down at herself. She was wearing nothing except her nightgown and apron, it was no wonder she was cold.

"Where are we?" she asked again, this time much more politely. "Over the 'edge, lass," said the first bogeyman, with a chuckle.

"You just wait till we gets back to the hovel," added the second, threateningly. "We's gonna sort you out, right good."

It seemed impossible, but the bogeymen seemed much more threatening now than they had in her loft back home. Their somewhat comical features, bulging eyes, misshapen mouths, squat, flabby bodies, all appeared to have changed the instant they arrived home. She still recognized them, for their forms were still very similar, yet now the shadows which blotted their features seemed sleeker, more menacing.

They were still shorter than her, but only just barely. Their overlong arms looked stronger and more sinewy. Their long-fingered hands now ended in sharp claws rather than chewed, uneven nails. Their eyes were still bulging, but sat normally in their sockets and gave off a faint, sickly, purple glow. Their teeth were most changed of all, though. They were no longer uneven, but sharp and identical and stood out pearly white against the blackness of their ebony skin.

Aisling was sure that the dark faeries had kidnapped her in order to eat her, or at least, she assumed they did. For what other purpose could teeth and claws like those serve if not to devour prey? Her mother, her nan, her sisters, and Jonathon, for all their stories, could never have prepared her for the reality of these creatures in the flesh.

"You're not going to eat me...are you?" she asked, almost impulsively.

The three bogeymen laughed at one another. It was loud, raucous, and wholly unsettling. It seemed that now that they were out in the open, they had no more need of whispers. The third bogeyman, when he was done laughing, proceeded to hack and sputter and cough for another full thirty seconds.

"An' why would we be eatin' you?" chuckled the first bogeyman.

Aisling had no answer for this. This dream, if it was one, was unlike any she had ever experienced and she had no frame of reference for dealing with creatures such as these. She shrugged.

"You ain't good for eatin', anyway. Too skinny," explained the second bogeyman. "Besides, we din't take you fer us..."

But the bogeyman never got the chance to finish his statement. Before he could even utter the next syllable, an arrow, which appeared to come out of nowhere, had pierced his throat.

Instinctually, he reached up and grabbed at his neck, but it was no use. Dark green, mucousy blood poured from the wound and the bogeyman choked helplessly on his final statement, his eyes still bulging.

The other two bogeymen turned in the direction of the arrow, but before they could dive for cover, a half dozen more shafts whistled through the air in their direction, littering the ground around them. Two of the arrows struck true though; one hit the first bogeyman in the left shoulder, and the other hit the third bogeyman's right knee. Both creatures fell to the ground in pain.

Aisling could hear rustling in the treetops above them. The sounds of nightbirds and insects had been replaced by the sound of hoots and hollers. All around her, Aisling could see shapes streaking through the dim glow of the twilight forest. She looked around at the arrows and immediately kenned that whomever was shooting them had not been aiming for her.

Ten or so figures appeared in the darkness of the tree line. Then, several more fell from the trees themselves. Aisling rubbed her eyes again and as soon as she took her hands away, found herself surrounded by a dozen or so human children, each one brandishing some kind of makeshift weapon.

The two bogeymen on the ground cowered in fear and pain, the glamour of their newly fiendish features had washed away again, revealing the sickly-looking, flabby something-or- others that had broken into her brother's home.

As the children stepped into the light of the clearing, Aisling could see that each one was dressed in a combination of rags, furs, beads, and feathers. Their skin and faces were covered in a mix of mud and what looked almost like war paint. Some of them had boots, others wore moccasins, and a few remained shoeless. Because of their strange dress, Aisling couldn't make out which ones were boys and which ones were girls, though she could tell that they were all different ages.

The children were wild-eyed and ferocious looking. As they approached, weapons drawn, Aisling got the impression that this wasn't the first time this particular group of children had been called to deal with monsters. They encircled the creatures and glared at them.

"Leave us alone!" pleaded the first bogeyman. "We wernt doin' nuffin."

One of the children, a tall, dark-haired boy dressed in what looked like a striped tiger skin and holding a rusty-looking sword, walked up to the first bogeyman and placed the tip of his blade under the creature's chin.

"You really expect us to believe that, bogey?" he said, confidently.

The rest of the children giggled at the statement. Despite her circumstances, Aisling couldn't help but feel a bit sorry for the bogeymen.

"Don't kill them yet, Christopher!" shouted a voice

from behind the other children.

The voice was high, almost singsong, and lilted with a bit of a brogue. The children parted ways, allowing the speaker to saunter ahead of them.

The young man who walked towards Aisling was shorter than she was by a good six inches. He had sandy blonde hair, piercing blue eyes, and a well-freckled, almost cherubic face. He walked with a air of confidence and a fluidity that seemed at odds with his obviously youthful features. If Aisling hadn't known better, she would have thought that he was walking on air.

Like his fellows, the young man was wearing what looked like the patchwork remnants of once-finer clothes. At his side, he carried a long, finely wrought cutlass with a gold-plated hand guard and pommel that had obviously been worn away over time. He winked at Aisling, almost offhandedly, then without missing a beat, bent down to stare into the bulging, quivering eyes of the bogeymen.

"You bogeys know this is our territory," he said coolly. "We've warned you before. Now you gotta pay the price."

The first bogey went to speak up, but the young man was too quick for him, he drew the sword from his scabbard quick as a whip, and slashed clean across the faerie's throat. In one gruesome, blood-spattered instant, the creatures head had been knocked off its body. The remaining bogeyman, who it appeared was about to say something prior to his friend's demise, swallowed his words.

"Take the other one back to the village, lads," commanded the leader. Then, turning to Aisling, he said, "It's ok. You're safe. We've rescued you."

It was strange to Aisling, that only moments ago the young man had appeared so much older than he clearly was. Yet there he was, tousle-haired and smiling a gap-toothed freckly grin, holding a bloody sword in his left hand.

"Um..." began Aisling. "Where exactly am I?"

The young man chuckled. It was an infectious, charming laugh, and his smile doubly so. "Oh yes, I had nearly forgot. You're from through the veil, aren't you? Well Miss, my

name's Peter Goodfellow and let me be the first to officially welcome you to The Seven Realms," he answered, with a slight bow.

"These," he gestured to the crowd of children around them, "are my Foundlings. Like you, they were stolen from their homes on the other side of the veil by these awful monsters. This is: Elizabeth, Sakiko, Michael, Jorge, Tom, Tommy, Orla, Danny, Sean, Gustav, Marcello, and that's Christopher. What's your name?"

"Aisling Mason," she replied, looking around at the many faces of the Foundlings and feeling for the first time how absolutely naked she was in just her night shift and apron.

"Could I maybe...do you have any other clothes?" she asked, sheepishly.

"Oh yes! Come on everyone, let's get Aisling here back to the village so we can get her some proper clothes and some food!" shouted Peter. "We have a great deal to talk about."

The walk back to the Foundlings' village was rather cold and rocky, but thankfully brief. As they walked, one of the young boys began singing a song Aisling had never heard. He was at about the second bar when the lot of them began to sing along with him. It went like this:

A stranger came from lands afar, he strode through hill and dale

He brought with him a special magic, he wrought beyond the veil, and used it to ensnare a love, a princess fair and pale.

The stranger walks, the stranger walks, and magic he doth bring, all to ensnare a princess and make himself a king.

He was not like the others here, his magic it was clean,

It was not marred by faerie dust, but from within his dreams, and so he gave it to the maid, so perfect and serene.

The stranger walks, the stranger walks, and magic he doth bring, all to ensnare a princess and make himself a king.

He walked the path to Gideon, upon that cobbled road,

And every stone the stranger touched, it turned from stone to gold, and wend it to the maiden, so on the stranger strode.

The stranger walks, the stranger walks, and magic he doth bring, all to ensnare a princess and make himself a king.

He never reached the castle, was lost and far afield,

The curse it struck him as he walked, his magic did not shield, but though he was affected so, the stranger would not yield.

The stranger waits, the stranger waits, he'll never do a thing, nor will he find his princess, he'll never be a king.

"What was that song called?" asked Aisling.

"It's called the Stranger and the Gilded Road. It's a story about a traveler who loved a princess and was cur because of it," explained Peter.

Aisling couldn't help but feel something for the tr She herself was a traveler, somewhere in a strange pla motivations were different, of course, but there was something familiar in the story and the song; something she wouldn't come to fully understand for some time.

As soon as they walked into the clearing, Aisling could see that this place was most definitely built by children. Ramshackle treehouses sat in some of the largest, thickest trees Aisling had ever seen. Unlike the tall, skinny timber on the Mason's tiny farm, these great oak trees seemed almost primordial. The walls and roofs of the smallish houses looked to be made of hundreds of repurposed wooden planks. The houses were high enough off the ground that they couldn't be reached except by the rickety ladders that leaned against their trees.

The houses had all been painted in wild, mismatching colors, which stuck out vibrantly amidst the browns and tans of the forest. Some of the houses had windows, others had shutters, even a few had makeshift curtains strung over the open sills.

A series of rickety rope bridges were tied between the houses on several of the trees, resulting in what looked like a network of above ground roads. It was a child's paradise; a cobbled village where orphaned boys and girls could pretend that they were still home.

Yet, as Aisling watched the Foundlings drag in the final remaining bogeyman and throw him into a stained, bamboo cage, she became keenly aware of something. Whatever these children used to be, whatever civilized part of the world they had come from, their time here had forced them to become something else entirely. She wondered if she, too, would end up like the Foundlings or if she perhaps would be able to find her way home; even when the rest of them plainly hadn't. She decided to hold her questions and her concerns for the time being. The first step was finding some decent clothes and God willing, a pair of shoes.

"Hi, there," said one of the girls, breaking Aisling's concentration. "I am Sakiko. You need a dress, right? Or would you prefer pantaloons?"

Though she clearly understood what she was saying, Aisling could have sworn that Sakiko wasn't speaking English at all. It must have been one of the odd things about this strange place, that no matter where the children were from or what language they spoke, they could understand one another. Aisling had never seen an Oriental before, though she had heard stories about them from her father's friends and the traders in the village.

The girl had a round, pale face and squinty eyes. Her hair was black as night and tied up in a sort of bun-like ponytail. She was shorter and skinnier than Aisling, but didn't look malnourished. If anything, she looked stronger even than some of the boys she had seen. She wagered that she couldn't be much older than Aisling.

"Yes, a dress please, if you have one," she answered, politely.

Sakiko smiled and led her towards a large treehouse to the left. She was wearing a dress herself, though it was cut oddly and made of the palest pinkest silk she had ever seen. The only other two girls, Orla and Elizabeth, followed them both. The girls continued on, urging Aisling forward. She stumbled slightly, tripping over a rock and stubbing her toe on it.

"Ouch!" she squealed. "I really hope you girls have some

shoes in there, too."

"You can have mine," said the girl named Orla, stepping out of her boots and handing them over to Aisling. "I don't really need them anyway, your feet get tough after living out here a while."

Orla, in direct contrast to Sakiko, looked older, stronger, and much less "girly". Where Sakiko looked almost like a doll, Orla looked like a little boy. Indeed she dressed so similarly to one that Aisling had thought she was a boy at first glance. Her hair was wildly unkempt, and stuck out at all angles. Her face was dirty and, in fact, there wasn't a single inch on her tanned skin that wasn't covered in a thin layer of dust or coated with grime.

When they arrived at the tree, Orla ascended the ladder first, followed by Sakiko and then Elizabeth, who Aisling noted couldn't have been much older than Thomas or Mary. She followed them up and into the treehouse. The ladder creaked on every other step, but felt sturdy beneath her. Clearly, whoever had built it had put in a bit more work than some of the others.

Its three windows, though grimy, were made of glass and framed by patched purple curtains. Three beds were spaced evenly about the one room and there was even a small table with three chairs near one of the corners. Each bed had a small chest at the foot of it, though each was of a different design.

"Do you like it?" asked Sakiko, still smiling. "It's lovely," said Aisling.

"Made it ourselves, Sakiko and me," said Orla, proudly. "You did? Really? How old are you?" inquired Aisling.

"Me, I'm twelve, Sakiko is nearly fifteen, and Lizzie here is six. As for building it ourselves, well you gotta learn to do things on your own here, s'not like any of the lads would help."

"They would if we'd asked," said Sakiko, pleasantly. "Well, I wasn't gonna ask, anyway," added Orla.

As the three were talking, Elizabeth went over to what looked like an old chest in the corner and shoved it open. She leaned into it, pulling out swatches of fabric and old, tatty clothes, and piled them one by one onto the adjacent table. When she had emptied the whole thing out, she walked back to Aisling, took her by the hand, and led her to table, gesturing at the clothing.

Aisling smiled down at her. Her sweet face, curly blonde hair, and big blue eyes reminded her so much of her niece. A pang of deep sadness sunk into her chest as she thought of how she may never see her beloved Thomas and Mary again. She pushed the feeling down and focused instead on something else, namely finding the perfect outfit in the mess of clothes before her.

In no time at all, she had settled on a slightly ratty blue dress, which she wore over her night shift, and a pair of simple brown breeches just in case. Orla's dusty brown boots completed the rough ensemble. It wasn't anything elegant of course, but in this company, she fit right in.

Just as she was about to take off her apron, she heard a weak *cheep* come from inside the pocket. "Oh, no!" she started, before gently lifting the nightingale out of her pocket and examining it to make sure its wing was still set.

"Thank goodness you're all right. Sorry about that, little

38

nightingale. In all the hullabaloo I didn't realize you were still in there."

The bird was unharmed, but wriggled irritably in her hand as if to show its disdain for what Aisling had put it through. It ruffled its feathers and sat back into a comfortable position once more. When Aisling was dressed, she tucked her treasured pouch into her right dress pocket and the nightingale gently into the left.

"How do I look?" she asked the girls.

"Pretty as a rose," came a haughty, familiar voice from the doorway. "Peter, I didn't hear you come up the ladder," said Aisling, blushing.

"I'm quiet when I need to be. I hate to take you away from the girls, but I imagine you're very hungry and that you have some questions," replied Peter.

In all the chaos, Aisling hadn't realized that she was indeed quite hungry. She nodded and followed Peter over to his own treehouse via a series of rope bridges. Whereas Aisling stepped uneasily on the bridges, theFoundlings walked about them as casually as if they were solid ground. Indeed, Peter himself had such a grace astride the boughs and bridges that he looked almost like he wasn't even stepping upon them at all, but gliding across them.

When they reached Peter's treehouse, the grandest and most well-built of the bunch, he stepped back to allow her to enter first. The inside was just as nice as the outside, and looked rather cozy. A dozen or so pillows were scattered about a common area and a large, finely crafted old chair sat at the head of the circle. A table had been set for two in the center of the pillows and had been laid out with a delicious smelling roast in the center.

Aisling walked over to the table to examine the crispy, roasted bird, crusty sliced bread, and bowls of fruits that accompanied it atop the small table. Before she could turn around to look for Peter, he was standing right next to her, holding out a stool so that she could sit. After he pushed her in, he walked around to the large chair and pulled it close to the table so that he, too, could sit.

"Eat up. You must be famished," said Peter, still smirking.

Aisling didn't want to be rude. In any other situation she would have waited for the host to eat first, but as he had given her the go-ahead, she decided she needn't stand on ceremony.

Within minutes she was stuffed to the gills on the sumptuous meal.

Peter ate as well, although not much slower. He ate like a teenager would be expected to eat, ravenously and with gleeful abandon. When they had both finished, they sat back happily in their seats.

"So, Aisling Mason. Where are you from?" Peter asked, picking his teeth.

"Norfolk, ehm, England. I suppose," she replied. "I notice that not all of your Foundlings are from there, but everyone seems to speak the language. Why is that?"

"People come through the veil in many different ways, though it's rare of course. My guess is whatever strange magic guides this place makes sure we can all understand each other. It also seems to slow down aging quite a bit. For us anyway," he explained.

"You mean people?" she continued.

"There are other people here, humans and other sorts as well, as you've seen with the bogeys. I mean people from your world," said Peter.

"How do…" she began, and her voice quavered slightly. "How do we get back through the veil, wherever it is?"

Peter's perpetual smile seemed to fade at the question. It was clear from his expression that not only was this was a question he had answered many times before, but that it was also one he never liked having to answer. Aisling knew immediately what that answer was going to be.

"You don't. This is your home now, Aisling. Forever."

Chapter Four

The Crones

hat can't be," said Aisling.

She said it before she even knew she was going to say it, the words spilling forth unbidden by her brain.

"How did the bogeymen get back and forth across the veil, then?" she added, while trying desperately to contain the panic now welling up within her.

"They have permission from the Queen of the Seven Realms. For their part in her ascension, she granted them safe passage to and from the mortal world," explained Peter.

"So, this queen…if I can get her to grant me her favor, she'll let me go home?"

Aisling was putting things together in her head. It seemed simple enough. Surely this queen, whoever she was, didn't want strange people in her realm. If she could only find her, she could prevail upon her to be allowed to leave.

"How do I find the Queen? If I want to meet her, that is," she asked.

Peter Goodfellow looked taken aback. Obviously, this girl didn't really know what she was asking. Nevertheless he had been through this before, with other brave Foundlings like the girl. One trip to the Crones and she would accept the reality of her situation.

"I have someone I think you should meet," he said, seriously. "But not now, it will have to wait until the quarter moon. That's in three days. In the meantime, try not to feel so down. The foundlings here, all of us, we're in the same boat as you. We've all found ourselves at this same point before. Everything will be ok, I promise."

Peter smiled, but as reassuring and impeccably charming as it was, it did nothing to cure the sudden nauseous feeling bubbling up in the pit of Aisling's stomach. She nodded and finished her meal. Then she scooped up the nightingale and made her way back to the girls' treehouse.

The other three girls were fast asleep when she arrived and it seemed they had put together a sort of small makeshift bed in the once empty corner of the little home. Aisling took off her boots and breeches then set the drowsy nightingale on the little shelf beside her. A sense of hopelessness surged inside of her then. It was something she had only felt once before, when her mother, after having cared for all the rest of her family, had finally succumbed to the Sweat herself. She felt lost and alone, even amongst the other children. It didn't matter that they were all in the same situation, none of them could understand her pain or her loss.

All of those feelings, the terror, the loss, the loneliness; they all began to well up inside her and soon, hot tears began streaming down her cheeks. Soon though, the long night took its toll and Aisling Mason, just another foundling, fell into a deep sleep. Her dreams that night were full of strange and unexplained visions, things that terrified her as she woke, but faded into nothingness with the morning light.

The next few days were, despite everything that had been going on, rather enjoyable. The other foundling children were wonderful to be around. They all seemed to know that they were in this together, and so they worked together on everything that their little village needed in order to thrive. They gathered fruits, and nuts, and hunted together. They did each other's laundry, collected firewood, cooked and built, sewed, and forged.

As Aisling explored the encampment in the company of the other foundling girls, she discovered that it felt almost like the village back home. Except, of course, for the fact that everyone, including the de-facto alderman, was younger than twenty.

All of the foundlings seemed to look to Peter Goodfellow for guidance and it was clear that he was the obvious choice for a leader. He was good at just about everything, from sewing to swordplay, and Aisling couldn't help but notice as she watched him spar with a few of the more burly boys, how handsome he was.

She still wanted to go home, of course, but each night as she sat around the table with the foundlings, laughing and eating, she felt more and more like this place could be her home, if it came to that. Nevertheless, when the third night finally came and Peter arrived to take her to meet the person he had suggested on that first evening, Aisling was more than ready.

He led her out of the village proper and through the woods. They traveled about two miles by the light of Peter's single torch until they came to a cave in a clearing. Inside the cave, a firelight was flickering.

"Peter, what is this?" she asked, nervously.

"I found the women inside this cave many years ago. They are...well, I suppose you could call them witches, for they dabble in magic..." explained Peter. Then, noticing the worried look on Aisling's face he continued.

"They aren't the bad kind of witches. They helped us by building wards around the village and even helped lead me to many of the foundlings when they first arrived here. In return, we help them by bringing them trinkets we take from the bogeys, items from the mortal realm that they seem to treasure. They know everything about the Seven Realms. If anyone can tell you how to meet the Queen, it's them."

Aisling swallowed hard and followed Peter into the cave. It turned and twisted only twice before opening up into a large chamber where three smallish women stood around a tiny table, fiddling with what looked like some sort of quilt.

The three women, if that was what one could call them, were squat and round, only about three feet tall. Their hair was gray and greasy and hung down over their eyes in lank curtains which hid them entirely. Giant, bulbous, warty noses took up most of their faces, but Aisling could tell that each of the women still had tiny, pursed lips hiding beneath their overlarge nostrils. They had small, pointed ears and heavily wrinkled faces.

They ambled over to Peter and Aisling on short stubby legs which ended in large, gnarled bare feet. Each of them wore a sort of gray winding sheet, tied in the middle with a simple rope to make it look like a dress.

"Peter Goodfellow, he is…" said one of the women and she sniffed the air.

The other two mimicked her, fervently sniffing the air with their enormous noses like a pack of hunting dogs.

"It is him…" said another one.

"'Course it is. Peter Goodfellow, come to get more secrets…" said another. "He knows he isn't supposed to know…" cackled another.

"Nosey…nosey Peter Goodfellow…" one of them teased. "What brings you for us, Peter Goodfellow?" asked the first.

At this point, Aisling couldn't really tell which of the three was talking at any given time. It almost felt like the three of them were speaking in one single voice with only slightly different intimations or changes in pitch, and it was giving her a headache.

"Tea, girl?" asked the woman closest to her. "Sit down for tea, follow we…"

The woman took Aisling's smooth hand in her own wrinkled one and led her over to a short table and sofa on the other side of the cave. Peter and one of the other women followed them over. The third one rushed out of the main cave and into a back room. Smoke began to billow forth from the room and no sooner had it appeared, than the little woman came back with five small cups on tiny plates teetering dangerously in her hands. Aisling rose to try and help her, but the woman to her right yanked her down.

"No need, girl…" she said scoldingly.

"She's got it. Just tea after all..." agreed the other.

The woman took one tea cup down at a time and placed it in front of each of them on the small table.

"We know why you're here, Peter Goodfellow..." "We always know..."

"Know why you brought the girl, too..."

"All questions this one..." said the one nearest to Aisling. "More tea, dear?" asked another.

As Aisling hadn't even had a moment to take a sip of the first cup of tea, she shook her head politely and tried to say 'no, thank you', but before she could even get the words out, one of the women was already coming in from the smoky separate room, carrying two more cups and saucers. She placed them in front of Aisling and continued.

"What do you want to know, Aisling Mason?" she asked.

Aisling put down the cup she had just picked up and moved to speak when she was interrupted again.

"She wants to know how to leave..." said the woman closest to Peter. "No leaving here no more..."

"The way is shut..." "Sure is..."

"More tea, girl?" said one of the women, while another simultaneously placed four more cups upon the small table right in front of Aisling.

"Peter knows it's true..." "Found out the hard way..." "So many come across..." "None go back..."

Aisling was getting dizzy trying to discern which of the three women were talking to her. She reached down and made an attempt to take a sip of tea to calm her nerves, yet as she moved to replace the cup upon the table, found that the table before her was now impossibly crowded by more than a dozen identical teacups and saucers.

"Nope…no way out of the Seven Realms…" "What about the Queen?" asked Aisling, irritably.

"What about her?" replied the three women in unison.

Aisling took a deep breath and put down her tea. It seemed her outburst had quieted the women's seemingly incessant jabbering at last.

"Peter told me that in order to be allowed passage through the veil, you have to get the Queen's permission. How do I get the Queen's permission?" she asked.

"You don't…" "You never will…"

"That's not the way for you to get home, Aisling Mason…" "Then how?" groaned Aisling.

The three big-nosed women looked at one another across the table of teacups. Peter meanwhile, sat placidly on the end of the plush chair, sipping his second cup of tea.

"So you come for knowledge not for yourself then, Peter Goodfellow…" "Surprise even us, that does…"

"Drink your tea, Aisling Mason…" said one of the women, who placed another four cups of tea atop the crowded table.

"We will tell you a story…"

At once, the three old women moved closer to one another and began to hum. It was a tune that seemed familiar to Aisling and yet she knew for certain that she had never consciously heard it before. Perhaps it was something she had heard in a dream. Before she could try to discern its meaning however, the story began:

"Long ago, the Seven Realms were separate and unruly.

Each of the realms, Stonewall, Verdenwald, Ondine, Gideon, Hikayat, Eissland, and the Sabbiaterra, were ruled by a king or queen of their own. Each one of these rulers believed that theirs was the ultimate rule and this belief led them to war with the other neighboring kingdoms. The lands and people of the Seven Realms suffered under the horror of all-out war.

The warring between the Seven Realms continued until one day, when marching to battle, a young farm boy happened upon a magical sword. The sword was unlike anything the world had ever seen and it granted its wielder indestructibility and unmatched skill in battle. The boy who would be king marched into battle and in a matter of hours, put an end to the warring between the realms forever.

The people called the weapon the King's Blade and granted the boy who wielded it complete power over all of the Seven Realms. The boy grew into a man and the man took a wife and in time gave birth to sons and daughters, who gave birth to their own sons and daughters. His line built the great castle of Caerleon in the center of the Seven Realms and his family ruled for over a thousand years.

It was in this immense and stately castle, that the king and queen appointed those who would serve as wardens to the lands within their realm. The Seven Realms were now ruled by a just king and a noble queen. Though each of the realms had their own lords and ladies, the true and ultimate seat of power lay in the lands nearest Caerleon.

All endings were happy. All dreams came true. The people of the Seven Realms prospered under the rule of the one true King and Queen. Peace, perfect and serene though it may be, rarely lasts forever, even in a place like this. Somewhere, deep in the darkest corner of the world, a dark power was waiting...watching...biding her time.

The great sorceress Maledicta, most powerful of her kind, believed that the great king's line had usurped what was hers by virtue of an ancient pact she had with the land itself.

Maledicta was the most powerful witch in all the Seven Realms, but even she knew that while the king held the King's Blade, she would never be able to take power.

Maledicta's power came from the land and she knew that deep within it, the Seven Realms had the power to make her dreams a reality in the same way that it had for so many others. So she began the ritual that would create the curse to end all curses.

Seven virgins were sacrificed with seven blades, over the course of seven nights during the seventh month. The curse was paid for in blood, seven times over. The dark forces of the world listened to Maledicta's whispers and accepted her offering.

The curse emerged and spread across the land faster than the fastest plague. One by one, each of the Seven Realms fell to its power. In their great fortress at Caerleon, the king and queen heard their people crying, but it was too late. Far too late.

As more and more people fell to the power of the curse, Maledicta's power grew and grew. She marched upon Caerleon with an army of dark faeries. Though he tried to fight back, even the power of the King's Blade was no match for her now. Maledicta used her dark powers to transform the king and queen into beasts and separated them to opposite corners of the world. The power they once held to protect the Seven Realms was gone. Maledicta, Queen of the Witches, now ruled all Seven Realms…"

The humming ceased and the story stopped. The smoke-like images that Aisling had seen during its duration dissipated entirely. She reached down to take a sip of tea. It was cold, but she drank it anyway.

"So, the Queen is a witch?" asked Aisling. "And she has taken over this land by cursing it?"

"The witch to end all witches…" said one of the women. "She is every witch…"

"Every warning and bad dream…" "Every hate and scorn and spell…" "Her power is absolute…"

"That can't be true though," surmised Aisling, who had heard a thousand stories about witches who met their defeat at even the simplest of contrivances. "In the stories, the witch is always defeated. They always have a weakness."

"What about your story, Aisling Mason?" queried one of the women, while taking Aisling's teacup from her shaking hands, dumping out the liquid, and turning it over onto its saucer.

"My story?" she asked.

"This is your story now…" replied the woman to her right, taking the saucer from the other old woman.

She turned the teacup right-side up again and peered inside, staring at the remnant tea leaves sticking to the bottom.

"When you enter, it becomes yours…" she said, before motioning over to her fellows to come look with her.

The three old women placed the cup before them and looked inside. As they did so, they muttered to one another in a strange language.

Aisling stopped for a moment and looked down at the nightingale, who was perched on the end of a teacup and gently poking its head in and out to partake. She felt terrible. She felt just like the nightingale, who was whisked along with her in her nightdress. Aisling hadn't asked for any of this.

She looked up at Peter, who stood exactly where he had been standing earlier. There was a look upon his youthful face that she couldn't place. If she had to guess, it would be one of regret, even envy.

"Why is it my story?" asked Aisling, breaking the strange old ladies out of their closed conversation.

"Always has been…" replied one of the women. "It was just waiting for you…" added another. "You are meant for great things, Aisling Mason…" "It is in the leaves…"

"You are to break the curse…"

The three Crones began to hum again, their otherworldly notes, transporting Aisling into a world of unseen possibility.

Peter Goodfellow looked angry beyond words. He had been through this with all the other foundlings. Each time, they drank their tea and found themselves resigned to simply being another member of his slowly growing community. None of them were destined for anything other than surviving, than following him. He assumed that once he had amassed enough of them, he would have enough clout to make a difference; for him and for them. But he had evidently been wrong.

How could this skinny little nothing child be more important than him? How could she be the one whom the

Crones sought all these years? He had done so much, saved so many. He had done everything the batty old faeries had asked him to do. It wasn't fair. Still, realizing what he must look like, he shifted his expression. He would keep his incredulity to himself, for now.

There would be time enough to discuss it with the old women later, after they sent the girl off. "We should, uh...we should go, Aisling..." he tried to say.

But Aisling couldn't hear him, she was too busy listening to the low hum of the Crones as its pitch began to rise once more.

"A girl who comes from 'cross the veil, she cannot leave, she must not fail, She holds the way to curses end, through force of will, with foe and friend, A Seventh daughter will she be, with scroll and sword, with bloom and key, To break the hold upon this land, with iron courage, gentle hand,

For she will be the witch's bane, return the worthy to their reign."

The humming stopped again and with it, so too did Peter's anger abate. The Crones had told him many things since he arrived in the Seven Realms, they had given him a life, a purpose in a place that would have otherwise been his grave. They fed him, taught him how to fight, how to use the magic of the Seven Realms, they guided him to the other foundlings and warned him of threats. In all that, they had never delivered a prophecy, or at least, not one like this. It occurred to Peter that if this Aisling Mason was the key to ending the Queen's dreadful dominion over the land, then perhaps she was also the key to him finding his own way home someday.

Aisling was speechless. She had been told many stories over the years and told many herself, but in all those tales, she had never envisioned herself as any sort of hero. For her entire life, Aisling Mason had felt like little more than a footnote in the story of someone much more heroic and much more deserving than herself; her brother, Jonathon.

Yet here she was, alone in a strange place where strange creatures, magic, witches, monsters, and all the fantastical things she had ever seen in her mind's eye actually existed. There was no brave Jonathon Mason here to save her and take care of her and make things better. Aisling was going to have to learn to rely on herself, and if what these women were saying was true, the whole world, the Seven Realms, were relying on her, too.

She knew one thing for certain about stories, whether good or bad, if your story has a prophecy, it's important. Even the old stories, the tales that went back to the days when the Romans lived in England, spoke of prophecy. If your hero is the subject of a prophecy, if they are spurred to action by the whims of fate itself, then they have no choice in the matter, they must act.

"All right," said Aisling. "But where do I even start?"
"With this…" said one of the women.

She hobbled over to a large, wooden chest in the corner of the cave and opened the top. The items inside looked commonplace and as the old woman began to rifle through it, Aisling began to suspect that it might be deeper than it appeared from the outside. A few moments later, the woman's torso, which had disappeared beneath the trunk's detritus, reappeared. She was clutching a foot-long wooden scroll in her left hand.

"This is the Prophet…" the woman said, handing it to Aisling. "It will help you on your journey when we cannot…"

"It gives knowledge…" said another.

"It gives clues…" added the third woman. "We've had it so long…"

"So long waiting…."

"But what do I do? How do I save Seven Realms?" asked a frantic Aisling. "So many questions…" replied the first Crone.

"Prophecy does not provide answers…" "It provides guidance…"

Aisling frowned and looked over at Peter, who didn't seem to know what to say either. "Can you tell me anything? Can you at least tell me about the curses?" she said,

desperately.

The women looked at one another and began to murmur, glancing over to Aisling every so often. Then, shrugging their shoulders, they began to hum.

Beast and briar, unchecked greed, headless queen of wanton need, Reprised hour, sunken love, one life stolen, axe above,

Snows as white as corpse's skin, curses come from deep within.

The Crones ended their second verse and looked expectantly at Aisling. The girl, even more confused than she had been previously, looked confusedly at them. Before she could speak again, however, the first of the women stood and spoke.

"Go to the West, Aisling Mason…" directed the first

woman again. "Peter Goodfellow will show you...."

"Go with our blessing..." the three said in unison.

A moment later, the fire that had been burning in the hearth suddenly went out and darkness filled the cave.

Aisling and Peter found themselves back at the village. In his hand was a burned out torch, in hers, a paper scroll with a gilded handle through the center. The two shook their heads and looked at one another.

"Was that...is this real?" she asked him.

"Yes, I'm afraid so. They do that. Get some sleep, Aisling. You're going to need it," replied Peter, and he walked her back to the girls' treehouse.

Chapter Five

Barnyard Stew

he next day, Aisling awoke to the smell of eggs and meat cooking on an open fire. She sat up in the small bed the other foundling girls had built for her and looked around the room, but there was nobody else there. The smell was coming from outside the treehouse. She looked over on the small shelf next to the bed and saw the nightingale, sitting placidly in a sort of makeshift nest made from a torn sock. The little thing still couldn't fly, but seemed to be quite content nonetheless.

"Well, little one, I guess we should get going," she said to the tiny bird, before petting it gently on the top of the head with one finger.

The nightingale closed its eyes and ruffled its feathers in appreciation.

Aisling got up and straightened herself out before putting on the clothes and boots the girls had given her. Then she placed the nightingale back in her apron, along with the rest of her belongings and went out to find breakfast.

As she descended the ladder outside, Aisling wondered if she had been dreaming the whole encounter with the three Crones. She didn't think so, though she couldn't remember if she'd had any other dreams during the night either. She shook off the strange thoughts and focused on finding out where the cooking smell was coming from.

Across the clearing, a large fire was burning brightly. Several of the foundlings, including the girl Orla, were cooking eggs and meat in large, iron pans. There was also a large cauldron bubbling in the center, which by the smell of it, seemed to be filled with porridge of some kind.

"Morning, Aisling!" yelled little Elizabeth, who came bounding over to her and gave her a big hug.

"Good morning," said Aisling.

She hugged the girl tightly. She may have been only a bit older than little Mary and Thomas, but her hugs felt the same. It pained Aisling to realize that she may never get the chance to see her darling niece and nephew again, but before she could dwell on it any further, a voice cried out to her.

"Breakfast, Aisling?" asked Orla, who was plopping a heap of porridge and eggs into a wooden bowl.

She gestured for Aisling to come forward and Elizabeth begrudgingly peeled herself from her. The porridge was hot and filling, but mostly bland. At home she would have added some honey to it, but she imagined such things were as much a luxury in this world as they were there. Her hunger soon got the better of her taste buds however, and before long she had finished two bowlfuls.

She and the other Foundlings sat around the fire and she listened to them talk about the fun and chores they had planned for the day. It warmed Aisling's heart to know that she would be leaving them in capable hands. The Foundlings had one another, and for children who had lost everything they had known in the blink of an eye, that was surely enough.

Still, Aisling was uneasy. The thought of what awaited her weighed heavily upon her mind. Before she had too long to think on it further, Peter arrived at the breakfast circle. Each of the Foundlings greeted him in their own way. Aisling could tell instantly how much they admired him, how much they respected him, and how grateful they were.

"Good morning," he said, merrily. "Morning," replied Aisling.

She hesitated to say anything about the previous night, but only for the briefest of moments. Finally, she found she could not hold it in any longer.

"Peter, about last night..."

"I know," he said, cutting her off. "After we eat, I'll show you what I've prepared for you. It's not much, but it's all I can do given our current situation."

When Peter had finished eating, he led Aisling back to his treehouse. At the foot of the tree sat a small, leather knapsack, which cinched around the top by way of a long strand of thin leather. He bent down and picked up the sack, then held it open for her to see inside.

"I've packed you a compass, some dry biscuits, some apples, and dried meat. I had the girls pick you out another pair of trousers and a clean shirt as well. There's also a thin bedroll in there, too. Sorry it isn't much. Honestly, I don't know that there's much else I could give you, besides this anyway…"

He reached over to the tree and picked up a small, leather scabbard that Aisling simply hadn't noticed before. He handed the bag over to Aisling, which she slung over her shoulder, then made to pull the blade from within its sheath.

The sword he drew looked as though it had been made for a child. The blade was not entirely sharp, but even a novice like Aisling could tell that it was by no means a child's plaything. It was simple and functional, and it was exactly what she needed.

"Thank you, Peter," she said, gratefully.

"I wish I could do more, or that you had more time. Unfortunately, the Crones are usually pretty timely with their prophecies. It's the only reason I've been able to save as many children as I have, by going where they tell me right after I've heard their warning. I hope you understand why I can't send any of them with you," he paused for a moment. "And why I can't come myself."

"I do. I've seen them with you, they need you here. They depend on you. I'll be ok. I'm not the damsel in this story," she said, smiling.

"No, you most certainly are not," chuckled Peter. "There's one more thing…" He took a small, brown leather parcel from his pocket and handed it to her.

"It's a deck of playing cards. They're nothing special, just something to keep you busy if you manage to find some people to play with. They've always brought me luck," he added with a wink.

"Thank you so much, Peter," said Aisling.

The two hugged again and soon enough Aisling was saying her goodbyes to the whole group. Though she had only known them for the space of a few days, she had come to quite like the Foundlings.

Ultimately though, she had resigned herself to doing anything and everything she could to get home to what remained of her family. If that meant breaking some kind of curse and defeating a witch, then that was what she was going to do. If she had learned one irrefutable fact about stories it was this: the hero always triumphs in the end. Little did she know, her own story was only just beginning.

At Peter's suggestion, Aisling began her journey by heading west, away from the small forest of the Foundlings and toward the Queen's great fortress at Caerleon, which lay in the very center of the Seven Realms.

Aisling had never really stayed out in the wilderness on a hunt with her brothers. After all, where she was from, little girls didn't do that sort of thing. Girls didn't hunt, or fight, or anything like that. They cooked, sewed, did farm work, laundry, and eventually gave birth so they could look after their children. Aisling was very good at a number of *those* things, but she had a feeling she was going to be pretty rotten at hunting; and she was right.

From the moment she left the Foundlings' village, Aisling was on the lookout for any small, edible creature she could find. She happened upon some squirrels, but was far too slow to catch any of them. Later, she saw a rabbit, a strangepurple-looking thing, but no sooner had she taken a step towards it, than it was off and running into the woods;

nothing more than a violet blur shrinking into the distance.

Birds were also completely out of the question. In the first place, Aisling assumed, and rightly so, that if a squirrel and a rabbit were too fast, a target that could fly would be utterly impossible. The real reason though, was because Aisling was still carrying the injured nightingale in her pocket and even if she had captured a bird by some small stroke of luck, she would have felt too guilty killing and eating it in front of her tiny companion.

The sun came down far quicker than she had anticipated. Aisling felt as though she hadn't made any progress at all. Peter had told her that there were many farms and small villages along the way where she might be able to stop if she needed, yet the edge of the tree line was nowhere in sight.

Aisling surmised that if there were farms, they would certainly be beyond that. She realized, with no small amount of dismay, that she might actually have to bed down early for the night and pick up her journey in the morning. Her belly growled as if in agreement.

She had no tent, but the Foundlings had given her a bedroll at least. She placed her pack and the bedroll down near a tall oak tree and went off to look for kindling. She wasn't sure she would be able to build a proper fire, but she had to at least try.

Trying was about all she could do. After an hour of unsuccessful attempts, Aisling threw her hands down in frustration. Her hastily collected twigs were no closer to sparking than they had been when she started the process, but her hands were so burned that they felt as if they might burst into flames at any moment. She sat back against the oak and looked up into the tree branches. Perched above her was a strange, purplish-looking cat.

She hadn't noticed it at first, probably because she had been so busy trying to light her own hands on fire. The cat, if that was indeed what it was, had longer ears than the cats back home, but she could tell by its feline face that it was, in some way, a cat. The eyes were wider though, more human, and its stare was at once both comical and unnerving. From her vantage point beneath it, she could see that it had lovely black stripes going down its back, flanks, and tail. She wondered if all the animals in this part of the Seven Realms were purple.

"Like you could do any better," she huffed.

The strange cat mewled and leapt away, disappearing into the twilit branches of the oak. Aisling let out a sigh. Her belly gurgled again and she reached in her pack for the dried meat and biscuits the Foundlings had given her. She hated to use any of the rations now, but she wasn't going to catch anything at sunset. The biscuit was hard and crumbly, almost rocklike, and she wished she had stew or something to dip it in. The dried meat was almost too tough to chew.

Still, a few difficult bites into both and she was feeling much better.

The sun set and she stood up to try and see the stars through the canopy. The forest she was in seemed old, but not so dense that it blotted out all light. It was strange that she could feel the age of the forest in that way. She had never felt that way about the forest near their farm back home. Sure, she knew a dozen stories about the trees and the treefolk, and how they are trees that come alive, that have lived for untold generations. The thing was, back home those were just faerie stories; in the Seven Realms, they could be real. She knocked gently on the oak behind her, waiting for some sort of response, but received none.

"This place," she whispered to herself. "It's likely to drive a person mad."

Aisling tried to sleep. She figured if she fell asleep early enough, she would be less likely to be terrified of what might be lurking out there in the dark. This tactic, however, rarely works, and it didn't work for her either. The minutes turned into hours and the hours flitted away and all the while Aisling Mason sat beneath the oak tree, eyes closed tight, trying desperately not to think of the horrors waiting for her.

It was a few hours before sunrise when Aisling's nostrils caught a whiff of something that was not just the damp smell of an old forest for once, but something much more enticing. It was the smell of cooking, the salty smell of a hearty stew, of boiled onions and celery. The delicious smell traveled unbidden down her nostrils and into her belly, which rumbled deeper and louder than it had all night.

Aisling got to her feet and sniffed the air again. A light breeze from the northwest had carried the smell to her. Maybe someone else was camping out, a hunter from one of the villages. She thought if she could find them, maybe prevail upon them for a spoonful, she would feel better. She might feel well enough even to sleep, especially if she was in the company of others and not alone amidst the shifting shadows of the deep wood.

The girl picked up her pack and her sword and headed in that direction. A few moments later, Aisling came upon a brightlylit clearing next to a large, stone outcropping of some kind. There, burning in the entrance of the cave, was a roaring fire, atop of which was a great iron stewpot filled with bubbling, orange liquid. Up close, it smelled even better. She looked around the clearing but didn't see anything, besides the cauldron and fire, that would give any indication that anyone else was camping there for the night.

Carefully, Aisling tiptoed into the clearing and made her way towards the pot of stew. The stewpot was enormous, bigger than her even. A huge ladle, basically a spear with a bucket on the end of it, leaned against the cauldron. Normally, Aisling would have considered all of this very odd, but the smell of the stew and her own starving belly and lack of sleep were proving to be an irresistible combination.

Aisling knew that she couldn't step onto one of the rocks surrounding the fire and get some soup, it was far too hot and she was far too small. It was then, at the moment that particular bit of logic set in, that Aisling realized she was in terrible trouble.

It occurred to her that whatever it was that was capable of even lifting a cauldron that big onto the fire, let along cooking food in it, was not the type of creature that she wanted to associate with. In her experience as a storyteller, things that cook stews in such large pieces of crockery are unlikely to be friendly.

Aisling decided that it was time to get out of that clearing, but just as she turned to walk away, she felt the ground beneath her feet begin to shake. She stood stock-still as the rumbling slowly approached her from behind. She heard the soft padding sound of large feet treading upon earth and slowly, tremulously, she turned back to meet it.

Whatever it was, it was huge; the largest being Aisling had ever encountered. The monster, for it was indeed a monster of some sort, was more than eight feet tall and covered in mottled green skin, pockmarked by all manner of warts and scales. Atop its large, unnatural looking head, a scraggly mop of dark brown hair hung down about its face and down its back. It wore clothes, or rather, it was draped in a number of pelts, some of which were animal and others of a more...questionable origin.

Aisling beheld the creature's long four-fingered hands, its long floppy ears, its gently wagging cow's tail, and its bulbous nose and realized with a pang of fright that she was now face-to-face with the scourge of children and goats alike: a troll.

The troll smelled old, like rotting wood and leaf litter, he smelled of morning breath and stagnant water, and the underneaths of things. She wondered if he could smell himself, surely he could with such a large nose. Aisling had thought the noses on the Crones had been big, comically so, but the nose on this immense creature seemed to take up most of its squat, angry- looking face, and there was nothing comical about it.

The other half of the troll's face seemed to be made of mostly jagged teeth, set haphazardly within a drooping maw of a mouth, and it had two beady yellow eyes.

"Looking for a bite? asked the troll. Its voice sounded deep and guttural.

"It's good stew," he continued. "Got sheep, horse, goats, onions, carrots, celery. Need the roots for a base. There's even a whole peck of chickens in there, too. I'll admit though, it's still missing something. One special ingredient."

The troll smiled, and for the first time Aisling could see every one of his gruesome, yellow teeth. It had far more than were necessary for a mouth. Even one so big as the troll's.

Aisling didn't know what to say. The bogeymen had been terrifying enough, but this monster, well, she doubted that her paltry little sword was going to do much against his thick hide.

"No…I uh…" she stammered, trying to back away. "I should be going. I must have just wandered off. Sorry to bother you, sir."

The troll took its overlong arm and reached over Aisling's head, casually and very clearly blocking her escape.

"Nonsense," insisted the Troll, still smiling. "You simply must stay for supper."

"If she's staying to eat," said a small, unfamiliar voice behind them. "Then I'm sure you won't mind if I join you, too?"

Aisling craned her neck to see who it was. She hoped that Peter had changed his mind and decided to follow her. Surely, he would know how to deal with a troll. She was most disappointed to find that the voice was coming not from Peter Goodfellow, but from the long- eared purple cat.

The troll, obviously just as confused as she was, gazed quizzically at the cat.

"I'm sort of in the middle of a thing here," he said, and he couldn't keep the slightly harassed tone out of his guttural voice.

"Well, you invited her for dinner," said the cat, obviously a bit hurt by the troll's non- invitation. "Surely, if you've got enough to feed human girls, you can spare some for a hungry cat in need. You've no idea how hard the rabbits around here are to catch. You know what I'm saying, don't you, girl?"

The cat had sauntered up to them, proudly, as if he hadn't a care in the world. He stared up at Aisling as he spoke, his amber eyes almost glowing in the firelight.

"I, um…" said Aisling, who it seemed was even more speechless in the presence of a talking purple cat than the troll.

"Not a bright one, this girl. Am I right, friend?" said the cat and though he was speaking directly to the troll, kept his eyes trained on Aisling.

"I guess so," replied the troll.

The purple cat leapt up onto the bucket of the long makeshift ladle and effortlessly climbed to the top of it. He perched there for a moment, taking in the delicious scent wafting from the pot, then climbed back down and shook his head.

"What's wrong?" asked the troll, concernedly.

"Well…I don't want to give offense of course…" began the cat.

"Is it the stew?" asked the troll, who seemed more than a little concerned with the quality of his cooking.

"It's just," the cat continued. "Well, like you said, I think it needs something else. It's not quite right, you know?"

The troll reached down without a second thought and hefted Aisling into the air. He pointed to her with his free hand.

"Human," he said emphatically. "It's missing human meat. I was trying to be funny before with the girl, but I don't think she got my joke. I was telling her that it needs human. Why don't I just toss her in? It could be ready in an hour or so."

"No, no," said the cat. "It's not human. A stew like this, with all the roots and farm animals and such, it doesn't need human. Human is such a strong taste, if you add a human to that stew, you're going to drown out all those flavors."

"Oh…" said the troll, and it was clear that he was considering the cat's words very carefully. "What does it need, then?"

The cat sat on its haunches and closed its eyes in a very cattish way. He sat that way for a long while, quietly contemplating the additional ingredients that would make the stew perfect, until finally, the troll's patience began to wear thin. He cleared his throat.

"Oh yes," apologized the cat. "I was trying to go through all the different stews I've had in my time. I'm something of a stew expert amongst cats, you see. Do we have any dill weed? Any potatoes or beetroot? I think a stew like this needs more root vegetables. It will thicken it up quite well."

The troll looked disappointedly at Aisling. She was still clutched loosely in his hand, loosely enough that she could have attempted to wriggle out if she wanted, but she had decided that it might be best to let the cat do most of the talking for the time being. She forced a smile and looked back at the troll.

"Potatoes sound good," she said, half-enthusiastically.

"I have some potatoes I think," said the troll. "And the

herbs, too. I have beetroot, also, but...I really kind of hate it. If it's bad I'm gonna add the girl to it after."

Then he added, somewhat abashedly, "I kind of like the taste of human."

"My dear troll. Who is the expert in stews here? Trust me, I would never steer you wrong when it comes to stew cookery," explained the cat.

The troll put Aisling down, then he wrapped a length of rope firmly about her body, tying her arms to her sides and her legs completely together.

"Don't go nowhere," he warned her.

He walked into the cave and began rustling around with what sounded like wooden crates and heavy sacks.

The cat didn't say anything to Aisling as they waited. She hoped that the animal might give her some indication that he was on her side, but it was almost as if he was going out of his way to disregard her. Only once, right before the troll returned, did he lift his head from his self- cleaning to meet her eyes again. The expression on his feline face was as implacable as ever.

"Here," said the troll, as he dumped a sackful of potatoes and bundles of herbs into the cauldron. "I have the beetroots, too. Are you sure?"

The cat nodded.

The troll dumped a small bucket of purplish beets into the pot as well.

"How long do we wait?" asked the troll as he took up the ladle to stir the stew. "Not long now," said the cat.

"I hate waiting," complained the troll.

Suddenly, Aisling had an idea. If she could keep the troll

busy for just a little while longer, perhaps she could find a way to convince him not to eat her. Perhaps the stew might even be as good as the cat said it would be and the troll would be content with it.

"Why don't I tell us a story?" she suggested. "To pass the time?" The cat's eyes lit up.

"That…is a wonderful idea. I love a good story. Don't you, troll?" he said. "Stories are good," said the troll, and he smiled.

It wasn't pleasant exactly, but it was more pleasant than any of his other expressions had been.

Aisling sat up straight and began to tell the longest story she knew. It was the story of Tam Lin, who was ensorcelled by the Queen of the Faeries and was eventually rescued by his true love, a maiden. As she spoke, the troll and the cat both became enthralled by her words. For a moment, Aisling felt like she was back in her little lofted bedroom, weaving a faerie tale to put Thomas and Mary to sleep. It took about an hour to tell the whole tale and by the time she was done, the troll was sitting cross-legged with his face in hands, and the cat was curled up by the hot rocks of the fire.

"That was a good story," said the troll.

Then, looking at the cauldron, he got to his feet and took in the smell. He wrinkled his nose slightly at the odor and grimaced a little.

"I don't know if beetroot was a good idea," he snorted angrily. "Try it," said the cat. "Trust me."

The troll dipped the ladle into the pot and pulled up a bucketful of stew. He brought it to his lips and blew on it to cool it down. Finally, he dumped the whole bucketful into his mouth. He chewed it slightly and swallowed it, licking his lips as if to retest what had escaped his initial slurp.

"Ehhh...I knew this wouldn't work," said the troll and then he said, "That's it, I'm adding the girl."

The troll walked over to Aisling and reached down to pick her up, before he could grab hold of her, however, the cat began laughing raucously.

"What's so funny?" asked the troll.

Aisling found herself both terrified by her imminent death and a little incensed by the cat's utter disregard for the severity of the situation.

"It's sunrise, troll. That's what's so funny," replied the cat, who was now on his feet and gesturing towards the slowly encroaching sunrise.

A look of terror spread across the troll's hideous face, and it was that look which would remain plastered upon the monster's face for all time. No sooner had the sun risen above the tree line, than the troll's green scaly skin began to calcify. It spread across his body in the blink of an eye. One second he was flesh and the next, he was a rather grotesque granite statuary.

The cat continued laughing for a moment more and then, without warning, he too transformed before Aisling's eyes. His sleek feline features morphed into a vaguely humanoid shape. His face elongated, along with his nose. His paws turned to fingers and toes. His eyes changed too, though they were still amber, they were now larger, wider, and more suited to a human's face. When he had finished his miraculous transformation, some features of the cat still remained. He was still purple, his ears were still overlong and sat atop his head, and his tail remained long and bushy, only now it was sticking out of a person's backside.

"Need a little help?" said the not-cat. Aisling nodded, slowly.

The strange creature came over to her and began to untie her. His long, spindly fingers were a little clumsy at first, almost as if he wasn't used to using them. After some effort, he undid the knots and Aisling got to her feet. Dusting herself off she said,

"I don't mean to be rude…and thank you for helping me, by the way,but what…" she stopped herself. "Who are you?"

"My name's Hoegabbler," said the creature. "I saw you come into the clearing and I had a feeling you might need help. Honestly, the people in Stonewall have been trying to get rid of that troll for weeks now. He keeps stealing from their homes and farms. As if they didn't have enough going on these days without also having to worry about trolls."

"What do you mean?" asked Aisling.

"Let's get some stew first," said Hoegabbler. "Trolls aside, I do love a good barnyard stew."

Hoegabbler and Aisling sat in silence for a few minutes, eating the stew and admiring their handiwork. Aisling had been starving and the stew, for all they had put into it, the troll had been right, the beets had been too much.

"What's your name?" asked Hoegabbler.

Aisling proceeded to tell the creature everything that had happened to her. Her life back home, how she had gotten there, how she had met the Foundlings, the Crones,. and finally, her mission.

"That's one heck of a story already. I bet once it's done you're gonna have enough to keep trolls distracted for a month of Sundays," he said, slapping his hand to his forehead. "You're gonna need help with something like this."

Aisling could easily place the meaning in Hoegabbler's tone. He was, at the very least, a fairly clever little fellow, whatever he was, and talented enough to be of use to her. He was also a native who knew much more about this strange world than herself. And one it seemed, who wanted to go with her. Aisling was not exactly in a position to refuse a friend.

"You can come along if you'd like. I'd be glad of the company," she said, smiling.

The changeling jumped up into the air and by the time he landed again he had transformed into the purple rabbit.

"You won't regret it!" he said happily. "So, you need to get to Caerleon? Well, fastest way there is through Stonewall."

"Is that one of the Seven Realms? Is it dangerous?" she asked. "Not at all," lied the changeling. "We'll be fine."

Chapter Six

A Big, Bad Wolf

oegabbler spent most of his time as Aisling's traveling companion in the shape of his purple cat. He had began the journey in his normal shape, but proved to be rather ungainly on his somewhat chubby, oddly-shaped legs. Aisling wondered if all of his kind were this way and if that was why changelings in her world spent most of their time in their secretive animal forms.

Aisling's other traveling companion, the still-injured nightingale, didn't seem to appreciate her new feline friend as much as Aisling did. Though it still spent much of its time in the pocket of her apron, it still appeared significantly ruffled every time Aisling peeked inside to check on it.

On one such occasion, Aisling had noticed something metallic shimmer slightly in the other pocket. It was her mother's thimble, fallen from her pouch. Until that moment, she had all but forgotten about it. She took it out and after threading it with a few loose threads from her newfound clothes, placed it around her neck as she walked. She made sure it was kept tucked beneath her shirt of course, for safekeeping, but it still felt good to have the necklace close to her heart. It felt like a constant reminder of home and the family that was still out there, waiting for her to return. She left the other two items, the lock of Abigail's hair and the gold coin that was her inheritance, safely tucked in her pouch.

Aisling and Hoegabbler kept to the woodland paths for the most part. The changeling was familiar with every part of the area and seemed to know intrinsically which paths to avoid and which were safe to traverse.

They had been smart enough to loot the troll's stores before they left and even managed to spoon a good amount of stew into a large, leather wineskin he had made for himself. It ran out in a day or so, but it kept them going. Five days later and the two of them found themselves on the border of Stonewall, the first of the Seven Realms.

It was, for all intents and purposes, a woodland realm. Indeed, the first village they passed was set so deeply into the forest itself that at first, Aisling didn't even realize it was a village at all. It seemed to Aisling, as she meandered her way through several of the small hamlets, that many of them wered somewhat bereft of villagers.

The villagers who remained were strung out and sad-looking. They were skittish and untrusting. It felt as if every person she encountered flashed her a nervous, suspicious look. Aisling was reminded of the way the villagers in her old home had looked when the Sweat first came down upon them. Every person seemed to think that everyone else was carrying the sickness and that if they so much as greeted them, they too might contract the fatal disease.

Aisling wondered if the villages of Stonewall were experiencing a plague of some sort.

Once they had successfully passed through the village and found a place to camp for the night, Aisling decided to ask Hoegabbler what was going on.

"It's a cursed place," he said shakily. "I mean, everywhere is a cursed place these days. Curses every place you go, really, but Stonewall is particularly cursed. It's not just the land that the Queen has affected but the people, too."

"Cursed in what way?" Aisling asked, as she finished building a fire.

She had become particularly good at doing this since her first day away from the Foundlings' village and with each successful fire she lit, she felt even better about herself.

Hoegabbler made to answer her question, but before he could even squeak out an answer, Aisling's pack began to shake. She rose to her feet and backed away. Hoegabbler arched his feline back and flattened his ears back against his head. His fur was standing on end.

"What are you carrying in there?" asked Hoegabbler. "I don't know," she said. "Whatever Peter gave me."

Then it occurred to her that she did have something in there that Peter had not given her. She was also carrying the wooden scroll from the Crones. Steeling herself, she walked over to it and pulled it out. It shook violently in her hands like a trapped animal trying to escape. Aisling took hold of the end of it, and pulled it down.

Suddenly, it sang in the voices of the Crones once more. This time though, it was a verse she hadn't heard before:

"A curse that lingers for all time, that's spoken of in song and rhyme. For love is but a myth you see, that cureth not, the beast is she. So she remains and rules this land, the people fear her beastly hand, her wolves and monsters crave their flesh, and one small nick, they're like the rest. We're naught but animals you see, and she will make a beast of thee."

A moment later, the singing stopped, and so did the shaking.

"So, um…you have a magic scroll that sings to you in rhyme," said Hoegabbler, matter- of-factly.

"So it would appear," replied Aisling. "I got it from these old ladies called the Crones. They told me that it would give me clues and assistance during my quest. Hoegabbler, have the people been cursed to become monsters of some kind?"

"That's the rumor. The thing of it is, most of the realms stay separate now, only a few people move between them since the Queen took over. Every one of the Seven Realms, and the lords and ladies who used to rule them, have been affected by the Queen's curses. But I really don't know the specifics of any one of them, other than the rumors anyway. Nobody does," he explained.

"Well, whatever this curse is, it's obvious the scroll was warning me about it." "It might perhaps be more useful if told you how to break the curse," added the changeling.

"I'm not supposed to break the curse on Stonewall. I'm supposed to speak to the Queen and convince her to release her hold on all Seven Realms, and I don't think I'm even capable of doing that," said the girl.

The two sat there for a long time after that. Usually they would spend time around the campfire before they retired, both of them weaving small tales to entertain the other. This night was different. They ate quickly, then set up Aisling's bedroll and decided to make it an early night.

Aisling didn't sleep well. She had stayed up most of the night just staring into the darkness and trying to understand what the Prophet's cryptic warning meant. The words on the scroll were no longer inscribed upon the parchment, but they were indelibly etched into her brain. She wished they had been more clear.

The next day, the two companions packed up in silence and made their way to the next village. Like the first, this village was quiet and unnerving. There were a couple small farm stalls set up and the people who manned them were selling all the basics: eggs, dried meat, fruits, and vegetables. Aisling decided it was time to learn a bit more about what was really going on and walked up to the friendlier-looking of the two stall owners.

"Good morning," she said, genially.

The woman looked to be in her late thirties. She was skinny and harassed-looking, and had bags under her red-rimmed eyes. She grimaced at Aisling's approached, but it seemed involuntary, and she managed a small smile as she replied, "Good morning, miss. What can I get you today?"

Aisling had no money yet. She wasn't even sure what sort of currency they used in the Seven Realms. She assumed it was like home and that gold and silver were the obvious choice, but she wasn't about to trade away her one gold coin for some eggs and potatoes.

"I apologize for asking, ma'am, but what seems to be the trouble around here?" she asked, trying her best to seem braver than she felt.

The woman's slim smile turned into a frown and her sad eyes searched the area rapidly for a moment. She looked down and began busying herself by rearranging some of the potatoes.

"Nothing," she said plainly. "Nothing's wrong here. Nothing at all. Would you be wanting some green beans? Two coppers for a satchel. It's a good bargain..."

Aisling looked plaintively at the woman. "Ma'am, please. I just want to help."

The woman closed her eyes and shook her head as if she were trying to get an insect off her face. Then, she slammed her calloused hands onto the stall table.

"No one can help!" she shouted.

She scooped what little wares she had into a bushel and then, picking up her dirty skirts, hurriedly walked off in the opposite direction.

"What is going on?" Aisling asked Hoegabbler, who even as a cat seemed flabbergasted by the woman's sudden outburst.

"She's just upset," said a deep voice beside Aisling. "The curse has already taken her husband and the life of one of their children."

Aisling turned to see the voice's owner, he was a broad man, not tall, but not short either.

His skin was deeply tanned and his hair was long, curly, and brushed back tightly in a neat ponytail. He wore a tan buckskin tunic, brown breeches, and scuffed leather boots.

On his shoulders was a thick, gray animal pelt, which was held across his chest by a buckled leather strap.

"Sad, sad story that one. These days, it's hard to believe how happy this place used to be.

You're new to this village, aren't you?" said the man.

His voice was deep and soothing, and had an almost relaxed air about it, which amidst the worried, shaky voices of all the other people Aisling had met in Stonewall so far, made it stand out. He smiled at her as he spoke and his teeth were gleaming and white. His nose was wide and squarish, but suited his broad face.

His eyes were his most striking feature, however. They were gray, like the pelt, but shone with flecks of dark and light. They reminded Aisling of the shadows that appeared on the moon on clear nights.

"Yes," replied Aisling. "I'm just passing through."

Believing that it might be prudent not to tell any large, burly-looking men where she was going, Aisling decided to omit any further information about her business.

"These are dangerous times for a girl like you to be traveling alone. Even one so armed," said the man, gesturing to the sword that hung at her side. "My name is Lucas Rogauru. I'm sort of the law around these parts, the unofficial sheriff if you will. What is your name, dear one?"

He smiled then. It was a leering smile, a predatory one, the type of smile that Aisling, young as she was, had seen on the faces of men like him many times before. She wanted no part of what was offered by that smile. Still, what was most important at that moment was getting out of that situation before things got any worse.

"Aisling Mason, sir," she replied politely. "And I really must be going."

She went to turn around and leave, but felt the man lay a forceful hand upon her shoulder.

At her feet, Hoegabbler hissed and spat angrily. The man released her.

"My apologies, dear one," he said, and there was a note in the apology that Aisling could tell was far from sincere. "I shall not keep you any longer, then. I do hope we'll be seeing each other again soon."

With that, the man gave a slight bow and walked over to the other stall, where he proceeded to help the elderly owner to carry her overlarge basket of meat pies. Aisling gave a slight shudder.

"I'd hate to run into him on a dark night," she said.

"Agreed. We should be going anyway, Aisling. We still have a couple more patches of forest to get through and a few villages before we get to the border," suggested Hoegabbler.

She nodded and the two kept right on walking. As they reached the village gates, Aisling noticed the man come out of a small shack set some distance into the woods themselves. The old woman followed him out and handed him what looked like a small, wrapped parcel before waving him goodbye. Aisling picked up the pace.

By the time the two had finished dinner it seemed the discussion from the night before had ebbed away along with Aisling's worries. Whatever the scroll's warning meant, it was no concern of hers, not really. She had to get home, that was the important thing, the only important thing as far as she was concerned.

If her "standing up" to the terrifying sheriff was any indication, she was not the hero the Crones believed her to be.

"Lookit that," said Hoegabbler, who had transformed into a sort of squirrel at this point. "It's going to be a full moon tonight."

"I've always liked the full moon," said Aisling.

The nights back home when the moon was full were always so much brighter. Even here, in the shadow of yet another strange, sad, cursed village, it was comforting to know there was a bit more light shining on their campsite. The two companions sat together, watching as the moon made its way over the trees and soon it become an illuminated circle in the star-strewn sky.

It looked almost exactly like the moon back in her world, and Aisling wondered if it was actually the same moon. She wondered if the worlds on either side of the hedge shared things like the moon and the sun and stars. She hadn't recognized the stars yet, but she assumed that maybe things were reversed here, as in a mirror. Aisling's concentration was suddenly broken, however, by the sound of something howling far away.

One by one, distant wolves began howling in the night, their cries echoing the first in rapid succession. Hoegabbler had jumped down from the tree and had turned back into the rabbit. He stood on his hind legs, his long ears perked up and listening intently to the echoing howls. Within minutes, the mostly silent night was awash with the sounds of braying wolves. The sound was unnatural and it made Aisling shudder. Inside her head, the Prophet's words repeated themselves,

...her wolves and monsters crave their flesh...

"Hoegabbler," she said worriedly. "We need to move. We shouldn't stay here."

The changeling nodded and transformed to help her pack up their small encampment. As he helped her stuff her bedroll back into her bag, his ears twitched. Almost instinctively, he transformed back into a rabbit, and scurried behind her legs.

Aisling looked around, trying to find whatever it was that had made him so frightened.

She drew her sword, rather clumsily and held it out in front of her, peering into the moonlit forest for whatever was lurking in the impenetrable shadows of the trees. There was a snarling from the grove in front of them, followed by the heavy breathing of something huge and predatory.

She had never seen a bear before, but Jonathon had described their size and ferocity to her in stories. She wondered if the hulking monster before them was a bear, but reasoned that even if it was, she didn't know what she could do about it either way.

Out of the woods the creature crept. It was large as two men, much bigger than any wolf Aisling had ever heard of, and yet it still looked lupine. Gobs of shimmering drool dripped from its long muzzle full of sharp teeth. The creature's arms ended in large, humanoid claws, but its hind legs were elongated like those of an animal. It looked somewhat crooked, like if it wanted to support its prodigious bulk, it had to walk on all fours. It had a long, furry tail and was covered from head to toe in thick, gray fur.

Its eyes seemed to glow with the same intensity as the

moon above, almost as if the moon itself was reflected through them. The wolf roared at them, a ferocious, inhuman bark filled with rage and hunger, and something else Aisling couldn't place. In seconds, the great beast was bounding towards them across the clearing. Hoegabbler, unable to stop himself, darted off in the opposite direction, scurrying through the dark woods at breakneck speed. Aisling spun around the tree, dropping her bag onto the ground.

The wolf's claws scraped against the tree bark as it missed her, sending chunks of wood flying in all directions. Aisling knew that even if she had been a skilled warrior, she would have no hope of fighting this creature. Whatever this wolf creature was, it was wild, unhinged, and it was hungry.

Aisling ran for it, ran deeper into the forest, deep in the darkest part of the woods she could find. Behind her, she could hear the wolf running, too, its great claws scraping up chunks of earth as it bounded after her.

She weaved and dodged around the trees, hoping the animal would become too entangled within them to keep going. The wolf's panting was still close to her though, and as she made her way over and under the tangle of branches, she could hear it crashing through them in her wake. It roared again, and Aisling felt flecks of its hot spittle smack against the back of her neck.

She turned left, ducking behind a rowan tree and trying to make her way back to where she had been. She was trying to lead the wolf in the wrong direction, hoping it would get too turned around to bother pursuing her. She heard a smack and the sound of a yelp, followed by an angry howl. Then, the sound of four running paws picking up speed behind her.

Despite her attempts to serpentine away, the wolf was still following closely. In her pocket, the nightingale was chirping worriedly. Aisling couldn't think, she had to keep running, but her own breaths were coming raggedly now. A painful stitch was growing in her side as she made her way through the forest, and she was becoming more and more lost with each passing second.

She tumbled out into another clearing and stopped for a moment to get her bearings. It was too late, the wolf appeared out of the forest, not ten feet behind her. It was panting and drooling, its eyes were burning. It shook its head and roared and leapt towards her. Aisling ducked and rolled just in time. The wolf had overestimated her location and missed her, but just barely. Unable to get to her feet, Aisling slashed at the animal's back leg, but missed as it turned swiftly to meet her gaze. She could smell its rancid breath.

She got to her feet and tried to run, but the wolf leapt again and cornered her escape.

Aisling braced herself for another attack, hoping that the creature wasn't smart enough to anticipate her using the same move again. All of a sudden, Aisling heard another strange sound echo through the night. It sounded like someone blowing a horn.

The sound of hammering hoofbeats sounded through the clearing and suddenly the two of them were surrounded by half a dozen people on horseback, each of them wearing a crimson cloak. Each of the cloaked riders held a bow, knocked and trained on the hulking wolf creature. The wolf let out another roar of anger and the riders loosed their arrows. In an instant, the monster was knocked onto its side, with half a dozen arrow shafts sticking out of its hide.

The wolf let out a whine of pain and anguish, and for the first time, Aisling felt a little sorry for it. She dared not move, however, but stayed kneeling where she was, sword tip pointed out, in case the prone wolf decided to go for one last grab at her. It wouldn't get the chance.

The riders had knocked their arrows again and were firing wave after wave of them into the wolf. After the third volley, they stopped, and the pincushion that was once the wolf lay bleeding on the forest floor.

Its breathing was coming in ragged bursts now and it moaned and whined as if it couldn't help itself. A moment later and the sound stopped. The wolf was dead. Aisling slowly got to her feet and stared at the beast, which now that she saw it up close, was almost as big as the troll had been.

Suddenly, the wolf began to transform. The girl watched in wonder as the beast's furry skin seemed to melt away before her very eyes. Its back legs became human legs, its back flattened and became a man's back, dark and deeplytanned. Its once-wolfish face slid away from its skull to reveal the long, messy ponytail, squarish nose, and impossibly white teeth of Rogauru, the man from the village.

"The curse..." Aisling whispered aloud.

"Yes," said a strict-sounding feminine voice atop one of the horses.

The crimson-cloaked figure stowed her bow in her saddle and jumped down. She walked towards Aisling, her face still partly shrouded by the red cowl attached to the cape. She was not as tall now as she had looked atop her steed, but though she was barely Aisling's height, she looked no less imposing.

She pulled down her red riding hood to reveal a headful of golden curls and a pair of intense blue eyes. She surveyed Aisling for a moment before motioning to one of the other riders to throw her something. The man atop the steed pulled down his own hood, to reveal what was plainly her blond -haired, blue-eyed, male counterpart. Then he reached back into his saddle, pulled out Aisling's bag, and tossed it to her.

"Put this on and let's go," commanded the woman. "We should not linger here during the full moon."

Aisling slung the pack over her shoulder and followed the woman back to her horse. After helping her up and onto the large, chestnut horse, the curly blonde-haired rider hefted herself onto the saddle as well.

"Let's go," she said.

And the group of them rode off into the darkness.

Chapter Seven

The Red Riders

hey rode through the night for a long time, the riders remaining completely silent the whole while. Though her mind was awash with a thousand questions, Aisling remained quiet as well. She hoped that Hoegabbler was all right. She didn't blame him for fleeing as he did. After all, he had already saved her life once since they had met, and really, what was he going to do against the wolf man?

Eventually, the riders left the forest path and made their way into an open field, it was the first field Aisling had laid eyes on since she had arrived in the Seven Realms. Like the moon and the people, the field reminded Aisling of the world she came from, the world she knew.

They rode over hill and dale, through farms and past distant villages, until they came to what looked like some sort of large encampment.

The camp was filled with structures that looked like a

cross between tents and shacks.

There were also a number of run-down wooden carriages there, too, their wheels too damaged to carry them any longer. It looked as though they had been there for some time, and many of them were slightly sunken into the muddy earth, or else listing at strange, though stable angles. Broken carts filled with barrels, bushels, and boxes could be seen here and there, though Aisling could not tell what their contents were.

The riders slowed to a trot as they entered the camp and those few people who had stayed behind regarded them with a cautious air, though it was not the slightly xenophobic air that Aisling had encountered in the other villages. The blonde girl and her brother stopped their horses beside a blacksmith's forge, and the rest of the riders walked on.

Aisling's escort hopped down from her saddle and extended a hand to help her down. She accepted and tried her best to climb down with even half as much dexterity, but failed. She slipped and fell hard onto her knees. Her legs muscles were still a bit wobbly and Aisling had never been good on a horse, even when she rode with Jonathon. The girl sighed and helped her back to her feet.

"What in the world were you doing back there, little girl?" said the blonde-haired girl. Her accent had a trace of something foreign to it. Aisling was never good with accents, but if she had to try and place it, she would have guessed it to be Germanic.

"I was..." began Aisling, and then she realized that she was slightly offended by the fact that the woman, who couldn't have been that much older than her, had called her a 'little girl'.

"I am traveling to Caerleon," she finished.

"Why in the world would you want to go there?" asked the blond boy, and Aisling could tell by his accent that he was most certainly related to the girl.

"I have my reasons," Aisling replied, defensively. "...thank you both, by the way. I don't know what would have happened if you hadn't showed up."

"You would have died," said the girl.

"May I ask who you all are?" asked Aisling. "We're the Red Riders," said the boy. "Who are the Red Riders?" she asked again.

The curly-haired blonde rolled her eyes and huffed. Then she began fiddling with her horse's saddle.

"Forgive my sister's rudeness," said the boy. "My name is Hans, she is Gilda. We, and those we ride with, patrol the countryside saving those like yourself from the cursed minions of the Lady of Beasts. We had actually been hunting the one who attacked you for almost two moons now. It's almost impossible to tell them apart from normal people during the day."

It occurred to Aisling that this might be the reason why the people living in the villages she had passed had been so wary of strangers, and indeed each other.

"So, during the day," said Aisling, knitting the whole theory together in her mind. "They look like normal people and during the nighttime they transform into...what, wolf people?

Monsters?"

"Not just wolves, but they are the type we have seen the most of. They turn into all manner of half-animal beasts.

They transform every night, but they are especially active and powerful when the moon is full," replied Hans, and he pointed up at the full moon.

"Who is the Lady of Beasts?" asked Aisling.

"She is the source of the curse that has affected all of the people in this realm. Somehow, everyone she touches becomes a monster, a wild, feral thing like her. Those who they injure in the course of their nightly hunts, whoever they don't kill anyway, become cursed as well. It's been nearly a decade since the curse began affecting our people," explained Hans.

...And she will make a beast of thee...

There they were again, the Prophet's words, echoing in her mind.

"It's been ten years since the curse took our parents away from us..." added Gilda. "It's taken a lot of parents, Gilda," said her brother. "And children, and friends. We do what we can to try and stop others from being affected by the curse, but nights like this are dangerous, even for us."

"And most of the time, the only thing we can do to help is kill the afflicted," said another rider, who had walked over to join their conversation.

"It's either that or they keep running rampant, hunting and killing and cursing everyone they encounter," said Gilda, and she could not keep the venomous tone from her voice.

It was clear that the loss of her family had affected her more deeply than it had her brother. Aisling was reminded of her own sense of loss and anger at the passing of her family. She remembered being angry at God, and angry at the people who might have spread the Sweat to them in the first place.

She was angry at her brother and sister-in-law for forcing them to leave, and even at herself, for having survived when the rest of them had died. She understood what Gilda was going through.

"Is there anyway to cure them?" asked Aisling. She felt foolish for even asking such a thing.

"There are rumors," replied Hans. "But if it all comes down from the Lady of Beasts, then the only way to cure the rest of them is to break the curse upon her first. And that would mean getting close enough to her to do it..."

"Which is impossible," added another nearby rider.

"It's not impossible. You cowards just don't want to try it," said Gilda, angrily. "How would we get close enough to the Snarling Manor even if we wanted to? If you

think the beasts out here are bad, you should hear some of the stories I've heard about the lands close to the manor," said Hans, with sufficient ire to match his sister's.

"That's enough for now. Girl, what is your name?" said another rider, who appeared to be the only one there with graying hair.

"Aisling Mason," she said.

"Where are you from, then?" asked Gilda. "You're obviously not from Stonewall. So where are you from?"

"Far from here," replied Aisling. "I'm very far from home. I was going to Caerleon in order to speak with the Queen and see if she can give me passage back to where I'm from."

Aisling wasn't sure they would believe her. Then again, these were people who rode on horseback and hunted wolf men, so they would probably believe quite a bit.

"Well, you won't be getting back there tonight," said the older man, kindly. "Gilda, she can stay with you and Hans for now. In the morning we'll take her to the nearest village. We can't take you much further than Mabaden, I'm afraid. As you can see, we have other things to tend to here. Rastel, Culver, and Chasseur, come with me, we need to finish the patrol. Hans, Gilda, you're off for tonight, take care of our guest."

With that, the elderly rider and three others jumped up onto their steeds and rode off into the night.

"Damn them," cursed Gilda. "Why do we have to babysit? We're the ones who tracked the big wolf. It's not fair."

"I know, Gilda. But part of why we're here is to help people and it's obvious our new friend needs some help," soothed Hans.

He smiled at Aisling. Hans was a round-faced young man, strong but not skinny, with crooked teeth and ample cheeks. His sister was his mirror image, only where Hans smiled, she scowled and where he was somewhat broad, she was only slightly curvaceous.

"Follow us, then," huffed Gilda.

The twins led Aisling to a sort of half-tent, half-shack at the far end of the encampment. They dropped their horses off at a paddock and removed their saddles, which they carried with them the rest of the way. The hovel was barely a dwelling, but it was more than enough for the twins. Once they moved their own bedrolls aside and made a place in the middle for Aisling, it looked practically cozy. It wasn't a problem, though, Aisling was used to sharing a small bedroom with twins who didn't exactly see eye-to-eye all the time.

Hans and Gilda removed their boots, weapons, and leather armor and set it just outside the shack, wrapping all of it neatly in their crimson cloaks. Aisling followed suit, though she didn't have a cloak to leave it in. She checked her pocket. The nightingale looked up at her and twittered quietly.

"Is that a bird?" asked Gilda, peering over Aisling's shoulder into her pocket.

"A nightingale," said Aisling. "It was injured when my nephew found it, so I was trying to nurse it back to health. I didn't mean to take it, but it sort of got pulled into this adventure same as me."

"It's a girl," said Gilda, laying down onto her bedroll with a hard thump.

Aisling hadn't even thought about what sex the nightingale might have been. In her mind, it was only with her until it got better. It wasn't like she was going to keep the poor thing as a pet or anything. She was going to get home and when she did, the nightingale would get home, too.

"The Queen isn't going to let you go home, you know," said Gilda, and there was a melancholy tone to her voice that Aisling hadn't noticed before.

"Gilda!" scolded her brother.

"Hans!" she returned, sitting up abruptly. "She might as well know the truth. There's no sense in having her go all that way for nothing. Even if you could get into the castle and see the Queen, which you won't, there's no sense in it. You might as well face the truth, Aisling. Like we did."

Aisling thought about retorting, but remained quiet. Then she said, "What are the rumors about breaking the curse?"

Suddenly, her satchel began to shake again. Hans and Gilda jumped to their feet. "What sorcery is this?" they asked, almost in unison.

"Hold on," said Aisling. "It's just trying to tell me something."

Aisling crawled over to the bag and opened it. Out flew the scroll, which floated this time and unfurled in the open air above them.

A blossom in a garden wall, that's guarded by a bramble sprawl, whose gentle touch will hexes break, or heal, or mend, or cure, or wake. Its petals an unearthly white, that fights the blight and blooms all night, and with it, you shall make things right.

The scroll fell to the ground and became inert. Aisling padded over to it, picked it up, and put it into her bag. Then, as if nothing had happened, she sat back down between the twins who had both drawn their daggers.

"Are you a witch?" accused Hans.

"What? No, I'm not a witch," replied Aisling.

"It makes sense now, that's why you want to go to the Queen's palace! You're a witch!"

Hans was shouting now, but rather than join in her brother's panic, Gilda walked over to him and placed her hand over his mouth.

"Hush now. We don't want to cause a panic. I don't think you're a witch, girl, butBut I wonder if you could explain what just happened," she said.

"When I arrived here from far away, another world

entirely, I was taken by a friend to these old women…I think they were faeries. They told me I was destined to help save the Seven Realms and they gave me this scroll as a guide. It speaks to me, unbidden most times, and tells me things it thinks I should know. The problem is, I don't know what the clues it gives me even mean. I wasn't lying before, I was going to the Queen because I want to go home…I just want to go home," Aisling explained.

Hans pushed his sister's hand down and the two of them looked at one another for a moment while they considered Aisling's story. It was an incredible tale, an unbelievable one, but the rhyme she had heard from the magic scroll had reminded Gilda of something.

"The scroll was telling you how to beat the Lady of Beasts," said Gilda, with a note of clear certainty.

"It's just a rumor, Gilda," pleaded her brother.

"It's magic, Hans!" she insisted. "It spoke about the flower that everyone has been whispering about; the one that can remove curses. This girl is the key to finding it. She came here for a reason. We found her for a reason. Don't you see?"

Hans looked worried.

"If what that little prophecy says is true, the flower exists and it's not far from here. It's in the woodland realm," Gilda continued. "Come on, Hans. I'm tired of all this. I want it to end, I want to save our people. If there's a chance it exists and this girl can lead us to it, shouldn't we take that chance?"

Her brother considered her words for a moment while Aisling sat between them, clutching her scroll and wondering if this was really all happening for a reason.

"How are we even going to do this? Verdenwald is as

cursed as everywhere else, isn't it?" asked Hans.

"It's cursed in a different way. It's the silent kingdom, the sleeping realm. We can go in, steal the flower from the Gardener's Tower and leave. It'll just be the three of us, after all. The girl's skinny, she can probably get in and out way easier," Gilda explained.

"My name is Aisling," she interjected, irritably.

"Sorry," said Gilda. "Aisling, will you help us do this? I know you've no reason to. I know you're not from here. But I promise if you help us do this, we'll take you anywhere you want to go, to Caerleon, even."

"I would be glad to help...if you told me what exactly you're planning," said Aisling. "We're going to break the curse that lays on Stonewall. We're going to find the flower that your prophecy talked about and save our people."

"First, we're going to get some sleep, though. Tomorrow we'll sort out this scheme of yours," said Hans, begrudgingly.

Gilda stowed her knife and sat back down next to Aisling. Hans did the same. "All right. Tomorrow, then," said Gilda.

Aisling lay down beside the twins. Between the two of them, they had both saved and threatened her life on separate occasions that night. In addition, her journey home had become much more complicated. She wasn't sure that she would even be able to get a lick of sleep that night. Then, whether it was from the exhaustive and confusing conversation, or the general exertion of running for her life, not a minute after she closed her eyes, she fell asleep.

She dreamt of her home and of a farm overrun with

weeds that choked out all other life and ruined the crops. The weeds eked up the sides of the cottage and snuffed out the fire in their hearth. It was a dream she would never remember the full details of, but one that would, like all the dreams she'd had in the Seven Realms, wake her in the middle of the night with a sense of fear and foreboding.

Above them, high in the boughs of the trees and unseen by the now sleeping occupants of the little shack, a raven sat and watched intently. Its eyes were no better in the dark than anyone else's, but it was not really the raven who was watching them.

Elsewhere, a queen gazed into a looking glass. Her hair was as midnight black as the feathers of her ravens and her alabaster skin was as pale as the coming snows. She watched the sleeping stranger through the eyes of her minions and as she did, her blood-red lips curled back into a wicked smile. Whoever this child was, she was certainly worth keeping at least one pair of eyes on.

Chapter Eight

The Gallows Tree

he next day, Aisling awoke to the sensation of something small and jittery walking upon her chest. She sat up with a start and felt whatever it was fly off of her with a loud,

"Eeeeeeeeee!"

Across the room lay a funny-looking purple cat, getting to its feet. "Hoegabbler!" shouted Aisling. "Thank God you're ok."

"You too, Aisling…I'm sorry I ran. I just kind of…panicked," he apologized, walking back over to her. "It looks like these folks had things well in hand, though. Have they been treating you ok?"

"I'm well," she paused and looked around the shack.

Apparently Gilda and Hans had woken up earlier to get things ready for their journey. "The scroll gave me another rhyme last night. It spoke to me and the two riders about a flower they say is capable of removing curses."

"That would certainly be something. Do you mind at all if I continue to come along?" he asked, awkwardly.

Aisling smiled and gestured for him to come closer. She picked him up and pet him

gently.

"Of course not," she replied.

Aisling got up and found the twins right where she thought she might, saddling their horses at the small, makeshift stables.

"What's with the cat?" asked Hans

"He's my...um...my pet," said Aisling, unconvincingly.

"No, he's not," said Gilda in an exasperated tone.

Sensing that the ruse was already up, Aisling made the proper introductions and the twins reluctantly agreed to allow Hoegabbler to accompany them.

Hans walked off towards a cook tent and came back a few minutes later with three plates of food piled high. Each contained an array of strangely-colored sausages, a flaky, heavily buttered bread roll, and halfanapple. The sausages, though odd-looking, tasted delicious, very much like the homemade links Eleanor used to smoke in the springtime.

It seemed silly to her, but the thought of those sausages, their taste, their smell, only served to remind Aisling how very far from home she truly was. Still the Seven Realms were not so unlike her own. There were even some moments where she felt as if she might just be in a different country, not another world. Everything about the the encampment, the clothing, and the accents she had encountered in Stonewall were familiar and foreign all at once.

When they were done, Hans took the plates back and

Gilda continued to secure their saddles. Aisling got to her feet, but as she did so, her hastily tied scabbard fell from her belt and hit the ground with a metallic clatter. As she struggled to pick it back up and retie it, she caught Gilda looking at her in a bemused sort of way.

"What?" asked Aisling, somewhat peevishly.

"Do you even know how to use that thing?" chuckled Gilda, her head inclining in the direction of Aisling's sword.

Aisling looked down at the scabbard, and in doing so, lost her grip on the knot and dropped it again. Embarrassed, she hastily picked it up and tried again.

"Here, let me," offered Gilda.

The Red Rider walked over to Aisling and took hold of the sword, deftly securing it to her belt in a matter of seconds. She stood back and looked Aisling up and down.

"Let me see how you hold it," she said.

Aisling yanked the sword out of its scabbard and nearly sent it flying pommel-first at Hans as he approached. She scrambled and took hold of it, then stuck it out in front of her defensively.

"Gods above, no. Not like that," said Gilda.

She walked next to Aisling and manipulated her hand so that she held a tighter grip on the sword. She then lowered her arm and positioned the sword point so that it was facing both up and away from her.

"If you'd held it the other way, you'd likely have poked your own eye out. Remember to always hold tight to it. Know where your sword is and where it's pointing at all times. A warrior who loses their weapon is of no use to anyone," explained Gilda.

"She'll be fine. I can see it in her. Aisling's a proper warrior," chuckled Hans from astride his horse.

He gave Aisling a knowing wink.

"You can ride with me," said Gilda, as she hopped herself up onto her own horse's saddle.

Aisling hadn't noticed it the night before, but both Hans' and Gilda's horses were a fair bit larger than the average steed. Both were over sixteen hands high, much bigger than Missy the Mare on the Mason's farm back home. They were chestnut throughout with black manes and tails, white around their hooves, and Gilda's horse had a patch of white on its face.

"Don't be afraid of him, Aisling. He'll know if you're afraid," scolded Gilda. "Karl won't hurt a hair on your head. Will you, Karl?"

Gilda patted the big horse on the neck and Karl snorted happily. Warily, but more bravely than she had before, Aisling climbed up onto the saddle and settled herself behind Gilda.

Hoegabbler, unsure where to stick himself, transformed into his squirrel form and clambered up onto Aisling's shoulder.

"What is this Verdenwald like?" asked Aisling, after they had walked for about an hour. "It's a cursed place..." replied Hoegabbler in a mock spooky voice.

"Every place is 'a cursed place'," said Gilda.

"They say the lady who rests there was once a princess and that when she was born, her royal parents paid a great insult to a faerie witch who lived in the surrounding forest," continued the changeling.

"What sort of curse?"

"Like the others, no one knows exactly what the curse is. All anyone knows about the curse on Verdenwald is that one day the kingdom was as bustling as ever, and the next, it was silent...as the grave. They call the princess who used to live there the Lady of Briars."

"Why do they call her that?" asked Aisling. Hoegabbler shrugged.

"They call her that because the whole realm has been affected by some sort of blight.

Great vines of briars have infested most of the trees there, and it is spreading rapidly. Some of it has even bled into Stonewall," said Hans.

All of a sudden, the horses became uneasy. Aisling could feel her pack shake. "Another clue?" asked Hoegabbler.

"I suppose so..." she answered, while reaching into her satchel to pull out the enchanted scroll.

"Asleep within her forest tower, a lass of Briars gains her power. For as she rests, her bramble tomb, it spells her people's certain doom. They do not work, they do not live, they cannot wake, they only give, their lives to make the thorns increase, to spread, to grow without surcease. Until the world is strangled tight, an endless weed, an endless blight."

When it had finished, the Prophet became inert once more.

"Well, that's an illomen if I've ever heard one," said Gilda, sarcastically. "I guess they can't all be hopeful," added her brother with a chuckle.

Aisling was unsure what the twins found so funny about the scroll's latest cryptic message. As far as she could tell, they were walking into something much worse than the curse they were leaving behind. It wasn't until a few hours later that this fleeting feeling of dread would increase another tenfold.

The forest around them seemed to go on forever. It appeared that the field the Red Riders had set up camp in was the only such place for miles around. Aisling didn't know why, but she could tell the very moment the horses stepped into Verdenwald. The trees were denser here, wilder, more dangerous. The paths within the forest realm were narrower and more overgrown. It appeared that Hans had been right as well. Each and every tree looked as though it had been affected by twisting wicked-looking patches of vines covered in thorny briars.

The blighted briars seemed to choke the trees from the roots up, but they hadn't killed their hosts. Instead, the thorny vines engorged the topmost leaves of the trees. This new thicker canopy was so lush and healthy that it blotted out the sun almost entirely. It felt like the woods themselves were shrouded in perpetual twilight and that this was how the briars preferred it.

Even the air was heavier there. It was a place of suffocation and pain and darkness. If Aisling hadn't believed it was cursed before, she did now. In the sunless grove that made up the forest of Verdenwald, Aisling was beginning to think she had made a mistake agreeing to help them find that flower, but it was far too late to go back.

The deeper into Verdenwald they went, the more the narrowing paths of prickers began to clip and snag the horses' hides and their riders' cloaks.

"Gilda, I don't think Erik and Karl are going to be able

to go much further. We'll have to go the rest of the way on foot," said Hans, gingerly pushing a particularly sharp tree branch out of his way.

Gilda huffed. She hated to admit it, but Hans was right. There was no way they were going to make it to the Gardener's Tower on horseback, not when the forest became denser and more dangerous the closer they became.

"You're right," she acquiesced. "We walk from here. Whoa, Karl. There you go, boy."

She hopped down from the horse and helped Aisling. She then walked over to Hans and proceeded to tie Karl's and Erik's reigns to the most accessible tree she could find. She patted both horses gently, and pulled a short sword from her own scabbard.

Gilda's sword didn't look like Aisling's did. It was about the same length, but the blade was more curved and was almost fat at the pointy end.

"What kind of sword is that?" asked Aisling.

"It's called a Kopet. It's used for cutting through brush. Hans and I started carrying them when we first joined the Red Riders. You spend a lot of time in wild places when you're a ranger. It's helpful."

Hans took his own Kopet and slashed it across the thorn-filled vine that crossed the path ahead of them. The blade sliced effortlessly through the thick vine and it fell to the ground limply.

"They're gonna be damned helpful here," he said with a smile.

They walked on from there for what felt like hours. At first, Hans and Gilda seemed to know which way they were headed, but before long, the beaten paths that wended their way through the forest disappeared entirely. At some point, Hans looked up to try and reorient them using the sun, but the canopy cover and the tangle of vines above them made it impossible to determine which way they were going, or even if it was still daytime.

"Admit it," grumbled Gilda. "You're lost, aren't you?"

"I'm not lost, Gilda," he returned sharply. "I just need to find the sun…then I can figure out if we're headed east or west…"

"Oh, for God's sake, Hans, just admit it. We're lost. There's no way to know where we're even going at this point. There's no sun to find."

Gilda's short temper was beginning to get the better of her. Aisling didn't blame her, of course. This forest of thorns was a sharp and sunless place where shadows and silence seemed to lurk around every tree. It put every one of them on edge. Even Hoegabbler, who was generally as chatty as could be, walked gingerly around the forest floor, avoiding the trees entirely. And despite his former expertise for navigation in Stonewall, he was as hopelessly lost as the twins were.

"Aisling…Does the scroll say anything about a way of navigating us through this maze of pricker bushes?" whispered Hoegabbler.

Aisling shook her head. So far all the Crones' gift had done was to give them useless clues and rhyming riddles. She knew what she had to do, sure, but she still had no idea how to do it. Inside her pocket, the nightingale stirred and poked its head out. It twittered slightly, as if to call out for other birds, but received no reply from the surrounding wildlife.

She hadn't noticed it before, but now that she had taken a moment to stop walking, Aisling could tell that there was something unnerving about the sound of the forest as well. Besides the bickering siblings and the random tweeting of the bird in her pocket, there was no sound in Verdenwald. No natural sound anyway. There were no birds or insects, no babbling brooks, or even the whispering wind rustling through the leaves. Aisling wondered if the others had noticed it as well.

"Please stop," said Aisling.

Then she walked over to separate Hans and Gilda, who were now mere inches from each other's faces, and said again, "Listen."

The twins stopped for a moment and tilted their heads. Hoegabbler mimicked their movements.

"There's no sound," said Hans.

"There are no animals," added his sister. "We need to go back," said Hoegabbler.

"Even if we decided to just turn around and give up," replied Hans, while sitting down on a nearby log. "I don't think I could get us back to the horses. Let alone Stonewall. We'll continue forward, we'll have to come upon some sort of village or shelter at some point."

Deeper and deeper they went, deep into the eerie forest. Aisling felt claustrophobic. The endless ranks of trees that stood about them were inescapable. They barred their way back and restricted the way forward.

"Hans, how big is this forest?" asked Aisling, hoping to break the foreboding silence.

"Larger than anyone would admit," he began. "The Woodland Realms, meaning both Verdenwald and most of Stonewall, is the largest forest in all the Seven Realms. It's so big that if you saw it on a map, you'd only be looking at a glimpse of a fraction of what its actual size is."

"How do you know where you're going if the map is wrong?"

"The map isn't wrong, exactly. There's just too much untamed forest to map properly.

Gilda and I can track because we've lived in the wild for years. That's how we get around. Also, we've been through a good deal of Stonewall's forest. After a while, you remember trails, landmarks, that give you an idea of how far you are from a place.

I suspect that's how the folks in Verdenwald do it, too. The main castles of the Realms are sort of like landmarks, they give mapmakers a clue as to the distance between them. Villages are the same way. It's only the untamed, unsettled places that remain a mystery, and there are plenty of those left; especially since the curses came down," Hans continued.

"Looks like they're all untamed now," said Hoegabbler, gesturing towards the thick, bramble-coated trees.

"Looks like..." agreed Hans.

Begrudgingly, the companions walked onward. They were looking for a castle, which they presumed had to stick out even in the gloom of the forest. If it was anywhere near them, they would certainly find it. What they found instead was a low rock wall, which jutted out of the ground out of nowhere and appeared to be the entrance to a strange clearing. It was the only such clearing that they had come upon since they had abandoned the horses, and standing menacingly at its center, was a great, leafless oak tree on a small hill.

The tree was the largest, most twisted-looking thing Aisling had ever set eyes upon. Even in a forest of gnarled, overgrown trees, this one stood out. Its bark was gray and lined, and pockmarked by knotholes. Its branches were bereft of even the smallest leaf, but they were long and strong, and tipped by sharp edges that curled downward like thin fingers. From a distance, they looked liked the long, fiendish legs of some giant oaken spider.

The most jarring aspect of this already jarring tree were the nooses, dozens upon dozens of them, hanging from its fearsome branches; the menacing reminders of hangings longpast.

Aisling had thought the tree was dead at first, but if it had served as a hanging tree at one point, then the boughs must have been mighty strong indeed. Still, she wagered by the state of the ropes, that it hadn't been used for that purpose in a long, long time.

"What is this thing?" she asked.

"It's called the Gallows Tree," said Gilda, nervously. "I'd heard of it, but I didn't think it was still here. I thought they'd cut it down ages ago."

"Looks like they tried," said Hoegabbler, who was running his paw along the roots and trunk.

He shivered and backed away from the tree. "Who did they hang?" he asked.

"Witches," said Hans, harshly.

"How many witches were hanged from this tree, I

wonder?" Aisling inquired.

"Not enough," replied Hans, and there were angry lines etched into his normally boyish face.

"Maybe that was the disrespect the Royals had shown the faerie witch. The killing of her kin," surmised Aisling.

"Couldn't have been. They hanged witches from this tree for hundreds of years before that. The way Gunter used to tell it, Verdenwald has never been fond of any magic in their realm," Gilda explained.

"There's magic everywhere though, how do you even manage to keep it away?" "You kill all the witches," said Hans.

Aisling tried to imagine what Hans could have been through to have developed such an intense hatred of witches. She had always been taught that they were not to be trifled with. Even in her world, where the witches were mostly just women who knew folk medicine and remedies, they were outcast, despised, servants of the Devil.

"Obviously that's not the answer," added Gilda.

Hoegabbler had transformed back into his changeling form and was kneeling in front of the tree, looking solemn and running his hand through the overgrown grass.

"A lot of blood was spilled here," he said, quietly. "Innocent blood." "If they were witches, then none of them were innocent."

Hoegabbler turned to face Hans. His overlarge eyes were brimming with tears, but he seemed more angry than hurt.

"Many of them weren't witches. They just thought they were, and they hanged them anyway."

All of a sudden, Aisling thought she saw something stir

out of the corner of her eye. The crooked, fingerlike tips of the Gallows Tree's branches seemed to twitch for a moment. At first, she thought it might be the wind, or a trick of the shadowy light filtering in from the thick wood around them. But there was no breeze blowing through the forest that night.

The sound of creaking wood echoed through the clearing. Above them, the skeletal limbs of the Gallows Tree began to shudder and strain as if they were waking up from a long sleep. At the same time, the nooses upon the tree began to shake and undulate like grayed, fraying serpents.

Hoegabbler jumped to his feet and transformed into his rabbit. Hans and Gilda each drew their swords and stepped almost reflexively in front of Aisling, who had drawn her sword as well, but was much less confident in her ability to use it than they obviously were.

"Stay behind us, Aisling!" shouted Gilda.

The many limbs of the Gallows Tree began to turn in their direction, but they weren't the only things. Even the roots of the tree started to shift position. They pulled themselves out of the uneven soil beneath it, breaking through the dirt and stone and pulling up chunks of earth as they made to drag the immense oaken monstrosity towards them.

"It can walk?" yelled Aisling, despite herself.

"It can do more than that," replied Gilda. "Back up and out of the clearing, we've obviously disturbed something here."

No sooner had she uttered the words though, than the brambles that had coated the rock wall rose up themselves to block their path. There was no way out of the clearing.

"How do we fight a tree?" said Hoegabbler.

The changeling had turned into his cat form and from what Aisling could tell, it looked as though he was doing his best to change into a slightly bigger version of it, but was failing to do so.

With each passing moment, the Gallows Tree was creeping closer and closer to them. Its branches had gone from merely looking like wicked spidery claws to becoming them. They reached towards the companions, grasping at them and trying to pull them towards the center of the tree itself. The Gallows Tree moved slowly, inching its way towards them. Behind it, massive roots dug long troughs into the earth, and it was inside those great trenches, that Aisling first saw the bodies.

Gilda and Hans began to fight back the encroaching branches, slashing at them with their kopets and hacking them off whenever they got close enough to snag upon a piece of cloak or clothing. Aisling, however, could only stare down in horror and disbelief at the countless skeletons being unearthed by the tree's slow egress.

Skulls, femurs, ribs, vertebrae, hands, feet, and teeth beyond counting, emerged from the ground where the Gallows Tree had once stood. They rolled from their burial places, down the eroded hill and towards the gathered companions. Aisling, terrified by what was happening and unsure of what she could even do to help, slashed wildly at the air with her short sword.

Clang!

The sword slammed into Gilda's kopet, knocking both

weapons to the ground.

"What are you doing, girl?" yelled Gilda. "Just stay behind us and don't bother. We'll get us out of this."

She rolled over to where the weapons had fallen and grabbed hold of both hers and Aisling's swords. She got to her feet just in time to catch one of the tree's wildly flailing branches right in the chest. It knocked her on the ground and the two swords once again tumbled from her grasp. The Gallows Tree had knocked the wind out of her and as she sat there, gasping for air, it reached down with a spidery, clawed bough and pulled her up into the air by her red cloak.

"Gilda!" shouted Hans, who was busy on his end of the tree, hacking off limbs as best he could.

Aisling knew it was her only chance to do something, to help. Steeling herself, she dove to grab the fallen swords. She rolled as she grabbed her sword, only narrowly missing the one of the tree's huge, grasping branches. She reached up while still on her back and slashed the branch clean off.

In the boughs above her, Gilda was being held by two separate branches, both of which were inching her towards one of the many hanging nooses. Hoegabbler, who had leapt upon the tree now, was still a cat, only a slightly bigger one. He was successfully beating back several branches, which seemed more concerned with the humans than himself. He noticed what was happening and with remarkable grace, the changeling ran towards Gilda, deftly dodging all the ropes in his way. He slashed at the boughs around her, scratching the spindlier ones and forcing them to relinquish their hold on the Red Rider.

Meanwhile, Aisling was on her feet again, and had

managed to flank the tree. It was now attacking them from both directions and its roots were moving along with it, frenziedly ripping in and out of the ground. Human remains littered the entire clearing and as the tree thrashed wildly, its stomping, pounding roots were making short work of the ground itself. Aisling narrowly avoided falling into a chasm of bones that opened like a sinkhole behind her.

"Aisling!" called Hans. "Move back towards me! Once we get it to the brambles, we can make our way back up the hill! Hoegabbler, get her down, we need her sword!"

"Working on it!" groaned the changeling, who was clearly growing more and more exhausted with each swipe.

Aisling did as she was bid and moved towards Hans, hopping her way around the roots as they flexed up and down. She heard a snap above her and watched as Gilda fell through the branches and back to the ground, landing with a thump on her behind. Her momentary distraction was her downfall, however. The root that Aisling thought she had bypassed lifted itself out of the earth and as she shifted onto her back leg, she tripped over it.

As she tumbled into the sinkhole, which appeared to be far deeper than even she could have believed, she tried to reach for the tree root. It was no use. She had fallen too far and too fast for her free hand to grab onto anything. She screamed, then took one last look at the world above before falling into the darkness beneath.

Chapter Nine

~

The Three Serpent Broach

isling awoke to a strange sensation on her face and a twittering sound in her ear. She was lying flat on her stomach on the cold, hard ground and the nightingale was perched upon her face, pecking at her cheek and tweeting dolefully. She shifted a bit and managed to get onto her hands and knees. Her whole body ached from head to toe. Once she managed to get into a sitting position, she patted the bird on the head, placed it upon her shoulder, and tried to get a better sense of her surroundings.

The chamber she was in was pitch black. She knew she was on some kind of stone floor, but she could not see what sort of stone it was. She looked up, hoping to see the chasm she had dropped in from, but found only more solid blackness through which not even a speck of starlight could be seen.

"Where are we?' she said aloud.

Her voice echoed throughout the cavern.

The nightingale on her shoulder twittered in response.

Aisling moved her arms around on the ground beside her, feeling for her pack and, more importantly, her sword. When she had found both she got to her feet. The cave around her smelled of damp and masonry dust. There was some other scent too, a tinge of something sweet and sour on the air. She hoped it wasn't what she thought it was.

The cavern around her was impossible to judge from her location, so she moved in one direction until she found a wall. When she was sure it was solid, she began running her hands along it, hoping to find some sort of indication that she was somewhere. It was cold stone, like the floor, and felt hewn, not natural. She hoped that there would be an opening soon.

"Help! Gilda! Hans! Hoegabbler!" she shouted.

There was no reply besides her own reverberating voice.

Aisling wandered in the dark for a long time. She took small steps, careful to detect any dips or holes in the stone floor beneath her boots. She moved slowly and as she did so, she thought dark, fearful thoughts; things she hadn't had much time to think on before that moment.

Everything about her situation had happened so quickly, one harrowing event flowing seamlessly into another, not allowing for any sort of introspection. There, alone in the dark, was the first chance she had found since she arrived in the Seven Realms to take stock of what had happened to her. All of the bleak emotions, all the fear, loneliness, sorrow, and confusion, came back to her all at once and Aisling found herself stopping.

She wanted to cry, to sob, to let everything out and just crawl into the strong, reassuring arms of her eldest brother until it all melted away. But Jonathon Mason was not in that dark place. Jonathon was home, in their cottage, with his wife and children, far, far away from any place Aisling could reach. She cried quietly to herself. Sobbing into the dark. Finally, exhausted by her ordeal, she slid down the wall until she was sitting, and fell asleep.

She awoke some time later, though she had no idea how long, and got to her feet. She continued edging her way in the direction she had gone in before, hoping to find something, anything that might give her a clue as to where she was and what she should do next. Finally, after a few more minutes of groping in the dark, she found a door-sized opening.

Aisling walked through it and along what felt like another hallway until she came to another archway into what felt like another room. She wondered if she was in a labyrinth of some kind. Grasping around the perimeter of the room, she felt what appeared to be rusted, iron sconces set into the walls. They held no candles, nor any torches that she could feel, but were clearly designed to have done so at some point. Eventually, after making her way around the room, she found another passage into a long hallway.

Her eyes had become accustomed to the darkness by then, but she still didn't know which direction she ought to go in. She assumed that going back would only lead her to the bottom of the unscalable pit she had fallen through, so she pressed forward. Even if she found a dead end, at least there would be an end. As she moved into the new hallway, she noticed something shimmering in the distance.

She rubbed her eyes and realized that it wasn't a trick, but flickering lights that appeared to have been set into the impenetrable darkness. She moved towards the lights, casually slipping the nightingale back into her apron as she did. Her free hand held her sword, which was drawn and ready to greet whatever she found in that dark, foreboding place.

As it happened, the light she had seen had come from a single guttering candle, set in a wax-encrusted sconce on the stone wall. The room that lay beyond the candle was well-lit by a dozen or so such candles, many of them burned down almost to the nub.

In the center of the room was a large, ornate casket, trimmed in gold and brilliantly painted. Beside it was a tall, wooden chair, almost like a throne. The rest of the room was a mishmash of chests, barrels, and baskets. An elderly-looking man, dressed in light armor and a fraying, gray tunic, was walking about the chamber reading a well-worn book by the light of the slowly burning candles. He did not bother to look up from his page as he said,

"Welcome, child. You can sheath your blade. I mean you no harm." Aisling did so.

"Pardon me, sir...I didn't mean to interrupt your, um...vigil. But I'm afraid I've been separated from my friends. We were fighting this tree..." began Aisling, but even she didn't believe the words she was saying.

"I heard a commotion near the Gallows Tree. Apparently your presence here has awakened something. It has been a long time since any of the trees stirred. The Lady of Briars must be sleeping restlessly."

"I am not sure I understand...ow," Aisling winced as she took a step towards the man.

Pain, which she hadn't noticed before, shot up from her ankle and into her back. A moment later and that one injury sparked the realization of half a dozen more. Her hands, her shoulder, even one of her ribs, all felt bruised. She wondered how far she had fallen into that pit.

"Please, Sir, I must get out of here...wherever here is."

"If there's a way out of this tomb, I'm afraid I don't know it. I am not supposed to know it."

Aisling was confused and a little irritated. The old man seemed pleasant enough, but like everything in the Seven Realms, he spoke in riddles. He, like so many others, seemed beholden to some sort of law or code that prevented him from pointing her in the right direction. Realizing that the old knight might have been affected by whatever curse had been laid over Verdenwald, she pushed down her agitation and took a deep breath.

She felt as though exasperation and injury were washing over her again and she stumbled slightly, but managed to grab hold of the wall to steady herself. The old man closed his book and shambled over to her.

"Come," he said gently. "Sit here."

The man led Aisling by the arm over to the chair and sat her down in it. He walked to a barrel, pressed the tap, and poured a measure of some liquid into an old cup, which he then gave to her. Aisling looked up into the man's eyes. They were gray and heavily lined. These were eyes that had seen many difficult years come and go, but there was an amiability behind them, something she knew she could trust. She took the cup and gratefully sipped down the clear, cool water.

"What is your name?" she asked, politely.

"It's been a long time since I've had need of a name," he chuckled. "They call me Ser Thomas, or rather, they used to. Though I suppose it would be Prince Thomas these days. What is yours?"

"Aisling Mason," she replied.

Aisling looked at the outfit the man was wearing. It was exactly what she expected knights to wear, what they always wore in all the old stories. His tunic and armor bore a strange insignia; an emerald three-headed serpent holding a dried, brown oak leaf in its central mouth. She didn't know what it meant, but she guessed it had something to do with his family.

"I thought there were only lords and ladies who ruled over the Seven Realms? That the king and queen sat at the center of it all and ruled the whole land."

"There are exceptions here and there. It's a long story," replied the man.

Aisling decided that she had time for a story. She wasn't going anywhere right away, not on that ankle. If Gilda, Hans, and Hoegabbler were alive, she would find them eventually. In the meantime, however, this Ser Thomas seemed more than glad of the company.

"I'd love to hear it…that is, if you're willing to tell it," she said. Ser Thomas smiled.

"I was a soldier, a hero. I fought bravely for the king of this land," said the knight. "This was a very long time ago, mind you, in the days when all the realms had their own kings and queens. We had been surrounded on all sides, many had fallen. I was the last one left to defend our king. I didn't care. I stood my ground, and the king stood his ground, and when the day was done, we two had prevailed. The war was won, and so the king told me I could have anything I wanted as payment for my good service. I chose his daughter, the princess."

Aisling was about to ask a question, but remembered how irritating it was to have people ask questions in the middle of a story. For the sake of politeness, she remained silent.

"The princess had her own stipulations for the marriage, though. I was a hero and a soldier, yet I had been born a commoner, and the princess did not think she should have to marry me. But a promise is a promise. She consented to the marriage on the condition that we loved each other eternally, with all our hearts, for all time. That we wake each day with love in our hearts, and bring that same love to our beds when it was time to sleep. That we give all of ourselves to one another so completely that should one of us die, the other would be buried alive with them to show their devotion. Smitten as I was with her grace and beauty, I agreed."

Aisling looked over at the ornate casket behind the man and she immediately knew how the story ended.

"How long ago did she die, your princess?"

"A long time ago, child. So very long ago that I've lost count of the years. When she died, many of those who knew us thought that I was mad to keep my vow. But a promise is a promise, after all. I consented to come down here, to be with her and live out my days in her service, just as I had vowed. My days just turned out to be greater in number than I'd anticipated."

The old knight chuckled.

"I'm sorry for your loss," said Aisling. "I know what it's like to lose someone you care about..."

"You're very young to have experienced such a loss."

"It was a plague that took them, my family. I think about it a lot, more than I should, considering what's been happening here. But I see so many in this place who have felt loss like mine. It's different, but it's not that different I suppose. Everywhere I go I find families who have been torn apart by calamities they have no control over."

The man was silent then. He got up and walked over to a large chest in the corner. Inside it were about two dozen or so wax candles, many of them already broken. It looked as though the chest had once held many other candles but was now down to a pitiful fraction of what he had once brought down there with him.

"What do you eat?" asked Aisling. She hadn't meant for it to sound so rude, but seeing the candles had put the idea straight to the forefront of her thoughts.

The man sat down and smiled. It was a grim smile, a platitude, and it didn't meet his eyes at all.

"I used to get supplies down here every now and then. But they stopped when the curse hit. I mostly eat insects now, rats, snakes, anything I can find. When they stopped coming, I planted some carrots and potatoes in a patch of dirt down that way. They have done well.

Problem is, I'm running low on steady crops thanks to the blight. I suspect my dearly departed wife and I will see each other soon enough."

Aisling tried her best to grin.

"The curse that has befallen this land is a severe one, and one that we truly deserved. My people did many terrible things before the new king and queen rose to power..."

"What sort of things?"

The knight looked ashamed, as if he didn't want to tell her what he knew. Aisling was certain that he was going to tell her about the hangings, about the witches they put to death and the blood that soaked the soil beneath the Gallows Tree.

"I understand," she said before he replied. She didn't need him to explain further.

"I heard rumors of the curse spreading long before it actually hit. Had I been there, I would have advised them to use the Remedy Bloom before it was too late."

"The Remedy Bloom? Is it a lily, by any chance?" asked Aisling.

"The most rare and powerful medicine in the entire Seven Realms. It sits in the Paradise Courtyard of the Gardener's Tower. It's the only one I've ever seen. It blooms forever, until it is used and then it won't bloom again for years. The king and queen who came after my bride's father, who took over when my beloved passed into the beyond, kept great care of it. He had been told a dark prophecy about his own daughter, the princess, Roselyn. He thought he might have need of it. I suppose the realization that the curse had happened came too late.

The prophecy revealed that the curse would come from, of all things, a spinning wheel.

He had them banned from the whole kingdom and so most of the people started getting their clothes imported from Gideon. It seems foolish, I suppose," said the mournful knight.

"Not so foolish. I take it she found a spinning wheel, then?" asked Aisling. "She must have, for the whole kingdom to have been cursed," he replied.

Aisling thought about destiny then. She looked down at her pack. Inside of it was a magical scroll that told her fortune. Well…what the scroll actually did was give cryptic clues about a destiny she had only just discovered was her own. Either way, it was not something she seemed to have much control over.

She wondered about the nature of the prophecies she had encountered, bout the Princess Roselyn who couldn't avoid the cursed prophecy, despite her father's intent to stop it. She wondered about self-fulfilling prophecy, about poor Ser Thomas, whose impossible promise allbut guaranteed his present fate.

She imagined destiny as some sort of raging, untamable river in whose current she was now caught. Maybe the truth of it all was that you can't avoid your destiny. All she could do was move with the flow of it and avoid the rocks. She stood up determinedly and hoisted the pack onto her back.

"Ser Thomas, I'm very sorry to have to do this, but I need to go. I have to find my friends. There has to be a way out of here. How did they used to bring your supplies down? Which way did they come from?"

"That hallway, but I've been down there many times before, there are no doors anywhere that I can see," he replied.

Aisling thought about it. Magic was plentiful here, it wasn't like back home. It wasn't a belief, wasn't disguised as religious miracles or strange happenstances. If the Seven Realms were what she was beginning to believe they were, then magic was imbued into all aspects of society. Even some of the lowborn folk could use it, or seemed to be products of it in some way.

She thought perhaps that if this knight and his princess were so important, then maybe they used magic to bring things down to the crypt. Of course, if that were the case, then she was trapped down there just like him. If it wasn't, she might still have a way out, so long as she found the door.

"Show me."

Ser Thomas lit two of the small candles and made his way back down the hallway that Aisling herself had passed through. Aisling looked carefully for any sign of a crack or space set into the stonework, but all she could see was the faint light of the candles shining upon the distressingly solid stone walls.

"They had to get down here somehow," she said aloud.

"There's a room up ahead," replied the knight. "Perhaps the servants came in that way."

They walked through the stone archway and into what Aisling could now see was a round room. It was different than the nearly identical hallways and the princess' crypt. She ran her hands around the perimeter, feeling carefully for anything that could help.

She almost didn't feel it at first, but there was an almost imperceptible differentiation in the stonework. Aisling brought her candle closer to it and examined the bump more closely. She brushed away the dust and to her delight, beheld the shadowy outline of a keyhole.

"It's a door!" she shouted, and it echoed throughout the empty catacombs. The old knight ambled up to the keyhole and held his candle closer.

"So it is…" he murmured.

"A key. Ser Thomas, did they give you any keys when they locked you down here?"

The knight's forehead creased. In the flickering, fading firelight, Aisling could see every line in his grizzled face. Then, recollection dawned in his faded eyes. He reached down to the worn, leather pouch on his belt and fished around inside of it.

"They said," recalled the knight as he continued to work his fingers through the pouch. "That I was only to use it in the most dire of circumstances. I had written it off as a bad joke and I'd allbut forgotten about it. Who needs a key when there's nothing to unlock? Ah! Here it is."

Ser Thomas was holding a small, metal key between his fingers. It was very old, and even in this light, Aisling could see that it was very rusted. If she wasn't careful, it might break off in the lock rather than open it. She didn't have a choice, though. Destiny was waiting for her, and hopefully, so too were her friends.

She took the key and placed it in the lock. Gingerly, as gingerly as she could, she turned it. The lock made a loud CLUNK and the wall before them opened up the space of an inch. A rush of cool, fresh air slid through the crack and into the hallway. Aisling slid her fingers in the space of the crack and pulled on the door with all her might. It was difficult, but after a few strong pulls, it came away from the wall, revealing an eight-foot space and a set of stone steps leading up. Aisling made for the stairs, then turned around to face the knight.

"Come with me," she pleaded.

"No, child," said the knight. "My place is here. I must keep my vow and you must find your friends."

"A promise is a promise, after all," said Aisling. The knight smiled.

"It was good to have met you, Aisling Mason." "An honor, Ser knight."

And with that, she walked up the stone steps and into the Gardener's Tower, to meet her own destiny head-on.

Chapter Ten

The Remedy Bloom

t the top of the spiral staircase was what appeared to be some kind of store room, though by the smell of its contents, it had been a good long time since any of it had been used. Crates and barrels of spoiled vegetables, rancid meat, stagnant mead, and weevil-infested grain were laid out all around her; each one having gone bad many years beforehand.

Aisling headed for the only door she could see, which thankfully happened to be unlocked. Before her was a great kitchen, the likes of which she had never seen before. Two hearths, each almost the size of her family's cottage stood like great, soot-filled caves set into the walls on either side of the room. A large, wooden table ran down the center, upon which were bowls and platters, plates, cups, jars, clay jugs, iron pots and pans, and woven baskets.

More jarring than the hundreds of abandoned cooking implements though, were the dozens of people slumped

beside them. Some of them had fallen asleep at the counter
and had the time and foresight to lay their heads down first.
Others lay sprawled on the ground, their limbs splayed out
at odd angles.

Aisling moved on through the abandoned kitchen and
out into the dining hall. The banquet hall was covered in
rotting food and there appeared to be at least a dozen diners
all asleep in their seats. Though their body parts did not
move at all, Aisling could see subtle changes in their
expressions. The cursed people of Verdenwald were sleeping
all right, but none of them were sleeping soundly.

She took a closer look at the sleeping denizens of the
Gardener's Tower and noticed that in addition to their
cursed and potentially nightmarish slumber, the people were
all covered with minuscule green vines. Each of those vines
was covered in hundreds of tiny, but very sharp looking
thorns. The wicked-looking vines snaked up and around
chairs, around limbs, across the floor, and back into cracks
in the castle masonry.

Aisling surmised that the brambles in the forest had
spread to the castle and that this was why the people
slumbered. Perhaps it was some sort of poison that coated
the vines. Whatever the reason, or wherever the origin of the
vines, Aisling decided that she ought not to touch them
lestest she too become cursed to sleep there forever.

Out in the main hall of the castle, Aisling heard the
sounds of movement. She tightened the grip around her
sword, and slowly made her way towards the large, wooden
doors. She peeked through the crack between them, hoping
that she could see something, anything before whatever was

out there made its way to her. A swath of crimson flashed before her eyes, followed by another. A second later and Aisling heard the familiar, slightly lisping voice of Hoegabbler.

"Do you think Aisling's ok?" he said.

"We can't worry about that right now," said a female voice.

Gilda's words were harsh, but felt right at home in her particularly tense tone of voice.

She sounded determined.

"There's no need for that…" said Hans' voice.

"We barely got away from that thing with our own lives, Hans," said his sister. "I can't worry about one little girl when the whole of our kingdom is dying. We know the Gardener's Tower has a garden in it. If there is a one-of-a-kind flower in Verdenwald, it must be here somewhere."

For a moment, Aisling considered not rejoining her comrades. She understood Gilda's reasons for saying what she did, but that didn't make it hurt any less. Shaking off her insecurities, she pushed open the door.

Hoegabbler jumped a full three feet up into the air and fell backwards onto his rabbity behind. Hans and Gilda, meanwhile, both had swords at the ready and turned to face their would- be attacker.

"It's me!" Aisling shouted, though she tried her best to keep her voice low. "It's just Aisling. I'm here. I'm safe."

Hans let his sword arm drop and Hoegabbler scampered over to her. Gilda, however, only allowed her arm to relax slightly. She was still very much on edge.

"What happened to you?" asked the changeling, while

simultaneously transforming into his humanoid form and pulling Aisling into a hug.

"I should ask you all the same thing," she replied with a smile.

"After you fell, we continued to fight the tree. Whatever curse had empowered it was strong. We were losing. After a few minutes of us losing actual ground, the earth gave way beneath it and it lost what was left of its root holds. Gilda, Hoegabbler, and I barely got out of the way before half the clearing fell into the same pit that had taken you. By the time the dust cleared, the entire clearing had caved in on itself," Hans explained.

"We couldn't even get down to look for you," added Hoegabbler, apologetically. "There was nothing to get," said Gilda. "We assumed you had been buried beneath the

tree and all the rubble. So we went towards the Gardener's Tower, which thanks to the tree being gone, was right through the next grove. We hacked our way through a veritable forest of brambles to get to it, but we finally reached the door. It was unlocked. As you can see, it's pretty easy to get into a castle when everyone is asleep."

Hans frowned at his sister and then looked back towards Aisling.

"Where did you go after you fell? How did you get into the castle?" he asked.

Aisling explained about the man in the tomb, the secret entrance and the Remedy Bloom and that they would find it in the Paradise Courtyard.

"I just don't know where it is," she added.

"Well," thought Hans. "We could head towards the

center of the castle. They call it the Gardener's Tower for a reason, right? Anything called 'Paradise Courtyard' must be central to a place like this."

The group moved forward, edging together into the ever-darkening castle. It seemed that the deeper they went into the keep, the more thickly the thorny vines clung to the walls. They didn't see many more people after that, but the few human beings they did happen upon seemed to be in much worse shape than the ones Aisling had encountered earlier.

These people were covered in blankets of briars blooming with tiny purplish flowers. They slept even more fitfully than the others, their heads and faces shaking and shifting into random, gruesome grimaces.

Hoegabbler stayed in his cat form for most of the trip, leading the way through the mostly dark hallways and indicating to them where the clearest footpath was. After a few minutes of walking in relative silence, Aisling could see a light in the distance.

Ahead of them was a portico into an open courtyard whose entrance was covered in long strands of hanging ivy. Unlike the wicked brambles rooted to the castle's walls and inhabitants, these vines were thornless and looked a healthy green color. Beyond the curtain of ivy, the sun shone brightly. Gilda, Hans, and Aisling stood before the vines, each of them unsure if they were safe to disturb. Finally, Hoegabbler swallowed hard and pushed his way through. A moment later and he was peeking his head back at them.

"It's fine, it's safe," he said, smiling.

Aisling and her friends walked through the veil of vines

and out into the courtyard.

Regardless of the state of the rest of the castle, it appeared that the garden that stood in the center of the Paradise Courtyard was every bit as beautiful as its name professed it to be.

Healthy oak trees, their deep leaves green as the first day of spring stood at various corners in the squarish courtyard. Unlike the twisted birch trees of the Verdenwald forest, every one of these trees was completely bereft of the blighting thorns.

The Paradise Courtyard was enormous, as large it seemed as even the largest farm. A wide expanse of healthy vegetables poked up out of rich, heady-smelling soil. Flowers bloomed on almost every surface. Roses and violets, posies, pansies, peonies, moon lilies and daylilies, bluebells and snowbells. If there was a flower somewhere in the world, it was there in that garden. It created a blended perfume that wafted about, different with each gentle blow of the breeze.

Then there were the groves of fruit trees. Apple trees, peach trees, pears, and plums; fruit the likes of which Aisling had never encountered, in all colors, hung fat and juicy-looking from strong, lively branches. The sweet scent of ripened sugars hung upon the air and it made Aisling's belly growl. She hadn't realized how hungry she had been. But the smell of such succulent treats was unavoidable.

Aisling marveled at the sight before her. Regardless of all the dreary, dreadful things she had seen on her way to that place, this view, this smell, this paradise, made it all worth it.

"Why isn't the blight affecting the garden?" asked Gilda, suspiciously. "It's enchanted," said Hoegabbler.

"Obviously," snapped Gilda. "But how is it enchanted? Where is the enchantment coming from? What happens to it if we try to take something out of this place, or if we try to eat something?"

At that moment, Aisling was walking towards a nearby apple tree. Its red, ripened fruit hung on low-hanging branches; the perfect height for a hungry traveler. Ignoring everything she knew about faerie tales and their lessons, Aisling reached up and took hold of one of the rosy-cheeked apples. It fell from its stem almost immediately. It was as if it had only been suspended there on purpose, waiting for Aisling to come along. She gazed down at its shining surface, and in its crimson sheen, her freckled face stared right back. She brought the apple to her lips.

Suddenly, the nightingale flew up and out of her pocket. It flapped and twittered madly in her face, forcing her to drop the apple on the ground. No sooner had the orb touched soil, than it rotted to the core. In the space of an instant, it had gone from rosy red and pristine to mottled gray and crawling with sickly-yellow grubs.

"What happened?" shouted Gilda.

"I was just...I couldn't help it. I was so hungry. I almost ate an apple. The nightingale stopped me..." replied Aisling.

Gilda shook her head and scowled.

"Smart bird. I'm not sure how, but I'm certain that the garden is as cursed as anything else in Verdenwald. Don't touch anything we don't have to. We're here for the flower, nothing else."

As harsh as Gilda's tone was, Aisling felt somewhat comforted by it. She reminded her of her older sister, Abigail.

Imperious, intense, and not at all to be trifled with when there were chores to be done. Even after she had gotten sick, she continued to push herself to care for the others and, of course, call out orders when she could no longer do things herself.

"Which one's the flower?" asked Hans, who was looking carefully at every flower as if he could tell from the outside which ones were magical.

When no one answered him, he directed the same question directly to Hoegabbler. "Why does everyone keep asking me this?" replied the changeling.

"I think that much is obvious," said Gilda. "If you don't know, then let's stop wasting time. Split up and look at each of the flowers."

And so they did, each of them taking it in turns to examine the countless varieties of flower within the courtyard's interior. Unfortunately for all of them, no one knew what a Remedy Bloom was supposed to look like. Hours passed and the sun began to set above the castle walls.

"We're never going to find it this way, Gilda," said Hans.

"Well, I can't think of a better way. Can you?" She returned irritably.

"What about your scroll, Aisling? Can't we just ask it what we're supposed to be looking for?" asked Hoegabbler who, now a rabbit, had bounded over to her.

"I don't think it works that way..." she began.

A sound echoed through the Paradise Courtyard then. A sad and beautiful song. Aisling felt a feeling of comfort welling up deep inside her. There was a longing in those twittering notes, something unspoken and familiar. It was a feeling that was bitter and sweet all at once. It crossed her heart half in hope, and half in despair. She had heard this birdsong before; on the day she had found the nightingale, the day before she had been brought to the Seven Realms.

Aisling and the others all looked up and around to find its source. The nightingale was sitting atop a branch above her, singing dolefully. Before she could move to say anything to it, the bird flew down and towards a grouping of flowering shrubs in the distance. The four of them chased after it, Hoegabbler leading the pack, until they came to the place where the bird had led them.

In the center of the small patch of vegetation, a flower bloomed. It was a lily, white and pure as fallen snow, with purple speckles dotting its pale petals. In its center, a sunbeam-yellow stamen gave off a faint golden glow. It bloomed full and bright on a single thornless stalk and stood out among the patch of crimson-red roses that surrounded it.

"That's it," said Aisling, breathlessly.

"How can we be sure, though?" asked Gilda.

"You said it yourself," replied Hoegabbler. "That nightingale is no ordinary bird. Maybe it knows something we don't."

"At this point, we have nothing to lose. We came all this way, Gilda," added Hans.

Aisling bent down and allowed the nightingale to perch itself on her finger. Then, deftly avoiding the thorny branches surrounding it, she plucked the white flower from its lonely stem. It glowed even brighter in her hand.

"I think we found our flower."

"Let's just get out of here," said Gilda. "What?" asked Aisling.

"We have to go, Aisling. We have a curse to end in our realm…"

"We have a curse to end here," she interrupted.

"Verdenwald is not our problem. There are people dying back home."

"Oh, my apologies, but did you not see the cursed people laying all over the floor here?

You know, the ones trapped in some enchanted nightmarish sleep?" said Aisling, defiantly.

Anger suffused Gilda's face and the grip on her sword hilt tightened.

"It's not just about us, Gilda. Or your people. If what the Crones told me, if what that stupid bloody scroll keeps telling me is true, then I'm here for a reason. There are so many people suffering out there. Seven Realms of people who are suffering because of these curses."

"Those people," stated Gilda. "Are not *my* people, little girl."

The two young women glared angrily at one another. Deep down, Aisling knew that she would never go home as long as the Seven Realms remained cursed. Yet, that wasn't why she was having this argument. She didn't want the people of Stonewall to suffer any further, but she couldn't call herself a human being if she left the people of Verdenwald to suffer in the bargain. Not if there was something to be done about it.

"I feel for them too, Aisling. I really do. But if we use

the flower to wake the Lady of Briars, then we won't be able to break the curse on the Lady of Beasts," said Hans, trying his best to calm the situation before it got out of hand.

"We'll find another way, then. The prophet led us here, there must be another way," said Aisling, with as much certainty as she could.

"And if we can't then we've lost our only chance at saving our own people," replied Gilda.

"Can you live with yourself if we just up and go? Because I can't," said Aisling.

There was silence then and Gilda and Hans exchanged a meaningful look. It was a soundless, significant look. Whatever it was they said to one another was said in the language of twins and was therefore completely imperceptible by anyone except those two. When it was done, Gilda slumped her shoulders and nodded to her brother. Her blue eyes would not meet Aisling's.

"All right, Aisling," said Hans, smiling. "What do we do next?"

"We need to find where this Lady of Briars' chamber is. I think we can get there by following the brambles."

"Why do you think that?" asked Hoegabbler.

"Something the knight told me. He said the 'lady was restless.' I would bet that like everything else here, she's sleeping; trapped in some nightmare. We need to wake her up. Wake her up and we wake them all up."

Gilda pushed past Aisling, then turned and grabbed hold of her shoulder with no small amount of pressure.

"I hope you're right about this."

Chapter Eleven

A Web of Thorns

ilda led the group out towards the main hall. She gritted her teeth angrily. Aisling was right, of course, but that didn't make what they had to do any more pleasant. To top it all off, she had no idea where they were supposed to go next. It wasn't as if she had ever actually been in a castle before.

"Which way do we go?" asked Hoegabbler, breaking the tense silence that had followed their departure from the garden.

Gilda scanned the main hall for anything of use. A grand staircase was off to the side, its marble steps coated in a fine layer of dust and like everything else, a healthy lattice of thorny brambles.

She began to ascend the stairs, careful not to touch or even tread on any of the vines. She motioned for the others to do the same. It was a long walk up the grand staircase and Aisling couldn't help but marvel at the scale of the place. Up until this point in her life, castles had always been nothing more than a faraway faerie tale. The derelict nature of this particular one, unsettling as it would have been under most other circumstances, did little to diminish the sense of wonder she felt.

As they reached the first landing, the staircase forked left and right. Aisling looked up to see an enormous oil painting hanging, slightly tilted on the wall. Its once fine, golden frame was wreathed in brambles, but the painting upon it seemed untouched by the cursed magic that suffused the rest of Verdenwald.

"Who is that?" she asked, quietly.

"Not sure," replied Hoegabbler. "It looks like it could be the king and queen and the Lady of Briars when she was a baby."

"Why isn't it crawling with vines, though? Like everything else?"

"A question for another time," hushed Gilda. "Come along, we're going to the right."

They followed. The group walked down the right corridor, passing what must have been dozens of rooms on the left or right of them. At the end of the corridor, far away, stood two large golden doors, and slumped beside them was the body of a man.

Suddenly, the vines that crisscrossed about the walls of the corridor began to shiver and shake around them. They moved and shifted, lifting themselves off the stone and shaking bits of decades-old grit along with them. A cloud of dust obscured the air, but Aisling didn't need to see to know what was happening.

The vines were coming to life, like the Gallows Tree before them. They reached into the center of the corridor, where the would-be heroes gathered close. When they found they couldn't reach their quarry, the vines started to twist around one another, thickening into wicked woven ropes. They added layer after layer onto one another, pulling roots and stems from masonry, thickening, molding, and becoming man-sized.

When it appeared they were strong enough the now man-shaped creatures pulled themselves away from the wall entirely. The sound they made was less a noise and more an inadvertent scratching and clattering. It was the noise that happened when strong winds blew through winter forests; the sound of dry foliage rubbing up against itself.

The tree creatures were tall and lanky and, covered as they were in thorns, untouchable.

They encircled the group brandishing their arms, for they didn't need any other weapons, and stared with hollow, lifeless eyes at their new prey.

Aisling stood there, sword held tight in her hand with her back against those of her friends, breathing hard.

"Just remain calm," advised Gilda. "Dodge their blows and only leave yourself open to strike back if you have an opening."

Aisling swallowed hard. "Do you hear me, girl?"

"Ayeyes. That is…I u-understand," she stuttered.

Hoegabbler was still in his true form, but he had drawn himself up to the same height and build as Hans. Indeed if it weren't for the skin, and the eyes, and the face, and the persistent potbelly, one might have thought him to be Hansfrom a distance.

A blur of brambles, a swish of steel swords, and the battle had begun. Swords slashed wildly, rending the creatures' dead, thorny arms into bits. Even Aisling, who wasn't particularly good with a blade, was easily dismantling the tree things with only the most glancing of blows.

"They're brittle," said Hans. "Could this be some sort of ancient trap to keep us from the lady?"

"If it is a trap, then it's broken, and it also means we're going the right way," replied his sister, gleefully.

Gilda, Hans, and Hoegabbler continued to slash and punch and all around dismantle the vine creatures. Aisling did her part too, albeit in a much sloppier, more haphazard way. It didn't matter though, the monsters were a shadow of what the Gallows Tree had been. Where the tree's bark had been as hard as iron, these creatures were brittle as dried kindling.

A few minutes later and they had rendered the once-frightening bramble creatures into nothing more than a mass of quivering twigs. Aisling felt somewhat less triumphant than her companions. Nothing was ever this easy in the stories.

"This was too easy," she said, nervously.

"The magic here is old," said Hoegabbler, who had settled back into his cat shape. "It could have just petered out. Or most of it could be directed towards keeping the princess and the realm's inhabitants asleep."

Gilda and Hans gazed down inquisitively at Hoegabbler. "You know an awful lot about curses..." said Hans.

"It's faerie magic...of course I do. I also know that these

things will likely reform if we don't move quickly."

The group continued down the hallway until they got to the door. The body on the floor was that of a man, dressed in a cape and half-plate armor. He looked as if he had once been a very handsome young man, but no longer. His face was heavily scarred and his severely scratched eyelids seemed to be clenched much more tightly than the other sleeping denizens of the castle. A sword, most likely his, lay nearby. Its golden hilt was stylized with the same rose- shaped sigil that adorned his armor. Hans bent down to get a closer look.

"He's asleep, not dead, and by the looks of it, he's been here a long while, too. My guess is he ran afoul of those things when they were in their prime and was just overwhelmed."

"They scratched out his eyes…" gulped Hoegabbler.

Hans nodded in agreement. Meanwhile, Gilda tried her best to push open the enormous door, but it wouldn't budge.

"You didn't think it would be that easy….did you?" said a gravelly voice beside them. Hans jumped to his feet and backed away, standing in front of Aisling and his sister both. "You're awake?!" he shouted at the man on the floor.

"In a manner of speaking," replied the warrior. "Where…where is my sword?"

Aisling grabbed up the man's rose-hilted sword and pushed past Hans to hand it to him, careful not to get too close.

"My thanks, good knight," said the man, clasping the sword and bringing it close to his chest.

"I am no knight, sir," she replied, meekly. The man tilted his head quizzically.

"A girl?" he asked. "What business brings you to this cursed place?"

"Yes," said Gilda, defensively. "Several of us are, as a matter of fact. We're here to help the Lady of Briars. What business has brought you here?"

"My apologies, good ladies. I am Ser Phillip, known to many as the Knight of Roses. I, too, came to save the lady from the curse. But I was waylaid and blinded when I arrived, by the creatures that guard this place. I fell into a fitful sleep, but I would wake from time to time, to find myself still here, unable to stir from my slumber and…"

A moment later and the Knight of Roses was asleep once more. "Ser Phillip?" said Gilda, then more loudly. "Ser Phillip!?" The knight stirred.

"I'm sorry. It's the curse. I can only go a few moments before I slip back into that nightmarish dream. I was saying the door, it can't be opened without…" and he trailed off again.

Gilda walked over and nudged him angrily.

"A key!" shouted the startled knight. "I have it here, it's in my tunic. Take it. End this…save her…"

He fumbled with the key in his tunic and it dropped onto the floor with a loud clinking sound. Hoegabbler scrambled to grab it, but no sooner had he touched it than he recoiled and dropped it again.

"Ouch!" shouted the changeling. "It's made of iron; cold iron." Aisling picked the key up and held it up to the lock.

"Faerie magic…they had insulted a faerie witch, right? And she gave them a warning about what would happen because of it?" she asked.

Hoegabbler cradled his slightly burnt hand and nodded.

"Of course...they would have made the lock and the key to her room out of iron, to keep the faeries out. It didn't do any good though, the whole castle was affected, the brambles were everywhere. Still, this has to be her room. The Lady of Briars is right through this door."

"Good. We can end this at last," said Gilda, reaching for the key. "Wait," said Aisling. "How did he get the key? Where did he get it?"

"Does it matter? You wanted to do this, Aisling. You wanted to waste our one cure on this kingdom. Well, here's our chance to do it," said Gilda, pointing to the key in Aisling's hand.

She wasn't wrong, but Aisling just didn't like the idea of finding the key at so opportune a time. Everything had fallen into place too easily, too readily. She looked over at her companions, all of whom looked just as exhausted as she felt. Maybe the Crones were right.

Maybe it was fate that she had found herself there, at that moment, with the very man who held the key to saving Verdenwald.

"You're right. Verdenwald has suffered long enough."

With that, she slipped the key into the lock and turned it. The tumblers inside creaked and clanked, before finally clicking into place with an audible thunk. Gilda placed her hand on it and pushed. This time, it easily gave way.

The room beyond was a complete circle, and all of its opposite walls were framed by wide mullion windows. A large, four poster bed stood in the center of the room directly across from the doors. A dusty wooden spindle and stool, both covered in cobwebs, sat near one of the windows. The needle tip at the end of the thing sparkled in the darkness. She had seen spindles before, even used them once or twice to make new clothes for the twins, but none of them possessed a needle that unnaturally sharp.

Ragged, pink curtains hung in tattered shreds atop the bed posts. Healthy, green vines, each covered in a hundred, red-tipped thorns hung there as well. Unlike the brown and brittle brambles that wove their way through the rest of the castle, the vines in this room were a brilliant and healthy green.

The vines crisscrossed over the tattered bedcovers, anchoring themselves to the bed posts and then to the ceiling above. To Aisling, it looked as though the wickedly sharp brambles had created a sort of verdant web about the whole chamber.

A young woman was suspended in the center of the vines. She was wrapped tight from head to foot, her arms bound close to her body in a sort of green cocoon. Her hair was the color of autumn wheat. It was long and it hung behind her sleeping head in lank, greasy-looking strands. Her skin was pale, and she had the look of someone who hadn't seen the sun in a very long time. She wore a pained expression on her face as she slept; the gruesome visage of one whose nightmare was never-ending. She moaned and cried in her sleep, her mostly silent sobs breaking the otherwise pervasive silence of the Gardener's Tower.

Hoegabbler's ears pricked up as they entered the room, but his pseudo-feline senses were too slow. Before any of them could turn to meet it, the door behind them slammed shut, trapping them inside.

The vines around the bed began to undulate, writhing and wriggling like great green serpents. They wound and unwound about the princess, pulling her formally horizontal form upright. The vines began to pull away from the walls then, twining around one another and thickening into eight arachnid-like limbs that dragged the girl from her bed. Chunks of masonry dust, splintering wood, and tatters of moth-eaten fabric clung to the quivering brambles.

At the center of the great green spider, hanging limp and lifeless as a rag doll, was the Lady of Briars. She shuddered tremulously before crying out with an ungodly sound. It was a pained and piercing wail, a terrible cry that echoed around the room and caused Aisling to shriek in alarm.

Hans and Gilda stepped in front of her, their swords outstretched, their eyes wide.

Hoegabbler stood stock-still, his back arched, spitting and hissing wildly at the monstrous thing before them.

It was bigger than the Gallows Tree, and thanks to the addition of a frail and crying girl suspended and swinging from its center, far more unsettling. It quavered momentarily on unsteady "legs", but soon righted itself. The Lady of Briars continued to wail.

Outside the bed chamber, Aisling could hear the feeble knocking of the Knight of Roses, though she couldn't make out what he was saying to them. The vine-creature charged at them, unwinding one of its middle legs into three whiplike tendrils as it moved. The loose brambles snapped at the companions, reaching out to grab hold and pull them towards it.

Gilda slashed down quickly, her well-honed blade making short work of even those healthy vines. A chunk of thick, knotty vine fell to the floor with a squelch, wriggling and disgorging a foul-smelling crimson liquid, while the other two tendrils pulled back. The Lady of Briars screamed even louder. She shook violently as tiny cuts began to form on the milk-pale skin of her tightlyclenched left arm. Beads of green-tinted blood appeared and dripped down her arm and onto the floor.

"We can't cut the vines!" shouted Aisling. "They're connected to her, to the princess!" "So?" replied Gilda. "What if killing her is what breaks the curse?"

Aisling didn't have time to argue, she jumped out in front of Gilda and glared angrily at her.

"There has to be another way!"

Meanwhile, Hans was doing his best to avoid the tendrils on the left side without slicing them all the way through. He hacked at the air, but the brambles were too fast. One of the vines whipped back and made contact, slashing against his cheek with an audible CRACK! Blood filled the ragged scrapes and he stumbled backwards.

"Hans, no!" yelled his sister, pushing Aisling to the ground and running to his side.

Hans managed to get to his knees, but before he could utter another word, his eyes rolled back into his head and he fell to the ground, unconscious.

"You stupid witch!" cursed Gilda, and she ran at the outstretched legs of the vine spider.

She slashed wildly now, fueled by rage and grief and frustration. Each deft strike hit home, and chunks of green and red plant matter began to fly in every direction. One of them flew directly at her and caught itself on the sleeve of her tunic. Without thinking, she grabbed hold of the vine and attempted to throw it away from her, catching her thumb on one of its red-tipped thorns. A moment later and she crumpled like her brother, prone and asleep on the stone floor.

Aisling was alone. Her two bravest companions had fallen to the curse, and Hoegabbler was cowering in the farthest corner of the room unable to defend himself, let alone her.

"Lady Roselyn!" she shouted at the now slowly encroaching Lady of Briars, but the girl couldn't hear her. Above the din of her own wailing, she couldn't hear a thing.

Aisling tried hard to think what she could do next. She pulled the Remedy Bloom from her pocket and held it out towards the sleeping princess, hoping that it would do something, anything to awaken her. It sat in her hand, beautiful, but utterly useless.

The vine spider was towering before her now, its loose vines whipping around her, threatening to do the very same to her as it did her companions. Suddenly, the nightingale flittered out of her pocket and up towards the dangling princess. The vines, too concerned to notice something as small and innocuous as a songbird, did nothing to stop it.

The bird landed on her shoulder, careful to avoid the thorns, and began to sing. It wasn't the same song as before, not entirely, but it hit all the same notes. It was a song that was bitter and sweet all at once, that rang out, half in hope and half in despair, and most importantly, it carried long and loud over the princess' crying.

The vine spider shuddered and ceased its movement. The princess stopped her crying, and a moment later, her eyes snapped open. Even from her vantage point, Aisling could see that they were the same verdant hue as the leaves on a rose bush.

No sooner had she opened her eyes, than a loud shriek echoed throughout the castle. It was a fierce, frightened, visceral screech and it moved as though it were reverberating through the brambles themselves.

The vines that held the princess began to sink to the ground, crumbling under their own weight, but letting her fall gently to the floor. Those that had bound her, loosed and fell around her like strands of broken thread, revealing the tattered remnants of a thin nightgown beneath them. Within moments, every scrap of bright green bramble had been rendered as dry and brown as the leaves in autumn.

The princess stood for a moment on unsteady legs, but before she could topple, Aisling rose to catch her. The nightingale flittered onto Aisling's shoulder and twittered triumphantly.

Hans and Gilda groaned and shifted beside them as they began to wake. Aisling wasn't certain, but she had a feeling that this was happening all around the Gardener's Tower, as people who had been asleep for years woke to learn that the nightmare had finally ended.

"Are you alright, m'lady?" said Aisling, gently.

"I...think so...am I awake?I can't remember what happened..." she replied, uncertain. "You've been asleep a long while," added Aisling.

"I remember the spinning wheel. I know I shouldn't have...I'd be warned. Then I was so tired, I was in a nightmare...it felt like it went on forever," she said, then, with a sudden realization, "you did it...you woke me up. You ended the curse."

"We did, m'lady. It's over."

"It's far from over," said a deep voice behind them.

The Knight of Roses was standing in the open doorway to the bed chamber. His sword was drawn.

Chapter Twelve

Awakening

hat do you mean?" said Aisling, while simultaneously pushing herself slightly in front of the Lady Roselyn.

"The Lady of Briars is only the first of many who need saving, Aisling Mason," replied the knight.

"She never gave you her name…" said Gilda, who was now flanking the knight to the left while her brother had moved surreptitiously to his right.

"Indeed, she did not. But though I no longer possess eyes, I do not lack vision. I can see many things in your auras, Gilda of the Red Riders. I can see much that even eyes as keen as yours cannot…"

"Ser Knight," interjected Roselyn. "As lady of Verdenwald, I bid you stand down. Stay your blade. These people have saved me and my kingdom. They have my thanks and are under my protection."

The Knight of Roses did as he was told. He placed his

sword back into his scabbard and fell to one knee.

"Of course, Lady Roselyn. As always, I am at your disposal."

The former Lady of Briars nodded. Then, realizing that the knight was blind, added hastily, "That will be all, Ser Phillip. Please go and take your respite. Take food, take drink, tell the servants to get you whatever you desire. I must speak with my saviors. I shall call for you later."

The knight bowed curtly and walked back down the long corridor.

"I wonder...might you all be able to come with me out to the Paradise Courtyard? asked Roselyn. "It's been so long and I wish greatly to be outside on such a fine evening. I feel as if I have been trapped in this accursed castle forever."

Gilda and Hans found the princess a new night shirt and a pair of slippers and the group helped her through the castle and out to the gardens. Everywhere they went, the denizens of the castle seemed to be rejoicing in their newfound wakefulness. All of them greeted her as they went, pleased to see that their lady had finally awoken from her cursed slumber.

When they reached the garden, the still groggy princess took a seat upon one of the sculpted benches to rest.

"I can never repay you for what you've done," she said to all of them. "But I would like to thank you for helping to free Verdenwald. Please, ask anything. If it is in my power to grant it, I shall."

No one spoke, all of them seemed uncertain as to how they should speak to a royal. Not wanting to seem rude, Aisling stepped closer, managed a slight curtsy and spoke,

"Milady, we've helped save Verdenwald, but there are other kingdoms that still need our help. Right through your forest, the realm of Stonewall is under their own curse," she gestured to the woods to the west of the castle. "We want to help them, and we were told that the way to do it was here, in the Paradise Courtyard. The Remedy Bloom, we need to know if it will work to cure the Lady of Beasts."

"It might," began Roselyn, considering the question. "But it works only in a potion. It must be stewed, its essence extracted, and drunk down. There are few left with the knowledge to brew such a potion…"

"Witches," replied Gilda and Hans in unison.

Aisling had never even considered that the flower had to be turned into a potion. Finding someone who could brew a curse-removing potion was going to be hard enough, but getting the Lady of Beasts to drink that potion was going to be downright impossible.

It was only then, as her mind whirred with these impossible notions, that Aisling suddenly noticed how exhausted she was. She hadn't realized it before then, but she had been awake for nearly a day and she hadn't eaten much in that time either. Roselyn must have noticed this because she said,

"We can discuss all this tomorrow. I will think of something, if not, my advisors will.

Rest for now. There is much work to be done here yet, but all that I have is yours."

The former Lady of Briars flagged down a servant who she politely asked to show the heroes to the finest rooms in the tower. The man led them out of the garden and into the main hall. To their surprise, the people of Verdenwald were not standing idly, talking and reminiscing, but working together to beautify the Gardener's Tower.

They hacked at the brittle brambles, pulling them away from the walls, tying them into great bundles. Those who weren't seeing to the brambles wiped, swept, and scrubbed the caked- on dust of several years from every surface. Aisling could hardly believe it. No sooner had these people woken from a cursed sleep than they had gotten right to work.

"Has the lady asked that these be taken down so soon after the curse has been lifted?

Don't you think they want to go back to their lives or else spend some time with their families?" she whispered to Hoegabbler.

The changeling shrugged then said, "I guess if you think about it, it's their home, too.

They just want to see it restored to the way it was before the curse hit. Besides, it's not like they are lacking for sleep or anything, they are probably itching to keep busy after such an energizing nap."

Gilda and Aisling were shown to one room, while Hans and Hoegabbler were given a room to share as well. No sooner had the door to their chambers closed, than Gilda rounded on Aisling.

"You....you said this would work! You and that stupid scroll of yours!" she shouted through gritted teeth.

"Hey!" replied Aisling, defensively. "I didn't make this decision! You're the one who assumed the flower was the cure. You heard the prophecy and you're the one who saw it as a way to save your own realm. I didn't even know about all this until you dragged me into it!"

"We saved your life, little girl…"

"I am *not* a little girl, Gilda!" she screamed, taking the Red Rider by surprise. "If you haven't noticed, I'm the one who got us through all this in the end. I didn't ask for any of this! I didn't want to fight magic trees or cursed thorn monsters, or wolf men, or trolls, or any of this! I just want to go home."

Then, whether from the stresses of the recent days, the exhaustion, or the emotional toll of it all, Aisling fell to her knees and began to weep. It was a cry that she had pushed back and pushed back each day since she had been taken. But she could bear it no longer. Every ounce of loss, fear, disappointment, and unwilling obligation came pouring out in great sobs and heaving breaths. Gilda stopped shouting and knelt beside her. Aisling looked up and saw that she, too, had tears in her eyes.

"I'm sorry, Aisling," she said. "I just…I want to go home…"

"I know you do."

And with that, she pulled the crying girl into her arms and held her tight.

In that moment, all of their frustrations were laid aside by the shared trauma of the past few days. They got undressed and climbed into the enormous bed together. Aisling's cheeks were still stained with tears, but as she lay there, Gilda stroking her hair and singing to her in German, she felt at peace for the first time in days. She missed her home, her twins, her brother, and sister-in-law, but at least she wasn't alone.

"Do you think the other children are all right?" asked Aisling.

"Which children?" Gilda replied, still languidly curling Aisling's hair between her fingers.

"The Foundlings, Peter's children. The ones I told you about."

"Well," began Gilda. "If what I've heard about this Peter Goodfellow is true, then they're doing fine. He'll keep them safe. Way I hear it, most folk have more to worry about when it comes to the Foundlings than the Foundlings have to worry about from the world outside their little piece of wood."

"I don't mean it like that," said Aisling, unsure of how she wanted to put it into words. "Do you think they're loved? That they are happy? I mean, I know I'm safe with you, Hans, and Hoegabbler around, but I also know that I'm not alone; that we have each other. Do you think they know that they have each other?"

Gilda smiled to herself. Aisling may have been a skinny little thing, maybe a bit of a whiner, but she had heart. She wondered if that was something she had been missing for a long while, too, and if Aisling had indeed come into their lives to reinvigorate that.

"I'm sure they do, Aisling," she replied.

Aisling turned to face her friend.

"I don't know how to ask this...but what's your family name? Please don't think me rude. I just, I know the royals have them and I'm sure the commoners do, too. But it seems like some people don't use them. I was wondering why that is."

"It's not rude. I don't know why other folks don't use them. As for Hans and I...we had one, I'm sure, at one time, but we've been tossed around so much, we sort of just lost it along the way. At some point, with everything we've been through, it stopped being important."

Aisling wondered if that was what would happen to her, if at some point she would stop being Aisling Mason and just be Aisling. She wondered when that point might come and how many people she would meet and adventures she would go on before something as trivial as a surname stopped being important.

"I guess it doesn't really matter," added Gilda. "It's our deeds and not our names that make us who we are in this world. The things we do, the people we save along the way, those are the things we ought to be remembered for."

Aisling considered this. In a way, Gilda was right, but her life had been very different than Aisling's. She realized then that it would always be important. If she lost her surname, if she stopped being a Mason, then she would have no reason to go home. She resolved then that no matter what happened, no matter how many trolls or curses she encountered, she would hold true to who she was. She would get home, she would find a way. And as she thought this, she fell asleep.

The breakfast they received the next morning was a repast worthy of an overnight stay in a castle. There were eggs, hard boiled and hard fried to their liking; bacon, burnt crisp and capped with juicy fat; and crusty fresh-baked bread with butter so creamy that it might have been churned that very morning. Then there were the variety of fresh blackberries, blueberries, raspberries, mulberries, and strawberries that decorated the long dining room table.

All of them had found fresh, brand new clothes outside their doors when they woke.

Aisling was most pleased about the boots, which fit much better than Orla's, though they felt just as worn in and comfortable. The castle interior, thanks to the overnight work of its many inhabitants, looked as if the cursed brambles had never crept their way into its cornices.

"You slept well, I hope?" asked Roselyn, as she tapped gingerly at the shell of her hard boiled egg.

She too had cleaned up in splendid fashion. Her dress, formerly a tattered night shift, was now a stunning gown made up of ruffled layers of pink, blue, and green. The skirts and petticoats flowed from beneath her waist, which, when she stood, gave her the appearance of a gentle pastel flower.

"We did," replied Hans, who then proceeded to wolf down a whole plate of fried eggs in one forkful.

Hoegabbler nodded, but his mouth was too full of food to even attempt a reply.

"Yes, thank you for the splendid clothing, Milady," said Aisling, flashing her boorish counterparts an exasperated look. "These are quite fine, as well. If I may, though, how did you manage to make them in our sizes so quickly? I was told that Verdenwald had no spinning wheels."

Roselyn smiled politely. Beneath it though, Aisling could see a hint of discomfort at even the mere mention of a spinning wheel.

"We didn't...for obvious reasons. Thankfully, my ladies are all dab hands at designing, cutting, and sewing any garment. It's become a skill we all had to cultivate after the…warning we received at my baptismal celebration," the lady replied.

It was a curt reply, but no less gracious.

Aisling knew she wasn't lying either. The clothes they had been given were some of the best she had ever seen. She had marveled at the stitching on them for a good few minutes before Gilda had snapped her out of it. As a seamstress herself, she always appreciated the intensive labor that went into making even the simplest of clothes. She recalled her mother, who had sewn nearly all the clothing for her and her six siblings. When she wasn't sewing new garments, she was repairing worn ones. It was a thankless, endless job, and Aisling appreciated it immensely.

"Your Highness…" began Gilda, stirring Aisling from her reverie.

"Please, Gilda, there are no need for formalities. You may call me Roselyn.. We are friends now after all," replied the lady.

"Roselyn, s there anyone in your realm with the skills to brew a potion from the flower? I'm very glad that we were able to help Verdenwald, but my people are still suffering greatly. My brother and I need to save our lands from the Lady of Beasts and….without the flower, we have no way to break the curse."

"I'm afraid there are no apothecaries in Verdenwald capable of brewing such a potion properly, nor any who couldwield the magic necessary to do it. I asked my advisors about it last night. They assured me that the only other people with the skills to do so left these lands long before the curse began. I wish I had another answer for you, but there's nothing we can do," replied Roselyn.

"Then it's hopeless. She's just going to keep turning my people until we're a land of beasts and monsters," said Gilda.

"Who were the other people who could have brewed the potion?" asked Aisling. "The witches?"

Roselyn bristled for a moment, but only slightly, before regaining her composure. "What happened to the witches was dreadful and before my time as lady of the

Gardener's Tower. Had I been here, I would have never allowed such barbarism. Unfortunately, what is done cannot be undone. All I can do is try and make amends to their descendants. But no dear, the witches are not whom I speak of. I am speaking of the elves. The first people of Verdenwald."

"What happened to them?" asked Hoegabbler.

"They say that my ancestors had an accord with them. They would keep to the untamed forest, the places where man ought never to tread. We would keep to the open wood and the farmlands. It was a pact that lasted for centuries until the king and queen united the Seven Realms. Before that, interactions between my people and the elves were rare, but afterwards, well it seems they just vanished altogether.

It was the elves who gave us the seeds to most of the rare flowers in the Paradise Courtyard. If there are any left in these woods who knows how to extract the magical properties from the Remedy Bloom, it's the elves," she explained.

Of all the stories she remembered from her gran, it was the tales of the sidhe, the elves, that Aisling was most fond of. They were the most mysterious of the fair folk, and the most capricious. They were as dangerous as they were beautiful, but the wisest of all the immortal beings. Part of her hoped that in this magical place, they still existed, but an equal, more wary part worried what might happen if they actually did.

"There is something I have that I think might help, but it's just a theory, based on what I know of the Lady of Stonewall," added Roselyn. "Before the curses came, when she was simply the Lady Isabelle, the two of us were friends. I only met her a few times, mind you, when our kingdoms needed to cooperate on things or when the king and queen required us to attend them at Caerleon.

She was a kind soul, of even temperament, and without an ounce of animosity in her.

Even her husband, who many would have described as a brute, seemed softened by her kindness. I don't know much about their relationship, but I do know that it was she who saved him from his own inner demons, and that was why he took her as his bride.

She was fond of roses, it was her favorite flower. She once told me that her dearly departed father would travel often and whenever he returned, he would bring with him a rose just for her. In fact, when she was first married to the prince and made the Lady of Stonewall, my kingdom sent over one hundred red roses as a gift."

She called over to one of the servants and motioned for the tray that he carried.

Removing the cloche, she revealed a stunningly red rose.

"This is the fleur de sangre, the blood bloom. It is the

most spectacular rose known to man and it grows only one place, in the Paradise Courtyard. It too has some manner of magical properties, though no one here seems to know what they are. Perhaps if you can reach her, if you can show her kindness and remind her of the person she once was, then perhaps she can be freed from the spell."

"What if we can't?" asked Aisling.

"You must," replied Roselyn. "You must reach her, the real her, the lady that lies inside the beast. I just know she has to be in there somewhere. She is trapped in her own nightmare, just as I was. You freed me from the nightmare. I know you can do it."

"Thank you," said Gilda, and there was a marked sincerity to her voice that Aisling hadn't expected. "I appreciate everything you've done for us, but we should be going."

Roselyn nodded, then rose to her feet with the rest of the group. She hugged each of them in turn and bid them farewell. In addition to the new clothes, the people of Verdenwald had seen to the twins' horses. The animals were fed, brushed, and their saddlebags were swollen with food for their journey home.

As they made their way through the open, shining gates of Verdenwald, Aisling thought about what awaited them back in the dark forests of Stonewall and the impossible task that loomed over her destiny.

Behind them, looming in the windows of the Gardener's Tower, the Knight of Thorns stood and gazed at them with sightless eyes. His time as Lady Roselyn's "Knight of Roses" was done. That ruse had run its course. He had more pressing matters to attend to.

He had been foolish and had allowed the curse to get the better of him. Yet, though he had failed in one of his tasks, the second had been a resounding success.

He took the pouch from inside his pocket and turned it over in his gloved hand, careful not to allow himself to be pricked again. A moment later, and he heard a fluttering of wings approach him. A raven had landed on the windowsill and cawed up at him irritably.

"The curse has been broken. It is as we feared," he told the bird.

The bird let out another doleful caw and attempted to snatch the parcel from his left hand.

He jerked it away, replacing the pouch back in his pocket.

"No. I shall bring it myself. Tell my lady that they are heading back to Stonewall, and that if she needs me, she can find me riding west."

One last time the raven cawed. Then, beating its wings furiously, it leapt from the window and out into the early morning.

Chapter Fourteen

The Long Way Home

he journey back to Stonewall was very different than the one they had made to get to Verdenwald. The brambles, that had previously seemed to be strangling the life from nearly every tree they passed, were now as brittle and broken as the ones in the castle. The curse's end saw life and greenery returning to the formerly gray forest.

"That's amazing," said Aisling as she and Hans rode past a newly blooming cherry tree. "How is it that it's all happening so fast?"

"Curses are terrible things and if they go unanswered, they can wreak havoc over an area or a person for decades, centuries even," explained Hoegabbler, who was in his squirrel form and riding on the back of Gilda's saddle.

"The thing about magical curses though, is that all that power that's been holding the curse in place the whole time dissipates when the magic of nature gets a chance to take over. That innate magic is the stuff that makes up people like me, and it's strong. It fights against curses, trying to return things to the way they ought to be, but it gets held back.

Think of it like a dam. When the dam finally breaks and the curse is lifted, all that water comes rushing back into the river bed. It surges through everything, returning it to normal just as it would have if it wasn't being held. It just does it all at once."

Gilda once again eyed the changeling suspiciously.

"You really do know a great deal about curses, Hoegabbler…" she said. "I know a great deal about magic," he replied, smiling proudly.

"Oh, really? Then how did Aisling's nightingale break the curse on the Lady Roselyn?" she said, smirking.

Hoegabbler's smile drooped.

"Honestly, I have no idea. I've been thinking about it. But that's some potent magic in that bird of yours, Aisling. A rare bird, indeed," he chuckled at his joke.

Aisling reached into her pocket where the nightingale was still sleeping, and stroked her head with a finger. The tiny bird ruffled her feathers happily and closed her eyes in pleasure.

"Then I suppose I'll have to take good care of her," she said.

They continued riding for a few hours until, without warning, Hans made them stop. "What's wrong, brother?" asked Gilda.

"This isn't right," he replied, anxiously. "This is the way back to Stonewall…isn't it?"

Gilda looked around for a moment, then turned Karl

around, treading back down the path a few feet and running her hand along a nearby elm tree.

"Something is wrong here. Hoegabbler, could the forest have shifted enough to bar our way back into Stonewall?" she asked.

"I don't think so. Not if there was always a path between the two realms before. It would have just returned to normal," said the changeling.

"Well, this is the way...so something has definitely changed. Hans, do you remember if there's any other way through to Stonewall?"

"We can try to go the long way, past the fields, but without cutting through the woods it will take an extra two days," he replied.

"Verdammt!" Gilda cursed. "It's like everything in this realm wants to stop us from getting back home. We'll make camp here tonight. We'll head back to the main road tomorrow at first light. Maybe we're just missing something."

While the twins unsaddled the horses and unpacked the bags, Aisling and Hoegabbler went about collecting kindling to start the fire. The dried brambles that littered the forest floor seemed perfect for this, but both of them were careful not to let themselves be pricked by the remaining thorns; just in case. With the fire started and the sun going down, the group sat to discuss what their plan of attack was.

"I appreciate what Lady Roselyn was trying to say," began Gilda. "But I've fought the beastmen of Stonewall. I've seen friends turn in the moonlight and lose all sense of who they once were. There's no more love or loyalty, no memory. They're savage animals, nothing more. If the Lady of Beasts is anything like them, then showing her some blood-red rose isn't going to do anything but remind her how tasty we probably all are."

"If only they hadn't killed all the witches all those years ago, then maybe there would have been someone in Verdenwald to turn the Remedy Bloom into potion," said Aisling.

Hans glared at her angrily for a moment and then got to his feet.

"I'm going to go check to see if I can find a way in before the sun sets all the way," he said curtly, before stalking off.

"I'm sorry," blushed Aisling. "Did I say something wrong?" Gilda sighed.

"It's not your fault. Hans has never been fond of witches. After our parents died, and before we joined the Riders, we were adopted by an old lady from our village. She was a spinster, she'd never been married, never had any children of her own. We thought, despite everything, that things would get better," explained Gilda.

"They didn't," added Hans, who was standing in the shadow of a nearby oak. "The woman was a witch. She didn't want to take care of two children, she wanted to use us in some insane ritual. We didn't know anything about any of it in those days, we were young. When she told us that our problems were over, that we could have anything we ever wanted, any treat, any toy, anything...well, what would any child do?"

"She stopped letting us go out to play. Then when we fought against it, she began locking us in. We escaped one night and as we made our way past the windows of her little cottage, we saw her performing some sort of magical rite. She had killed a calf and was spreading its blood all around this painted circle on the floor," said Gilda.

"She spoke in a strange language," added Hans. "She was naked."

"The calf shriveled up into nothing and when it was finally gone, the old woman looked different, younger. In the circle, we saw a few of our belongings, things she had given us to play with and we knew…we were next," Gilda explained, shuddering at the thought.

"We locked the doors from the outside and barred the window. Then we set fire to the house. We burned the witch alive," said Hans, and his expression was harder than Aisling had ever seen it.

"It was the only way," assured Gilda.

"Witches are no good, Aisling," said Hans. "The Queen, a witch…she's the reason for all of this. She's the one who cursed our realms, probably the one who dragged children from their beds in your world to use in her own dark rituals here. It's good that they killed the witches.

We'll find another way to save Stonewall."

Aisling and Hoegabbler, now a cat curled up on Karl's back, remained silent. When she was sure that the twins had finished their story, Aisling said,

"Well, then I guess I wish we knew where the elves had gone. They're the only other ones who know how to brew the remedy."

"Can't trust elves either," said Hoegabbler. "Really now!" shouted Aisling.

"What? I'm just saying…"

Hans agreed to take the first watch and the group of them settled down for the night. In the orange glow of the firelight, Aisling could swear she saw humanoid shapes standing behind the trees. She knew that it was probably the night playing tricks on her eyes, but part of her imagined that they were the fair folk, hollow and hiding between the veil of reality and dreams. She wondered if the sidhe really did exist anymore. So far, she had encountered dozens of things from her gran's old stories. If trolls and changelings existed, then why not elves?

Aisling awoke with a start to the sensation of something cold and sharp on her neck. "Don't move, Aisling," warned Gilda's voice.

"What's happening?" replied the girl.

"It's all right," said Hans' voice. "This is just a misunderstanding." "Is it?" said a male voice that Aisling was not familiar with.

Aisling opened her groggy eyes and stared up at the figure of a tall man whose long, thin blade was pointing precariously over her throat. Her eyes searched the area for any sign of her friends, but all she could make out in the dim firelight was the man's shape. He was lean and lanky, almost waif-like, and he seemed an unusual shape for a man. As he shifted his head, Aisling caught a glimpse of the long, blonde hair cascading halfway down his back, and the pointed elfin ears sticking out from underneath it.

"Get up," commanded the elf.

Slowly, the man pulled the sword away to allow Aisling to get to her feet. Standing, Aisling could make out much more detail. A group of elves, maybe five or six, had come upon them as they slept. Two of them were holding knives to Gilda and Hans, while two more had their bows trained on Hoegabbler, who seemed stuck mid-transformation between humanoid and rabbit.

The sidhe were every bit as beautiful as they were in the stories. The majority of them had handsome, angular faces punctuated by either strong cheekbones or cute dimples. They had long, sleek hair, pointed ears, full lips, and straight teeth. Their most striking feature however, were their eyes, which were gleaming, colorful, and almond-shaped.

Their expressions didn't appear as she had thought they might. They weren't haughty, they didn't look cruel. Part of her assumed that was by design, that it was how they manipulated people. No, the elves before them looked more or less sorrowful. They had a peaked, dejected look about them. It made them no less beautiful, but it did make them far more relatable.

"You are not safe in these woods, mortals," said the blonde elf. "Clearly," returned Gilda, sarcastically.

"You are not safe anywhere," seconded a redheaded female, and she pressed her elegant knife even closer to Gilda's throat.

Gilda, who had apparently had the foresight to grab her kopet before she had been accosted, lowered the weapon. She was exhausted, her brother was exhausted, Aisling and the changeling were exhausted. She had always been taught that a good leader thought of their people first and picked their battles wisely. None of them were in any kind of shape for a fight.

"You're right," she acquiesced. "Listen, we're sorry if we intruded, but we need help.

We're just trying to get back to Stonewall and needed a safe place for the night. If you can help us get back, we'll leave these lands. We can't offer you much else in return, I'm afraid…"

The elf at the head of the group nodded to her.

"Come," he said, and all the elves lowered their weapons.

Hans eyed his sister warily, but a lifetime of being her sibling and brother-in-arms had taught him to trust her judgment implicitly. They stowed their own weapons and Hoegabbler turned into a squirrel, jumping quickly onto Hans' shoulder.

"Our horses?" asked Hans.

"They will be safe," said a gray-haired elf.

From there, the elves led them north, deeper into the woods. When they had walked for about an hour, they stopped before an unusual and moonlit clearing. A circle of toadstools could be seen there, tucked slightly behind a man-sized hillock.

"A faerie ring!" exclaimed Aisling, momentarily beside herself with excitement. "That's what mortals call them, yes. They are places of power for my people. The only such places left to us in this age," replied the blonde elf. "Step inside the ring, do not be afraid."

Gilda led the way, followed closely by Hans and Aisling. There was a flash of light and a loud popping noise. When the light faded, the four companions were in a great, underground chamber. Before them stood an immense, subterranean world. It was a city, larger by far than Aisling had ever seen in her world. But instead of stone buildings or houses of crossed timber, each of the buildings in this city was built into an enormous array of roots.

Despite the fact that they were very clearly underground, light shone out from within the root structures. It was a pale blue-green luminescence, the ethereal light of the fair folk. Aisling knew from the stories that this was the light of the piskies, of the will o' the wisp. It was the light given off by the spirits of nature itself, and it illuminated the city of the sidhe as brightly as the sun.

Aisling had seen many remarkable things since arriving in the Seven Realms, but it was this place, a world beneath the world, a place she had only ever seen in her own imagination, which took her breath away.

"Where are we?" asked Gilda.

"We are in the fae realm," replied Hoegabbler, almost reverentially.

"Welcome, mortals, to Avalon; the court of the Elven King," said the blonde elf. "I don't suppose that you invite travelers down here very often..." said Gilda, the

suspicion obvious in her tone.

"We do not, but my king has a special interest in your young companion," replied the red- haired elf.

"Me?" asked Aisling.

The elf girl nodded.

"I wished you were around and you appeared. Is that why?"

"We have been watching you for some time, girl. Since the boggarts brought you to our world. When we reach the palace, my king will explain everything, I promise. Follow me please, and stay on the path. It is a long walk to the palace yet."

The elves led the way across what appeared to be an enormous bridge. A lattice of thin, filigree-like roots crisscrossed above the main path, giving the impression of a canopy. It pulled her back in and shook her from her momentary daze.

"Be wary," said the blonde elf. "Stay on the path."

Beyond that bridge, the world of the elves rose up out of the darkness. Despite her own misgivings, Aisling looked over the side, but the pit was impossibly deep, far too deep to see anything. Its inky blackness seemed to swallow all light, extinguishing it completely in its bottomless depths.

It was so dizzyingly deep that Aisling found herself losing her footing as she stared. She teetered slightly, then felt a strong hand on her upper arm.

"Be careful, mortal. It is a long way to the bottom," said the blonde elf.

The closer they got to the castle, the darker it became outside the path. It seemed as if the city proper, and all its dazzling faerie lights, was now miles behind them. Though they had been walking for very long, the fatigue of their journey was beginning to weigh upon them. Even Gilda and Hans, who were no strangers to long walks in the wilderness, seemed to be moving much more slowly than usual.

The path they tread on became thinner as they went. In no time at all, they had gone from walking two by two, to moving single file along the bridge. All around them, the darkness of the pit spread upward, encompassing everything around them, even the formerly bright lights of the palace in the distance. In that darkness, Aisling could hear all sorts of things: laughter and crying, shouting, whispers; all coming from voices that some part of her seemed to recognize.

She listened more intently, trying to discern one or two voices amongst the cacophony of whispers. Suddenly, she latched onto something, something haunting. She heard what sounded like her niece and nephew, Thomas and Mary, crying out for her in the darkness. She had heard those cries before, whenever one of the twins had a nightmare.

She hated when the children had nightmares. It wasn't that they were inconsolable. A lullaby from either her or their mother would usually placate them fairly quickly. No, it was just that their nightmares always reminded Aisling of her own bad dreams. The ones that came in waves following her parents' deaths, and haunted her incessantly for months afterwards.

She remembered dreams of her mother and father, moldering and sticky with sweat, rising from the plague pit they had been buried in to reclaim her and pull her in with them. It had been years since she'd had that dream, but the memory of it still sent shivers down her spine.

The further they went down the path, the louder the children's screams became. The more she focused on it, the more the other sounds seemed to fade away. Soon all she could hear was the wailing of her beloved twins. She wanted to turn, to run the other way, but there was nowhere to go but forward now.

She turned to look behind her, to see if Hans and Gilda and Hoegabbler were experiencing the same thing, when her foot slipped suddenly on a root. The elf beside her reached out to grab her, but she fell too fast, and his hand missed her own by mere inches. Hoegabbler leapt from Hans' shoulder, plunging into the darkness after her, and a moment later they had both disappeared.

Chapter Fifteen

Off The Path

isling did not fall unconscious as she plummeted downward. It wasn't like the last time, when the ground crumbled beneath the roots of the Gallows Tree. This time, she didn't fall into something, she fell into nothing. She tried to look around her, to see if anyone was coming after her, but could see only darkness. A moment, or perhaps a lifetime later, and she was standing in front of the cottage.

It was her home, her farm, she would know it anywhere. It was daylight and the sun was sitting high in the sky. She looked around for any sign of her family, then, hearing what she thought were the sounds of plates and cups being moved, she ran to the front door.

"Eleanor!" she shouted as she pushed open the door. "Jonathon! Thomas! Mary?"

She called for everyone, but there was no answer. The house looked as it always had, but no fire burned in the hearth. The furniture looked lived-in, the same as it always did, but there was no one living in that house. Not for a long time.

How long had she been gone? How many years had passed between this moment and the night she had left?

"No, not left," she thought. "Taken."

Aisling feared that the few weeks she had spent in the Seven Realms had amounted to much longer in the real world. She knew about the faerie lands, the lands of eternal youth, and never-ending midsummer. She knew that some, like Thomas the Rhymer, had gone away for what felt like the space of a week or a month, only to return to the mortal world as an old man, in a time when all he knew was already dead and gone.

She called out again for her family, but still no one called back. Nervously, she climbed up into the loft, into her old bedroom, to see if there was any sign of where the twins had gone. They had been so young when she left...

The only thing left in the loft was her straw mattress and a crumpled mess of old blankets. She rifled through the covers, looking for anything, and suddenly, she felt it. It was round and cold, her gold coin. Her inheritance. Without thinking, she checked in her apron pocket. The nightingale was in there, still snoozing as it had been when she fell.

Her mother's thimble was still around her neck, but felt cold, unnaturally so. She checked the other pocket. The lock of hair was still in the purse where she left it, but the coin was absent. She looked at the coin in her hand. That was her coin, she knew it for certain. She had seen it a hundred times. She knew its slight weight in her hand. So how had it gotten back here before she had?

"Hey, little one," she said, picking up the nightingale and prodding it gently. "Wake up, little one. I think we're home."

But try as she might, the bird would not stir. It was still alive, she knew that for sure, but she couldn't wake it. She gently replaced the bird in her pocket and put the gold coin back into the other. Then she made her way downstairs and out the cottage door.

Sitting outside the door was a small, black cat.

"Hello, there," said Aisling. "Where did you come from, ey?"

The cat said nothing in reply. Aisling surmised that if she was still in the Seven Realms, the cat would have had the power of speech.

"I must be home then..." she said, though with no small amount of uncertainty.

The cat gave a quizzical look and tilted its head, then it mewled and darted off towards the barn. Aisling, recognizing that the cat was the only other living creature she had encountered besides herself or the nightingale, chased after it. As she rounded the barn, she saw two young children playing in a pile of mud.

"Thomas! Mary!" she shouted, and she ran towards them.

The moment that she said their names, however, the children vanished. She turned, thinking that she had ran past them, but could see no sign of them.

"No!" she shouted, frustratedly.

A storm began to roll in overhead. Clouds, darker than

any she had ever seen, began to blot out the warm afternoon sun. She looked up to see what was happening and heard what sounded like Eleanor, frantically calling for the twins to come back to the house. She sounded terrified.

Aisling turned around and saw two shadowy shapes running pell-mell towards Eleanor, who was crouched by the cottage door. When the shapes hit her, they resolved themselves into the children or, at least, what looked like the children from behind. She couldn't see their faces from her vantage.

There was a crack of thunder and a flash of lightning, followed by the sound of crying.

Thomas and Mary were wailing, Eleanor was sobbing. But where was Jonathan?

A shadow slid across the sky then, a massive winged shadow, that blotted out the sun and moved the clouds. Thunder and lightning followed in its wake and Aisling felt the sensation of intense heat all around her. As it passed over the house, the heat intensified. Thomas separated from his mother and his shape blurred again. He turned and ran towards Aisling, and a moment later, before she could make out his face entirely, he was engulfed in flames. Aisling screamed.

She blinked and she was no longer on their family farm, but was standing in a gray field at sundown. Aisling swallowed hard. She had been here before, so many times before. This was the field they had buried the dead in, when the Sweating sickness took her family.

The plague pit they had dug was open and the smell of body odor, of sickness, of death, and decay hung on the air like a noxious miasma. She was dreaming. She was sure of it now. But how in the world was she going to get out of the dream before what was going to happen, happened?

"How, indeed," said a voice behind her.

Aisling turned to see a man standing a few feet in front of her. He was dressed very plainly, in a hooded cloak. She couldn't make out much else about him except the thin lips and dimpled chin revealed beneath his hood.

"Who are you? What is this?" she asked.

"You fell from the path," replied the hooded man.

"Is this…is this Hell?" she asked, certain that the answer would be yes. "No, child," assured the man. "This is a dream."

"If it's a dream, how do I wake up?"

"That is up to you. It is your dream after all," he said, unsmiling. "Can you help me?" she pleaded.

"No, as we said, it is your dream. Only you can wake from it."

Behind them, Aisling could hear the earth begin to shift and move. She knew that sound as well as she knew that place. Any moment now and the desiccated, putrefied bodies of her family were going to emerge from that pit and come for her.

"I don't have much time," she said. "Please, tell me what I need to do."

"You have all the time in the world," he said.

"If you help me," she said, considering it for a moment. "I'll trade you something. Maybe we can strike up a bargain. I don't have much…"

"No, no," said the man, his dour expression turning

harsher. "We have seen how your bargains work out. We have seen what happens to those who deal with Aisling Mason."

Aisling couldn't help but feel a bit insulted by the man's implication, then, considering her situation, she chose not to rise and remained calm. Wheezing groans and the sounds of shambling feet began to stir behind her.

The man smiled, revealing a mouthful of sharp and crooked teeth. All of a sudden he was shorter. It looked as if he were hunching over, and his limbs had become elongated, distorted.

Before going to the Seven Realms, Aisling would have backed away from such a man, but she knew what stood behind her, and she was more afraid of that than any hooded stranger in a dream. Instead, she moved towards the man, placing her hand on the hilt of her sword as she did so.

"I think you want to strike a bargain," she said, threateningly.

"Ohh, such bravery. We can see why they chose you in the first place. If you're so brave, then why not turn around and face mummy and daddy?" he teased.

Aisling sneered at the man and drew her blade, but before she could say anything else, she heard a sound to her right that sounded like a cat's meow. She turned to look and saw the black cat from earlier, standing in front of a small, wooden gate. The cat mewled again, beckoning her to go that way, to follow it. When she turned back to see to the hooded man, he was gone.

"Aisling…" said a gravely familiar voice behind her.

Without looking back to see whose voice it was, she ran

towards the cat. No sooner had she gotten past the gateposts, than she found herself standing at the entrance to a cave she had seen only once before. The cat was there too, and it mewled at her before padding swiftly into the cave.

"Bloody cat..." she cursed and, sword in hand, followed it into the darkened cave. She had no torch this time, but somehow, in the manner of dreams, she knew the way.

The cave opened up to the same unusual sitting room she had been in the day she met the Crones. They were there too, ugly, identical, and batty as ever.

"Come back this way again?" asked the first, who was knitting in one of the old armchairs.

"That's odd, then," said the second, who was polishing a silver kettle.

"Aren't you supposed to be on a quest, girl?" asked the third, who had been reading a very large book.

"I followed the cat," replied Aisling. "Always a wise decision."

"They know their way through the world, don't they?" "Through all worlds."

"Is this still a dream?" she asked. "Oh yes, all a dream." "Such a dream." "Just a dream."

It hit her then, if it really was a dream, it was her dream and she could direct it where she wanted it to go.

"I want to make a deal," she said aloud.

The crones cackled and suddenly the dim light that had illuminated their cave went out.

Aisling found herself sitting in another room, this one full to the brim with an unusual assemblage of objects. All of it, the buttons and baubles, broken toys, battered books, and torn blankets, seemed to be little more than junk and yet they felt significant somehow. She saw splintered hobby horses, chipped ninepins, dozens of well-weathered balls, toy soldiers, and tattered dolls. She walked past them all, barely registering how similar many of the toys looked to her own hand-me-down ones.

The cavern was damp, and even just standing there, amidst all the bric-a-brac, she felt almost as if she herself were as lost and forgotten as those things; but not so lost as to not be able find her way home.

Out of the corner of her eye, lurking in the periphery behind a broken hobby horse, was the black cat. It eyed her warily, slinking into the shadows.

"What can you offer me?" said a gurgling, phlegm-choked voice. "I know that voice," said Aisling.

"You do, do you?" it said, and Aisling could hear it moving now, shuffling through the piles of trash around her. "Do you know us, then?"

"You're a bogeyman."

"We are the sluagh. These are our treasures," it said, its guttural voice sounding reverential as it reverberated around the room.

"They're wonderful," said Aisling. "Where did you find all of them?"

She looked around the darkened chamber making sure to keep an eye on the sluagh's shadow as it passed from pile to pile.

"The children," it whispered.

There was triumph in that statement that worried Aisling. This was no bumbling bogeyman, this faerie was not to be meddled with.

"If you let me go, I'll give you something dear to me," she pressed, her fingers running over the coin in her pocket.

"Trinkets and trifles," it said, and the sluagh's mucousy voice was right next to her left ear now. "We've plenty of those."

"These are valuable though..." she said, trying her best not to sound frightened.

"You have something of much greater value to us," it cooed. "If you're willing to part with it."

Aisling didn't know what it was, but she was certain that whatever the sluagh wanted from her, it was something she did not want to part with.

"What is it you want?" she asked.

"Your dreams, Aisling Mason. We want your dreams."

"And if I give you my dreams...you'll let me out of this one? You'll return me to the path?"

"If that is what you wish," it replied.

Though she couldn't see it, she heard the smile, what she imagined to be a grim unpleasant smile, implied by its statement.

Aisling, who knew the ways of faeries, understood the importance of distinction when it came to bargaining. If she struck a bargain with the sluagh, then she would have to be very careful about specifying the terms of their agreement.

She felt the creature's shadow loom over her. "And if I want you to return me to my home, to the mortal world?" she added. "Then you will return to the mortal world," answered the sluagh, matter-of-factly.

Regardless of her misgivings about dealing with the

faerie, the thought of being able to finally go home was very tempting indeed. No more trolls or brambles, no more curses and swords and faerie magic. She could go home and see Thomas and Mary. She could see Jonathon and Eleanor. She could be free from the prophecy that loomed over her as surely as the sluagh now did.

She wondered how many of these deals the sluagh had made in the past. How many lost children it had promised to love, or care for, or to return home.

"So many," said the sluagh. "So many have wanted so much, and they will trade us anything to get it. Everything."

"But you didn't give it to them. You lied," she accused.

Aisling heard a crash of falling wood and clattering beads, followed by the sound of footsteps running towards her.

"You accuse us?!" shouted the furious sluagh, now inches from her face. "We gave what we promised! We keep our promises! Can you say the same, Aisling Mason?"

And it was there, standing in that dark place, and hearing it said in the sluagh's hacking, terrible voice, that Aisling knew the truth. She wanted to go home more than anything else in the entire world, but she couldn't, not yet anyway. There were people depending on her in the Seven Realms, people in the grip of a curse that, as far as she knew, only she could help them lift.

If she agreed to go home now, then who knew what would happen to the people of Stonewall, to the other kingdoms she hadn't even been to yet...to Gilda and Hans, and Hoegabbler.

Suddenly, the black cat darted out from under a fallen

rocking chair and stood between Aisling and the sluagh. It hissed at the monster, who backed away slightly. Now that Aisling could see it more clearly, she understood why it had glamoured itself and hid in the shadows. In its true form, the sluagh looked much like the bogeymen, but taller, thinner, more skeletal. Yet rather than appear more fearsome, its slenderness only served to highlight the faerie's frailty. It gazed at her with sunken malevolent eyes and said,

"Your dreams for your freedom from this one. That is our bargain."

"Very well," said Aisling. "If you return me to the path, exactly where I fell, then you can have my dreams."

The sluagh smiled and held out a long-fingered hand. "The coin, Aisling Mason. Your dreams."

Aisling took the golden crown from her pocket and held it between her thumb and forefinger. She had lost much already on her journey through the Seven Realms, and she was certain she would lose much more before it was done. What was a gold coin in the grand scheme of things, anyway? People gave them away all the time. And with that, she handed it the coin.

Chapter Sixteen

Fairest of the Fair Folk

isling…are you ok?" said a voice she recognized.

Aisling awoke from her dream to a place she had never seen before. She was lying in a large bed wearing only a nightshirt. Hoegabbler, in his cat shape, was lying next to her curled up in a ball. She looked around the room. Gilda and Hans were standing above her, looking worried. On the other side of the bed stood a female elf in a long, flowing green dress; she was holding a bowl.

"I think so. I fell from the path," said Aisling, wearily.

"We know," said Hans. "Hoegabbler tried to come after you, but you both disappeared. The elves told us to keep moving and when we got here, there the both of you were, sleeping soundly and safely."

"I wasn't safe. I was trapped inside a dream. It's difficult to explain."

"There is no need," said a heavily accented voice at the end of the bed.

An elf stood there, but he was unlike any of the elves she had encountered. He was tall and lean, yes, but he did not appear young. His clothes looked as though they had been woven from dried leaves and leather. They flaked as he moved and gestured, crumbling to the ground in dried bits, yet replenishing themselves a moment later.

His long hair was white as the first snows of winter as was his beard, and both fell in cascading tresses to his waist. His pointed ears were longer, more definitively elfin than those of the elves who had led them there. His smile was warm and inviting. His eyes, like all the sidhe, were his most striking feature. They were a pale green, the same color as the grass at the end of a summer; the same green as Aisling's.

"Your dreams are your own, Aisling Mason, and you have come through them unscathed," said the old elf.

At that moment, Aisling remembered the end of her dream and the bargain she had struck with the monster inside it. Her dreams had indeed been her own, but now they belonged to someone else.

"I am Auberon, King of the Sidhe. You and your friends are most welcome," he added. "Thank you, Your Majesty. And thank you for saving me," said Aisling.

Hoegabbler shifted in his spot and opened his eyes, letting out a great yawn. Then, blinking groggily, he looked around the room and upon seeing the elf king jumped from the bed and into a kneeling position before him.

"My lord, Auberon. I am most humbled...I am,.my

lord…uh, Your Majesty…" he stammered.

"It is all right, Hoegabbler. You have done well. You brought her safely to us," said the elf king, smiling.

"You..you were the cat in my dream, weren't you, Hoegabbler?" asked the girl.

"Yes. I couldn't let you go alone, Aisling. Not after the last time. I won't abandon you again," he replied.

Aisling got to her knees and scooped up the feline Hoegabbler, hugging him tightly to her.

"Thank you."

"Your Majesty, the girl still needs to rest. I insist we let her sleep now," said the elf woman with the bowl.

"Yes, yes," agreed the king. "Gilda, Hans, if you would follow me, we can find you both accommodations. Your friend does indeed need to rest."

Gilda nodded, then, after placing a hand on Aisling's shoulder, beckoned Hans to follow her out.

"We'll talk tomorrow," he said, and he leaned over to give Aisling a hug. "May I stay?" asked Hoegabbler.

"Of course," said Auberon. "Rest now, little mortal. We have much to discuss. Sweet dreams."

The elf king smiled then, it was a knowing smile, and in it Aisling understood why her grandmother had warned her so fervently about the fair folk.

Try as she might, Aisling couldn't sleep after that. Once Hoegabbler was asleep again, she hopped out of the bed and padded across the dusty castle floor to the terrace outside her room. She leaned upon the wooden railing made of knotted roots and stared out into the distance. Miles from them, the city of the sidhe gleamed and glimmered in its own light.

"It's beautiful, isn't it?" said Hoegabbler, who was now perched on the railing beside her. "It is," replied Aisling. "I can't sleep."

"I know," said the changeling, and his rodent-like face was a mask of uncertainty. "You were there, in the dream. Weren't you?"

"I was. I couldn't let you fall, not again. You've given up something great, Aisling, greater than you realize. And you did it for us. Why?" he asked.

"Because like it or not, this is as much my home now as the mortal world was. Seeing the Crones again brought it all back to me. What if by breaking the curses, we restore this place to the way it was? What if, in doing so, we break the spell that binds the Foundlings and the other lost children to this realm? Thomas and Mary have their mother and father still, but the children here, the ones in pain, they have no one else. It was the only thing to do."

Hoegabbler nodded, then scurried back to the bed. A few minutes later and Aisling followed. She lay down and turned on her side, still staring out at the terrace window. Then, either a minute or an hour later, she fell into deep and dreamless sleep.

The next day, Aisling awoke to several beautiful sidhe handmaidens standing at the end of her bed next to a basin. They explained that king Auberon had sent them to bathe her and dress her wounds. Aisling, who hadn't bathed in she couldn't remember how long, took one look at the steaming bathwater and hopped in.

When she was clean and dressed, Aisling was escorted down to the dining hall, where the elves had put out quite a sumptuous feast. The sheer volume of food laden upon the table was enough to make their breakfast banquet at the Gardener's Tower look like little more than meager scraps.

The long, wooden table was covered from end-to-end in the most exquisite foods imaginable. There were fresh fruits, each one so perfect and ripe that their sweet scent wafted about the room. There was roast duck, roast pheasant, roast turkey, a dozen roasted quails, and an enormous suckling pig. There were stewed root vegetables, mashed potatoes, garlicky green beans, and sugary glazed carrots. Loaves of crusty breads, braided in the most intricate shapes imaginable, sat next to pots of creamed butter and golden honey. Jugs of wine, mead, and warm milk had been placed on the table at various intervals.

Gilda and Hans sat next to one another at the far end of the table, Hoegabbler was seated adjacent to them. Auberon sat at the head of the table and next to him, to his right, was a gorgeous sidhe woman, more beautiful than any person that Aisling had ever laid eyes upon. She wore a dress of green silks and seedpods. Her hair was the color of a wheat field and her eyes, as Aisling found out when she sat, were evergreen.

"Welcome to my table, Aisling Mason," she said as a servant pulled out the chair for Aisling.

"Milady," said Aisling, curtsying before she took her seat.

"Such manners, my love. You were quite right about this one," said the elf woman. "Indeed, my dearest one. Aisling, this is Titania, my lady queen. Is she not the fairest in all the land?" said the king, sipping at the milk the elvish attendant had just poured for him. "Oh yes, truly the fairest, Your Majesty," replied Aisling, nervously.

"Now that we're all here," said Auberon. "Eat and drink your fill. Attendants, strike up the band."

Aisling, having heard the stories too many times to count, reached for a succulent looking chicken leg and then put it back on the plate.

"Aren't you hungry?" asked Titania.

"I am...starving actually, but no offense, I've been warned about faerie food," said Aisling.

The elf king chuckled.

"My dear Aisling, if we wanted to poison you or bewitch you into staying here with us, we would have done so already. We have no need of you or your companions dead, nor do we need you here to 'dance the faerie reel' or whatever you quaint mortals call it these days. I promise you, the food is safe to eat, and you'll find no finer meal anywhere in the Seven Realms."

Aisling blushed. She felt foolish for having doubted them. Thus far, the sidhe had been far more decent than any of her grandmother's stories. She wondered if it was all a matter of misinterpretation. Of course, having insulted them quite enough already for one night, she guessed that might be a discussion for another time.

The four of them ate with gusto, as if they hadn't eaten for days. Auberon had been right, the food was better than anything Aisling had ever tasted. The wine was sweeter, the meat was juicier, and the mashed potatoes even creamier than she had thought possible. She wagered that the food was imbued with some kind of magic, but once she'd had her first taste, even that thought didn't slow her down.

"So," said Gilda. "Not to sound ungrateful, Your Majesty, or to you, my lady, but why have you invited us here? I'm not one to look a gift horse in the mouth but even I'll admit that we wished for elves and suddenly elves appeared. It's definitely far too convenient for my liking."

"We also know that when it comes to the fae, you can never get anything without giving something up," added her brother. "We've accepted your meal and your hospitality. You helped rescue Aisling and Hoegabbler. So, what do you want in return for all this kindness?"

"Your help in defeating Maledicta, of course," said the king, sipping his wine. Hoegabbler dropped his fork, then scurried to quickly pick it up.

"I beg your pardon?" asked Gilda.

"It might come as a surprise to you, Gilda, that my people are not content to live as we currently are; trapped beneath the world in the halfway point between realms. It was Maledicta's rise to power that pushed us here, and it is only by her death that we will be free once again," explained Auberon.

"But the elves were never part of the Seven Realms, you were never involved in any of the wars. Why would she have banished you here?" asked Hans.

"Because we were the ones who gave one poor farm boy the keys to the kingdom. It was my queen, Titania, who first reached out to the last true king and gave him the King's Blade.

With it, he would have the power to end the wars of men and bring about an age of peace and prosperity.

During his rule, we were given the forest of Verdenwald to rule over. Soon though, the sons and daughters of the true king and queen moved into the area. We offered to share with them. They accepted. In time, we decided to push ourselves back between the worlds. It was easier to go between the Seven Realms and the mortal world. My queen and I left for some time then, to live amongst the mortals of your world, Aisling, and learn your ways.

When we returned, we found ourselves trapped in the space between worlds, and our enemies, the Unseelie, had now taken our spot in the Seven Realms."

"What are the Unseelie?" asked Aisling.

"Bogeys, hobs, goblins, trolls, and…sluagh," said Hoegabbler, shooting Aisling a look. "The Unseelie were now in control of the gateway, and we were shut out. We could send a few elves here and there, but only into the Seven Realms. As for me and my wife, we were trapped here, along with most of our people.

Maledicta had chosen her allies well. With my people, the Seelie, out of the way, there was no one left to challenge her magical power. She released the great curse upon the land and it cemented her power even further. For years, we thought all hope was lost…and then you came along," said the elf king, looking at Aisling.

"Me? Is this part of the prophecy?" she asked.

"In a manner of speaking, yes. You are a very special child, Aisling Mason. In the mortal world, you're the seventh child of a seventh child, a rare and beautiful occurrence. It happens rarely, so rarely in fact, that even those who are looking for such a person fail to find them. We came looking for you, several years ago, but you and your family were suffering so greatly…and you were not yet of age. You could not help anyone as you were. So, we waited. But Maledicta's minions found you first," explained Titania.

"They took you," added Auberon. "Her Unseelie minions took you and brought you to our world before we could stop them. They knew you had to come willingly, so they attempted to take your niece and nephew first, knowing you would trade yourself to keep them safe. When they got you here, we lost track of you for a time, until Hoegabbler found you for us."

Aisling flashed Hoegabbler a quizzical look.

"The king asked me to keep you safe. To make sure that you got to where you needed to go. All they told me was that you were a mortal girl, I never expected that you were some sort of chosen hero," said the changeling.

"Neither did I…" she said, smiling warmly at him.

"So, Aisling really is some sort of prophetic hero then? She's the chosen one?" asked

Hans.

"Yes. As a seventh child born of a seventh child, she is the only one capable of saving the Seven Realms. Aisling Mason holds the key to all our salvation, and we must do what we can to help her," said Auberon, and his tone was less genial now.

"What about Stonewall, then? Will she really be able to help us break the curse on the Lady of Beasts?" asked Gilda, hopefully.

"I cannot see the future," said the sidhe king. "All I know is that she is the key. If she breaks the remaining six curses, then and only then, will she be able to face Maledicta. Until then, her power is too great."

"But if she's after me, won't she try and stop me first?" asked Aisling.

"The bogeymen who brought you here failed to bring you directly to her. Since then, they have been unable to track you down. You carry something very special on your person, Aisling Mason, the gift from your mother is no mere trifle," said Titania.

"My thimble? It's just a thimble," replied Aisling, taking the small, metal thimble from her pocket.

"As long as you carry it, Maledicta will be unable to touch you. Keep it safe."

"We have a way to break the curse on the Lady of Beasts," interrupted Gilda. "Lady Roselyn says that your people can help turn the Remedy Bloom into a potion to cure the beast curse. Please tell me you can…"

Auberon smiled. "We can indeed."

Gilda and Hans grinned at one another.

"Your Majesty…when can I go home?" asked Aisling.

Everyone at the table fell silent and all smiles faded. The king looked down at his plate, then sighed. When his eyes met Aisling's again, they were solemn. In them, Aisling could see the wisdom of the ages; a thousand years of experience and knowledge, a thousand years of pain, joy, and sorrow. She knew what the answer was even before he said it.

"When you have done what fate has chosen you to do, and the rightful king and queen once again sit upon the throne at Caerleon, then will the way to the mortal world be open to those such as we. When you have freed this land,

Aisling Mason, I promise I will take you home."

They sat in silence for a few minutes after that. Tears welled up in Aisling's eyes. She knew what he was going to say. She had heard too many stories to believe that she would be any different than all of those other heroes. She took a sip of wine and swallowed hard, pushing back the pain.

"All right," she said. "Let's start with the potion, then. Once we have that, you'll return us to Stonewall?"

"Of course," said the king, his infectious smile returning at last. "And you won't be going empty-handed."

They finished their meal and handed over the Remedy Bloom. That night, Aisling slept alone. She lay there, in her plush bed on silken sheets, staring up at a fresco of the stars on her bedroom ceiling. They were not the stars she remembered, but she was sure that she would soon learn their names as well as she knew the names of those back home. There was a knock at the door.

"Who is it?" asked Aisling, sounding startled. "King Auberon," replied the elf.

Aisling pulled the blankets up a little higher, then bid him to enter. "Having trouble sleeping?" he asked.

He strode in and sat at the end of her bed. "A bit."

"That will happen when one has no dreams."

"How do you…?" Aisling began.

"The realm of dreams is as much my home as this castle, child. More than that, though, I can sense it in you. The fair folk, as you call them, we subsist on the dreams of mortals. If I were to find you in your world, you would appear just as you do now, hollow, bereft of the dreamstuff that we need to empower our magic and immortality. I understand why you made the bargain, but I'm afraid that the full ramifications of that bargain will only reveal themselves in time," explained the king.

Aisling frowned. She knew what she wanted to ask the king. It had very little to do with the state of her dreams, but with the reality of her current situation.

"Your Majesty," she said, taking care to phrase her question very carefully. "Am I really trapped here until I save the Seven Realms? Is this really my destiny? I mean, I'm nobody. I'm not some hero of legend. I'm just a farmer's daughter. Why in the world did destiny choose me?"

"Destiny doesn't pick us based on how we see ourselves, Aisling. It has a greater plan in mind than we, limited in thinking as we invariably are, can ever truly comprehend. Frankly, destiny itself is only part of it. Fate will undoubtedly put you into its path, but only you can choose to run alongside it," he replied.

"What if I choose to walk down a different path? What if I don't want to play this game?" asked the girl.

"Well," considered the old elf. "If you don't, it can overtake you. Then again, if you're lucky enough, you can narrowly escape it...for a time, anyway."

"I'm rarely that lucky..." Auberon chuckled.

"I know I said that I'd accept my role in all of this. It was the whole reason I didn't accept the sluagh's offer," she said, pausing slightly.

"I understand what I need to do. At least part of it, anyway. I know that I'm expected to help save this place, my friends, and all those poor souls trapped inside the Witch's curse. How could I be so sure in the dream and yet so unsure now?"

"You're thirteen years old, Aisling. After all that you have seen, I am more than a little surprised that you're even this calm, and I don't surprise easily," he explained. "When it concerns the meandering river of your destiny, you've barely gotten your feet wet."

Aisling thought about the elf king's metaphor. Not so long ago, she too had thought of her prophesied destiny like a river. It was odd that he, too, saw it that way. Then, remembering what Auberon had told her at dinner, she turned to him once more.

"The farm boy, the one you gave the King's Blade to what did he think of all this?" she asked.

"He thought much the same as you. He was just a boy himself," replied the elf. "Did he try to avoid it?"

"No, his situation was a little different. He had seen what war was doing to his country, his friends, and his family. We were offering him the tools he needed to stop all of that death and destruction once and for all. If you think about it, it isn't all that different than what fate is asking of you. Much as you try to avoid it, Aisling, it will always catch you in the end. One way or another," said Auberon.

"But I thought you said I can choose..."

"Yes, you always have choices. There are always two paths. Fate will put you at the crossroads, but only you can choose which path you take."

Aisling thought she understood. It wasn't a good choice either way, but at least it was hers. A long silence stretched between them as they stared out into the starless underground of the faerie realm.

"I've dreamed about this, you know," said Aisling,

breaking the silence. "Being here, with the faeries, and learning these things. I never thought it would be anything like this, though. I never imagined it could actually be real."

"Certainly you did, it's why I kept an eye on you," said the elf king. "If things here hadn't gone as they did and fate hadn't snatched you up so quickly, I would have done so myself. Not one child in a hundred generations is as fortunate as you are, Aisling."

"I'm not a child," she replied reflexively. "No. Not anymore," he said.

Still smiling serenely, Auberon walked over and patted her on the shoulder, bid her goodnight, and exited the room. No sooner had he closed the door, than Aisling turned over onto her side, shut her eyes, and fell asleep.

Chapter Seventeen

A Bloody Business

he next morning, the four companions met their hosts at the castle gate. King Auberon and Queen Titania were waiting for them when they arrived. The only way back to the Seven Realms was to walk past the bridge of dreams once again, but this time, Aisling was ready.

"I suppose that this is goodbye, then?" asked Aisling. "For now, Aisling Mason, for now," replied Auberon.

"We have some parting gifts for you," added Titania, and she beckoned over one of the elvish handmaidens.

The elf girl was holding two ornate bows and matching quivers full of arrows, which she handed to her mistress.

"For the two rangers, elvish bows. They are carved from elder trees and strung with spider silk. The arrows are fletched with the feathers of dream grouses and tipped with elf shot, silver arrowheads. I suspect they will be instrumental in dealing with the threat to your homeland. May they ever strike true."

Hans and Gilda took the bows graciously, running their hands over the ornate carvings. "Your Majesties...I don't know what to say. I, that is, my brother and I...we are most grateful," stammered Gilda.

Hans nodded in agreement, still marveling at his new bow.

"That isn't all," added the queen. "As requested, here is the essence of the Remedy Bloom. Whatever led you to the bloom was correct, one sip of this potion will break even the strongest of curses, including the one upon Lady Isabelle. There isn't enough for the remaining six realms, I'm afraid, only three doses. Keep it safe. There is no potion like it in the entire world and the Remedy Bloom will not bloom again for another thirteen hundred years."

She handed a small vial of pearlescent liquid to Gilda, who took it reverentially. "Thank you, Your Majesties. You have no idea what this means to us."

"As for you, Aisling, you have heard quite a few stories in your time, have you not?" asked Auberon.

Aisling smiled.

"And told my share as well, Your Majesty."

"Indeed," beamed the king, "so you know then that every hero of legend must have a weapon, to fight the forces of evil so that good may triumph in the end. My smiths took a look at your sword, and frankly, that is no weapon for a hero with a destiny like your own. I had my finest smith work through the night to craft this for you."

From his robes the king drew a sword. The blade was sharp, Aisling could tell even at a distance, and it gleamed in the verdant light that surrounded them. The pommel was carved to resemble a four leaf clover. Other than that, it was not an ornate thing, not nearly as ornate as the bows the twins had received.

"I don't know how to use a sword like this..." said Aisling, nervously.

"Your friends can teach you. This is the blade of a hero, Aisling. It is rightfully yours," said Titania, placing a soft hand on Aisling's own.

Aisling took the sword. It was larger than her last one, and heavier in her hand, but even a few moments of holding it and it soon felt lighter. She hefted it higher, gazing into the shining blade and her own green eyes reflected there. It was indeed the sword of a hero, and it was her sword.

"Thank you, King Auberon...for everything," she said, strapping the sword and its ornate leather scabbard to her back.

Hoegabbler stood next to them, each of his companions appreciating their new gifts, and the changeling couldn't hide the look of longing on his face.

"We have no such gifts for you, Hoegabbler," said the queen, leaning down to meet his large, watery eyes. "All that I can offer you is advice. You ought not limit yourself to the shapes you have chosen thus far. You are more than a cat or a squirrel; far, far more."

The changeling smiled at his queen and nodded his head.

"My scouts will take you back across the path and out into the Seven Realms. I wish you all good fortune on your journey and in the tasks ahead," said the king.

The four companions stowed their new weapons and

walked out of the castle gates. No sooner had they begun to traverse the dark road back to the sidhe kingdom, however, than they suddenly found themselves standing in a grove of Rowan trees; their two horses were hitched to a nearby sapling and grazing placidly.

Aisling turned to say goodbye to the elves, but they had already gone. "What do we do now?" asked Hoegabbler.

"We head back to Stonewall, towards the Snarling Manor. With any luck, this potion should be able to break the curse on the Lady of Beasts…providing we can get close enough to her to use it," replied Gilda.

Suddenly, the nightingale flew out of Aisling's pocket and began to tweet in alarm.

Aisling and the twins could hear the familiar sounds of hoofbeats closing in all around them. A moment later and they found themselves surrounded by four red-cloaked riders. The man at the head of them, a burly, rough-looking fellow astride a giant dray, gazed down at them with the utmost disdain.

"Well, well, well, look who decided to show their faces again," he stated, "got tired of living it up in Verdenwald, then?"

"For your information, Chasseur, we were in Verdenwald helping to save them from their curse and gather some important allies," replied Gilda, angrily.

"Oh, have you? That's wonderful, they must be very grateful. In the meantime, Gunther has been turned. He was turned the night that you three rode off towards Verdenwald, when you abandoned your brothers and sisters to save another realm."

"We went to Verdenwald to find a cure for the curse affecting our people, and we have," replied Gilda, holding out the vial of pearlescent liquid.

"That? Some small amount of magic potion is going to stop the lady's minions from overrunning our remaining fields and villages?" laughed Chasseur.

Chasseur had a broad, chiseled face complete with a perpetual seven-day beard. He had thick eyebrows, pouty lips, and obvious dimples. He had a face that many a maid, Aisling included, would have found handsome in any other circumstance. His speech was hard, and his hands were rough, his frame was bulky and well-muscled.

His horse, a large, dusk-colored dray was as fierce, beautiful, and unapproachable as his rider. Chasseur's most striking feature, however, was not his horse, nor his face, nor even the bastard sword at his side, but his cloak. It was red like the rest of the riders', yet unlike theirs, Chasseur's cloak was made up of half a dozen pelts, all of which had been dyed crimson before being sewn together.

Aisling, having been chased by one not long before, could tell by the muzzles and ears and tails that made up the patchwork garment, that Chasseur's cloak was made of the formerly cursed citizens of Stonewall; cut from their bodies before they had even turned back to human.

"Who's left, then?" asked Hans, obviously trying to change the subject.

"Me, Ruger, Gilles, Emmanuelle, Sophie, and Fenton…and now you two," replied Chasseur, taking great pains to ignore Aisling entirely.

"That's it?" said Aisling "That's it."

Suddenly, a caw echoed through the clearing. Aisling looked up to see a flash of fluttering darkness swoop towards her briefly, then perch itself up onto Chasseur's outstretched forearm. A raven the size of an eagle had landed on the hunter's glove. Its beak was sharp and its great talons looked wicked enough to draw blood if they needed to.

With his free hand, Chasseur pulled a chunk of something red and dripping from the pouch on his saddlebags and handed it to the bird. It gobbled up the wet meat with great relish, its keen eyes surveying Aisling the whole time.

"Good boy," said Chasseur, stroking the bird's sleek head with his ungloved hand. "No sign of them?"

The great raven cawed, then chirruped in reply. Despite the fact that the animal clearly couldn't talk, it somehow made itself understood to Chasseur.

"Excellent. Go ahead and let the sentries at the camp know we're on our way."

The raven took one last quizzical look at Aisling and with one great flap of its wings, took off and headed east.

"If you want to help, then keep up. We're going to meet up with what's left of the Red Riders and the townsfolk who are willing to fight," said Chasseur.

With that, he turned his horse violently and galloped down the woodland path. Gilda and Hans looked at each other and followed.

"Did you see his cloak, Gilda? Doesn't he know those pelts belonged to people...his people?" asked Aisling, while struggling to hold on to Karl's saddle.

"He knows. He just doesn't care," she replied. "Chasseur is the worst example of a human being I've ever met. He's absolute troll dung, but he's also a damn fine hunter and he's saved our lives more than once. If Gunther has been changed, then Chasseur is the only chance we have left of turning the tide."

"Besides, we need him and the other riders to get us to the gates of the Snarling Manor. The villages closest to the manor were the first ones turned by the Lady of Beasts, they hunt in greater numbers there, and there are rumors that they don't just transform with the moon; that they've been monsters so long, they remain beasts at all times," said Hans.

Aisling swallowed hard. Perhaps she should have taken the sluagh up on its offer to send her home. At least in England she wouldn't have to worry about packs of angry beastmen.

"I wonder, though," Hans added, "how long do you think we were gone? I thought it was only a few days, but Chasseur said we rode off for Verdenwald weeks ago."

"We were in the faerie realm," replied Aisling, proud and confident that she knew the answer to something for once, "time passes strangely there. We may have felt like we were there for a day or two, but weeks, months, even years can sometimes pass in the outside world during that time."

Hans and Gilda nodded in understanding. Hoegabbler just smiled. "You do know your stuff, Aisling," he said.

As they did traveled, Aisling rifled through her satchel and took stock of her belongings. She still had the prophet and lock of her sister's hair. Her mother's thimble still hung around her neck, right next to the scabbard for her new sword. The coin was gone, but she had assumed this to be the case.

She reached into her bag again and felt something prick her finger. She yanked it out to find a bead of crimson forming from a minuscule cut. Looking into the bag, Aisling saw the rose that Lady Roselyn had given her. It seemed that the flower was as unaffected by their time in the faerie realm as they had been. It was as fresh and red as if it had just been picked.

They rode for miles until they reached a large farmstead on the outskirts of the forest. Two sentries, both of whom were plainly peasants in borrowed armor, stopped them for only a moment before Chasseur waved the rest of the group forward.

Dozens of people were there, almost all of them adult men and women. They were a scraggly lot, skinnier than they ought to be, but there was something extremely threatening about them. They had a determined look about them that Aisling had seen before. It was the same look she had seen on the faces of the remaining villagers after the Sweat had taken most of the population. These were people at the end of their ropes who were going to go down fighting if it came to it.

A couple blacksmiths in heavily burnt leather aprons stood working out of a makeshift forge in the center of the camp. Villagers were walking up to them in lines, handing them all manner of weapons and farm implements and waiting as the smiths dipped the weapons in a shallow crucible of what appeared to be rapidlydwindling silver. Aisling saw one of the Red Riders hop off her horse and hand the smith a leather pouch, which he then dumped into the crucible. A dozen or so shining silver coins fell into the molten liquid and melted away a moment later. The villagers were truly giving everything they had to this one last attempt at freedom.

Chasseur deftly dismounted and swept his way towards the largest tent. Hans and Gilda followed close, trying their best to keep up with his great, determined strides. Inside the tent were four other red-cloaked rangers, all of them standing over a map. For the first time, Aisling saw the immensity of the Seven Realms displayed for her. The world she had found herself in was far larger than she had anticipated. The sheer scale of it, coupled with her own uncertainty about the apparently forked road of destiny that lay before her, made her feel very small indeed.

"Where are we on the siege?" asked Chasseur, brusquely.

"It's hardly a siege…but we're ready to march on the new moon. That will ensure that the beasts will be at their weakest," replied a skinny, dark-haired female rider. "I want to say it again in your hearing Chasseur, we're most likely not going to win this one."

"Then we go down fighting," said Chasseur.

Aisling was not ready to die fighting. Yet among this group of people, those who have come to this by desperation, she knew that might not be a popular position to take.

"Has it really come to this?" asked Hans.

"Why, boy? Does the prospect of battle frighten you? Your sister always had more guts than that," Chasseur teased.

"What else do we know about the beasts nearest to the manor?" asked Gilda, breaking the tension.

"They're nothing like the curs we've found in the lower forests. The people from that village are all manner of monsters, bears, boars, cats, and bulls. They say the Lady herself is a mix of them all; a monstrous menagerie folded into one person," replied the rider named Fenton.

"So, why assault the castle directly? What does that get us or the villagers? Except killed, of course," said Gilda, sarcastically.

"We've all discussed the risks. This is the only chance we'll have to stop this before it gets any worse. I suppose you'd rather keep skulking about, killing her minions one at a time, then? That plan worked out so well for Gunther and his predecessor," Chasseur snarled.

"Of course not, but the fact remains that none of us will survive if we don't get to the Lady of Beasts and stop the curse at its source. It's how Hans, Aisling, Hoegabbler, and I did it in Verdenwald. We woke the Lady of Briars and the curse upon their lands lifted entirely. If we can get to the Lady of Beasts and administer the potion, then the curse will be broken. All of her minions will change back to the men and women they once were. That's the only way we're going to win, and I think despite your misgivings, you know it to be true."

Chasseur grimaced. He didn't want to admit it, but it was clear by his expression that he knew Gilda was right.

"What do you suggest then?" he replied.

The rest of the Red Riders looked at her expectantly. Gilda had not been prepared for this. She looked to Hans, then to Aisling, but neither of them had the answer either. She thought for a second, and then it came to her.

"Well," she began, "you were all prepared for a frontal assault on the manor, right? What if we use that to our advantage? If you lot and the villagers can draw her forces away from the castle proper, then Hans, Aisling, Hoegabbler, and I can sneak in and find the lady. We can give her the potion and end this once and for all."

"And what if 'the lady' won't take your magic potion?" asked Chasseur.

Gilda had considered this. It was a thought she had grappled with a thousand times before, though one she had never actually put into words.

"Then we take her down and hope her death ends the curse," she said.

Aisling winced. Gilda's admission was a grim truth and she wished that they could find another way, but Chasseur and the Red Riders were not looking for a peaceful solution. Her friend knew that, and had chosen her words very carefully.

Chasseur considered Gilda's plan. He looked around the tent, taking in everyone, including Aisling. His obsidian eyes met hers for the briefest of moments, and Aisling felt like a fawn staring down the length of his arrow.

"What about you?" he asked the gathered riders, "do you agree with the girl's plan?"

The Red Riders nodded. They had fought alongside both Chasseur and the twins. They trusted them all with their lives.

"It's not like we have a lot of time to decide," said Fenton, "the new moon will rise tomorrow night. We may not get another chance. We'll follow you into battle, Chasseur, and trust that Gilda, Hans, and their companions can do the deed."

Chasseur nodded and swept out of the tent. That night,

Gilda and Hans chose to find their own accommodations, but not before pitching a small tent for Aisling and Hoegabbler to share. It was a dreadful night. Storm clouds rolled in around sunset and they grew in gloom and menace as the evening progressed.

Aisling and Hoegabbler had little chance to discuss their part in the plan with the twins.

Nevertheless, both of them trusted Hans and Gilda enough to lead them in the right direction when the time came.

The camp was reasonably quiet that night. Aisling suspected that everyone was trying their best to get a good night's sleep before they marched off to face whatever awaited them the next day. She also suspected that most of them were, like her, staring up at the underside of their tent and absolutely unable to sleep.

Aisling wandered about the camp, taking in everything she could. After a while, she came to what looked like a small, makeshift graveyard. Dozens upon dozens of tiny gravestones were set in rows upon what had obviously once been a planting field. In the distance, kneeling over one of the many graves, was Chasseur.

Aisling, keen as she was not to disturb a man like Chasseur, made to move back towards her tent.

"Where do you think you're going?" he said, not looking up from his vigil. Obviously the hunter's senses were far too attuned for her to sneak away unnoticed. "I was just...I didn't mean to disturb..."

"Don't apologize. I was already done," said the man, getting slowly to his feet.

Above them, a sliver of the waning moon shone through the gathering gloom. The man slowly made his way over to Aisling. Chasseur was a big man, but up close and with no one else around, he seemed bigger somehow. He walked up to Aisling and glared down at her.

"So, you're the orphan girl Gunther was talking about?" he said. Aisling nodded.

"Can't sleep either?" She nodded again.

"Come on then, I've got something for that back at my tent."

Aisling wasn't quite sure she trusted Chasseur. In truth, he had done nothing to inspire any sort of trust in her since their first meeting. But, as that first meeting had only happened a few hours earlier, she realized that might not be fair. Reluctantly, she followed him. No one stopped them as they made their way through the camp and to his large tent on the far end.

Chasseur's raven was perched atop one of the crossed tent poles that stood above the entrance to the tent. He cawed down at them as they entered, first Chasseur, then Aisling.

Chasseur stepped over to a small table and uncorked a potbellied bottle of burgundy liquid. He poured a small amount of the liquid into a silver cup, then brought the bottle to his lips to take a swig.

"You don't look old enough to drink," he said, setting the bottle back down and bringing the cup over to Aisling. "Then again...what does it really matter?"

He handed the cup of wine to Aisling and she took a sip. It was far less sweet than the wines she had tasted so far, and much more potent. She coughed as she tried to swallow it.

"It'll put hair on your chest. Mark my words," he chuckled, taking another swig. Chasseur took off his cloak and threw it onto the bed. He sat down.

"The twins have taken a shine to you and your little changeling friend."

"They saved me. I saved them. We've been together a while now," she replied, still coughing a little.

"Are you frightened of me, girl?" asked the hunter.

Aisling's eyes shifted uncomfortably to Chasseur's grim cloak. He followed their movement.

"That's what frightens you, then? That I'm not afraid to do what needs to be done?" he asked.

Aisling didn't need to answer.

"It's a bloody business, that much is true...I never asked for this either, you know. My father was a tanner, my mother was a seamstress. My brothers and sisters grew to be farmers, shepherds, hunters, mothers, fathers..."

Chasseur took another great glug of wine, finishing most of the bottle.

"But like everyone else in this gods-forsaken place, they fell, onebyone to the curse. It was slow at first, it only happened during the full moon. We didn't even notice the patterns when it began. Then the livestock began to suffer and villagers began to disappear. Then my niece went missing..."

He stopped and shook his head.

"I'm sure the twins told you all of this already. Anyway, the point is...I do what has to be done to protect those who are left. It's not me you should fear, girl, nor the duties I carry out in service to our people's safety. You should fear what happens if we fail tomorrow. That's all I fear anymore."

Aisling nodded. She didn't know what else to say. "Finish your wine, it will help you sleep."

She finished her wine, then handed the cup back to Chasseur. "Thank you," she said, forcing a slight smile.

"You're welcome. Go get some rest, you'll need it for tomorrow."

He didn't smile, but Aisling suspected that wasn't something he did easily. She left the tent and headed back to her own. No sooner had she lay herself down onto the bedroll, than rain began to patter upon the top of the tent. Hoegabbler moved closer to her and curled up into a tight ball at her side. The nightingale, who had been slumbering in a small pile of clothes, fluttered its way down and nestled itself on her pillow.

As she lay there, listening to the rain beat a persistent tattoo on the canvas above her, Aisling thought about tomorrow. Chasseur was right. She was certainly going to need her rest.

Chapter Eighteen

Beasts in the Garden

hey awoke the next morning after a scant few hours rest. The day Aisling had been dreading had finally arrived and just as the storm clouds had foretold, it was pouring

rain. Outside her small tent, the Red Riders and the army of peasants were bustling about, all of them heedless of the persistent rainfall and all readying themselves for the battle to come.

Hoegabbler was sitting at the end of her bedroll as she dressed, looking nervous. "What if I can't face them?" asked the changeling.

"If I can do it, you can do it. We'll face them together. Besides, our job isn't to fight the lady's beasts, but to get inside the manor and face the lady herself. The less time we spend in the battle, the better."

She stared outside of the tent, at the people bustling to and fro, gearing up with makeshift weapons and armor to fight their cursed countrymen. In that moment, Aisling realized that this was the first time she had even seen rain since she came to the Seven Realms. She stuck her hand out into the rain and felt the drops fall lightly upon it. The rain, like so much else in this place, was the same.

"Let's go," she said.

The two companions walked out to meet Gilda and Hans, who stood amidst their brethren, waiting for Chasseur's arrival. The caw of the giant crow heralded his approach as the large bird swooped into the clearing, alighting onto the top of a nearby tent.

"Are you ready for this, Aisling?" asked Hans. "You don't have to go with us this time.

We have the cure, we can breach the castle ourselves."

"No," said Aisling. "You heard Auberon, this is my fight as much as yours. It's my destiny and I can't run from it any longer. Besides, you're my friends, I couldn't let you do this alone."

"You're braver than I took you for, girl," said Chasseur's gruff voice, "here, this will keep you a bit drier."

His horse trotted into the clearing and as Chasseur approached Aisling, he tossed her down a rolled up patch of red fabric. She unfurled it to find a hooded crimson riding cloak, just like the ones Gilda and Hans wore. Aisling grinned from ear to ear. She turned to Gilda, who helped her put it on.

"Now you look like one of us," she said, smiling.

"All right, rangers!" boomed Chasseur. "We all know the plan. Our job is to ride in and make sure the beasts stay off the girl and the twins both! The villagers will do their best to create a barricade around us, but most of the fighting is going to fall on us! We get them into the castle and it's up to them to find the Lady of Beasts and end this thing once and for all!"

The Red Riders all grumbled in assent.

"I have no illusions about surviving this day, and if I'm not making it, neither are any of you!" he chuckled. "I suggest the lot of you make your peace with whatever gods you hold to and give your all, because that's the only thing that's going to get us through today!"

The riders and assembled villagers all laughed and cheered. Even Aisling felt somewhat comforted by Chasseur's ability to joke in such a dire situation.

Aisling wondered if war was always like this. She wondered if King Henry had made such brazen pronouncements in France. Perhaps joking about death somehow lessened the tension, alleviated the fear.

Gilda helped Aisling onto Karl's back and Hoegabbler, a purple cat once more, sat behind Hans. Chasseur's raven flew onto his arm as he made his way over to the four companions. He leaned over to them and whispered.

"If you don't succeed by nightfall…if your remedy doesn't break the curse, then I'm coming in after you. I'll cut out the bitch's heart myself, if it comes to it. One way or another, we're ending this today. Do you understand me?"

Gilda glared at him, her blue eyes never wavering from his own dark ones. "We won't fail, Chasseur," she said through clenched teeth.

The hunter nodded and turned his horse.

"To the Snarling Manor!" he shouted to the crowd.

Their cheers echoed through the pelting rain, and over the crash of thunder in the distance.

Chasseur kept his forces on open ground for most of the journey. Numerous as they were, a rain-soaked trudge through the rowan trees would have forced them to walk mostly single file, making them perfect targets for the Lady's beasts to pick off one by one. Even so, the road they walked towards the Snarling Manor was sodden and slippery.

Behind the riders, the peasants trudged slowly through the deepening mud. As they neared the castle, the rain redoubled and many of their "army" had pulled up their hoods and collars, but shivered nonetheless in the ceaseless rain. It was a few hours later before Chasseur gave the signal for them to stop. He lifted his hand up into the air, then whispered something to his raven, which flew off ahead of them.

"Poe will return soon with word about what awaits us. The village of Racine lies just past this copse of trees. It was the first one affected by the Lady's curse and no one's been here since then. We'll take the main road through town, which will lead us directly to the gates of the Snarling Manor. Stay close and be mindful of your surroundings," he warned.

A few minutes passed before the raven came back. It landed, cawing its message to Chasseur. He motioned to the riders, who moved back amongst the throng of peasants, directing the lot of them to move forward. It was barely noon, but the skies around them were as dark as if dusk were already gathering around them.

"Leave your steeds and go around the troops. The beasts may have more acute senses, but the rain should be dulling even those. Just keep out of sight and make your way to the door.

Once the fighting starts, that will be your chance," explained Chasseur, who had rode back to speak with Aisling and the twins.

Gilda nodded and dismounted, helping Aisling off Karl's broad back. Hans and Hoegabbler did the same. The three of them drew their swords. As she held it, Aisling could feel how different this blade was than her last one; it made her feel stronger somehow. The four companions moved into the surrounding wilderness, making their way through the rain-soaked undergrowth as slowly and as silently as they could. Chasseur gave the order to march on and Aisling could hear the communal groan of the waterlogged army.

While the army moved through the center of Racine, Hans and Gilda led them around the perimeter of the village, which was small, derelict, and wholly abandoned. In the distance, past the fog and driving rain, Aisling could see stone spires emerging from the cloud cover; the Snarling Manor was a stone's throw away.

A long drive lay before them and surrounding it on all sides stood the remains of a once beautiful garden. Trees and trellises, scrubs and bushes, stood unkempt beside many a fallen marble statue and crumbling fountain. And there, wandering aimlessly around the former finery of a once grand estate, roamed the beasts.

The beasts that prowled the overgrown grounds were monsters of all shapes and sizes.

Some of them had the heads and hooves of boars or bulls, others were like the wolf man Aisling had faced the night she arrived in Stonewall. There were cat people, rat people, even a few that looked like strange spotted dogs. The most ferocious looking of them all by far, however, were the bears. They stood several heads higher than even the largest of the other beasts, their fur black as night, their eyes like pools of obsidian.

As Aisling gazed upon the Snarling Manor in the distance, she knew immediately how it had earned that name. The castle, for it was truly a castle, was made up of four great stone towers attached in the middle by battlements, hall, and ornately covered keep. The tops of each tower, as well as the cornices, parapets, walks, and ramparts of the castle were adorned with the most fearsome stone statues Aisling had ever seen.

Gargoyles guarded every free section of the manor. They were fanged, clawed, winged monstrosities, and they stood watch, scaled and snarling over all the manor's spacious grounds. Her eyes scanned the broken statues in the garden and saw that they too, angelic as many of them were, seemed more threatening than serene.

A ranger's horn blared in the distance. At once, the beasts turned their attentions towards the sound and the shouting that proceeded it. The hair on the back of their necks stood on edge and they began to move towards the noise. Thunder crashed and the beasts let out a collective roar.

Hans grabbed hold of Aisling and pulled her behind a nearby tree. He held a finger to his lips, indicating that she should be quiet. It was a warning he needn't have issued. Aisling was already too scared to speak. She peered around the tree and saw the Red Riders charging up the drive towards the grounds. The beasts, monstrous and soaking wet, lined up and stood their ground. Animalistic as they undoubtedly were, they still knew that their first duty was to protect their Lady. A flash of lightning as bright as the sun itself illuminated the scene and by the time Aisling had rubbed the spots from her eyes, the battle had begun.

The Red Riders were the first to meet the monsters. They rode unerringly towards the horde, loosing arrows as they galloped ever forward. Arrow by arrow, each one of their shafts hit home, sinking into the furry hides of the beasts before them. Some of the smaller beasts shrieked and made to find cover, but the larger ones seemed undaunted by their wounds, and howled with rage.

Behind the rangers, the few villagers who still had horses of their own galloped forward. They rode less gracefully than the red cloaks, but no less fervently. Behind them, the remaining peasants ran through the mud, their spears and pitchforks held high in the air. Most of them knew that they would not survive this day, but welcomed the chance to die fighting for the ones they loved, for their homeland and their way of life.

Meanwhile, the beasts moved to meet their attackers head-on. The largest and most fearsome among them were unperturbed by the ferocity of their mounted opponents. Indeed, it appeared as though the riders' red cloaks were actually seeing to draw their ire and their attention away from the weaker unmounted villagers.

The three great bears moved effortlessly through the throng of oncoming riders, wading through them as if they were nothing but wheat grass. They slashed at the riders with claws like savage shovels, hooking into the sides of horses and pushing men and women to the ground. At the same time, the Red Riders kept to the outskirts of the battle, firing their bows into any patch of fur they could find.

One of the bears, the largest of the three, ran towards Chasseur. Despite the brute's clear size advantage, the hunter was much faster and much smarter. He rode beneath an ornate villa perched on stone columns. The bear was too large to pursue him and roared in frustration as he tried to tear down the roof of the already crumbling structure.

Meanwhile, a smaller bear gave chase to one of the other female riders, who led the beast towards a small moon bridge. The wet ground beneath the bridge proved firm enough for the galloping horse, but too soft for the bear, who sank to her knees in the mud.

The third among them, smallest by far, proved fast and agile enough to outpace the rider he was chasing. He leapt from the top of an overturned sundial as Ruger rode past, crashing into him hard and sending horse, rider, and bear into a nearby topiary.

Despite a few hiccups, Chasseur's plan to herd the beasts away from the doors was working. The fight was giving Aisling and her friends just enough time to sneak around and enter unimpeded.

Aisling saw the wolves among the Lady's beasts gather together and growl to one another. Then, at the direction of the largest, they separated from the pack and ran towards the outside of the ensuing army. They were moving to flank the villagers, to take out the remaining riders and cut them all off from their escape.

"We have to warn them!" she whispered frantically to Hans. "They're going to trap them!"

Hans and Gilda shook their heads.

"We can't worry about that! We need to move towards the doors, now!" said Gilda.

She grabbed hold of Aisling's arm and the four of them ran away from the battle and towards the castle. Behind them, Aisling could hear snarling and screaming; the scraping of swords and the sickly squelching sound of flesh being torn asunder.

Hoegabbler, now a rabbit, bounded ahead of them, signaling to them as he went that the way ahead was clear. Suddenly, he stopped short and ducked, narrowly avoiding the grasping claws of a lone boar man.

Hans, who had since drawn his bow, raised it and took aim at the creature. His silver- tipped arrow hit the beast in the chest. It threw back its head and squealed in pain and anguish. It was hunched over, scraping at the wet earth with hands that looked more like sharpened hooves than anything else, and a second later it was off and running towards them.

Aisling could see the boar man's hot breath steaming in the rainy air, could smell the foul odor of its filthy matted fur, and she readied herself for the charge. She gripped high on her sword and despite the chilly, pelting rain, the blade felt warm in her hands. Then, even as she stood there facing down death, she realized that she had not yet named the sword. In her experience, all the best swords had names, all the ones from the stories anyway. She resolved that if she survived this experience, she would think up an appropriate name for her gift.

Behind her, Hans and Gilda launched another two arrows, which hit the beast square in the head, causing it to stoop over and crumple into a pile before them. Aisling jumped back as the creature made one last attempt to get to its feet and failed.

As she beheld the slowly transforming dead body at her feet, Aisling said, "It's…it was a little boy…"

"We need to keep moving," said Gilda. "We're running out of daylight."

Aisling didn't want to tear herself away from the boy, but she forced herself not to look back. She wanted to bury him, to do something, anything, but she knew Gilda was right. The only way to avoid any further bloodshed was to break the curse at its source.

Thunder and lightning continued to crash all around them, but even louder than the storm were the cries emanating from the battle. As they ran, Aisling kept trying to look behind her to get a better look, but it was no use. The rain, the mist, and the ever-widening gap between them blurred the battle so much that by the time they had reached the castle doors, all Aisling could see were flashes of brown and crimson in the distance.

The great carved wooden doors of the Snarling Manor were broken at the hinges and hung open like a gaping wound. Gilda stowed her bow and drew her sword, but quietly signaled her brother to knock his bow and be ready for anything. Hoegabbler transformed into his purple cat and shook out his fur.

"I'll go in first," he purred, and padded cautiously into the darkened castle.

Gilda followed him in, then Aisling. Hans stood behind them all, his bow trained on the battle in the distance.

"Godspeed, riders," said Gilda, frowning.

With that, she closed over the doors as far as they would go, sealing herself and her friends inside the dark and desolate palace.

Chapter Nineteen

The Snarling Manor

The inside of the Snarling Manor was just as unpleasant as the outside. Sculptures of horrific monsters ranging from more fearsome gargoyles to sickly-looking, emaciated cherubs, seemed to perch upon every plinth and pillar. Torches hung on the walls in spiked iron sconces. The eerie light they gave off fell across a number of ornately-sewn but heavily tattered tapestries, upon which were gruesome scenes of war, death, and unspeakable acts of torture.

"Good lord!" exclaimed Aisling, "it's as if every corner of this place is meant to be upsetting."

"That's because it is," said Hans, wincing as he walked past a particularly disturbing scene painted on a wall, "Gilda, do we think that there are any more of the Lady's beasties lurking inside the manor itself?"

"I would assume so. She had to have servants, vassals, even her consort might be lurking around here somewhere, just waiting for unwitting prey to come wandering into their nest. We need to move fast. It looks like the manor has four wings: north, south, east, and west."

"You're not suggesting we split up, are you?" asked a nervous Hoegabbler.

"Good lord, no. We stick together. We'll be harder to pick off that way. Let's head north, we can circle back around if we don't find anything there, but we need to make some ground before nightfall."

Gilda led them towards the north side of the manor. Just off the foyer was a long torchlit hallway, lined on either side by dozens of suits of armor. Each of the suits was different, some were spiked, others plated, and many appeared to have helmets in the shape of the monsters engaged in battle outside. Yet all of them looked as though they had been wrought by someone deeply disturbed.

Their wet boots squeaked against the marble floor as they crept ever forward, careful to watch for even the slightest movement from the unnerving suits of armor.

"Are we sure these are all empty?" said Hoegabbler.

"Perhaps? But just in case, Aisling, hold on to your sword," warned Gilda.

Hoegabbler, unable to help himself, walked up to one of the suits and batted it with his paw. A moment later and the lupine helm upon it swung downwards, gazing with sightless eyes at its awakener. It clanked and banged, shifting its indeterminate weight as it tightened its grip on the spear in its hand.

"You had to touch it?" shouted Hans, and as soon as he said it, all the suits of armor turned their helms to face him.

"I knew it couldn't have been that easy..." muttered Gilda. "Run! Now!"

The four companions took off down the hall. Aisling hoped that the formerly inert suits of armor were sleepy enough for them to outrun. When they reached the end of the hallway, they closed the door, but even as they did so, they saw the awakened armors stepping off their pedestals and turning sluggishly towards the door.

The room they were in was covered wall-to-wall in oak panelling. In the center of it, a grand marble staircase led to an upstairs corridor. On the side of the polished wooden railing stood a handsome, though slightly unnerving statue of a male angel wielding a spear. Its wings, scarf, and the point of its spear were all painted in gold. Aside from the staircase, the only way out of the room was back the way they came.

"Where do we go next?" asked Hoegabbler, anxiously. "I don't know," replied Gilda. "I need a second to think."

"Well, we can't go back that way," said her brother, turning towards the doors and the clanking sounds beyond them.

"Then I guess we just head up the staircase. She's gotta be in here somewhere," replied

Gilda.

A loud bang erupted from behind the doors. It sounded as if one of the armored guardians had collided with another and sent both suits clattering to the floor. All four of them turned to gaze at the wooden doors.

"We'd better make a decision quickly, sister," said Hans.

"All right, we'll go up the stairs and hope we don't run

into any more surprises before we find the Lady of Beasts."

There was a groaning sound by the staircase. It was the unmistakable sound of wood straining against something much stronger than itself. The four of them turned to see the angel statue beginning to stir. Its stone and metal body moved slowly, but each tiny shift of its form shook the wooden plinth and railing it was attached to.

With one swift and terrible motion, it pulled its great wings away from the railing entirely. Splinters of polished wood went flying in every direction as the angelic guardian hopped off its former pedestal.

As the four companions gawked at the statue, they could hear the slow clanking of armored feet making their way towards them. The hollow knights were still on their way.

"These are some persistent curses, ey?" laughed Hans, "it's like they don't want to be lifted."

"Aisling, Hoegabbler, bar the doors as best you can. If we can cut down this angel then all we have to do is head up to reach the Lady… presumably," said Gilda.

She put her bow away and drew her kopet. Hans did the same. A moment later and the two had engaged the angelic statue.

The twins were surprised to find that the statue was more swift and skilled than they had previously assumed it to be. The angel wheeled about, blocking and parrying Hans and Gilda's every move as quickly and effortlessly as even the most well-trained warrior.

Meanwhile, Aisling and Hoegabbler did their best to drag pieces of furniture in front of the doors. Unfortunately, as neither of them was particularly brawny, the process was arduous and not especially effective.

"I don't know if this is going to keep them out," said Hoegabbler as he heaved his hardest at an apparently immovable armchair.

"Well, we don't have a lot of options," said Aisling, who was doing her best to help her friend to move the chair, and failing.

The sounds of clanking, marching feet moved ever closer. Gilda and Hans were still deftly moving around the angel, but the statue only seemed to be getting stronger as they began to tire. Suddenly, Hans' sword made contact and he severed one of the angel's arms. It fell to the ground with a resounding CLANG, and Aisling and Hoegabbler both wheeled around to see what had happened.

"It's a good thing we laced these with silver and iron," said Hans.

The angel lifted its golden wings and brought them down in front of it like a shield.

Gilda's sword banged against them as she brought it down, but she failed to dent the gold, much less penetrate it. The moment her sword touched the metal, the angel lifted its wings violently, knocking Gilda to the floor and forcing Hans to dive sideways out of the way.

"Hold on to this!" Aisling shouted to Hoegabbler, and she ran towards the fight.

The angel saw her coming and before she could get close enough to swing her sword, thrust its spear in her direction. Reflexively, she skidded to a halt and swung sideways at the spear, parrying the statue's strike as if she had been doing it her whole life. Her unforeseen showing of skill stunned

Aisling long enough that the angel latched on to the momentary distraction and pulled the spear in for another jab. Aisling shook off her astonishment and ducked beneath the spear, but only barely.

Hans' kopet slashed downward then, slicing off the angel's spearhead near the tip. It responded angrily, knocking the remaining length of the spear into his solar plexus. Hans clutched his chest and fell to the floor, gasping for breath.

Hoegabbler shrieked as sword points, axe heads, and the jagged tips of spears came thrusting through the wooden planks of the door. Panicked, Gilda rushed to her brother's side, but was rewarded for her lack of awareness with a smack to the face by the angel's broken spear. She fell to the ground with a loud crash, her kopet sliding across the floor and away from her.

Undaunted by her fallen comrades, Aisling moved in closer to the angel. She circled it for a moment, moving towards its armless and vulnerable left side. The statue swung at her again and she blocked it with her sword. She gripped the sword tighter in her hand as the blade reverberated off the angel's spear.

"Hoegabbler, you have to try and get Gilda up! We need her! Hans, focus, I can't do this alone!" she shouted.

She was surprised at how naturally it came to her, this shouting of commands. But she was even more surprised by how readily she engaged the enchanted statue, and how well she seemed to be doing.

The angel, bereft of a left arm, bent down and slashed at Aisling with a razor-sharp wing.

Aisling slashed downward and cut across the golden

feathers. This time, instead of banging against the gilded stone, the sword passed through it like a hot knife through butter. Bits of broken feather tumbled to the ground, leaving a clean cut across half the wing tips.

As Aisling dueled the angel, Hans got to his feet. He was still mostly out of breath, but had recovered enough to at least move. He sheathed his sword and carefully walked to the half- moved armchair, pushing it the rest of the way to the door. Through the ever-growing slits in the wood, he could see that every single suit of armor was now standing just beyond it.

"Aisling," he breathed, heavily. "We're outnumbered. We need to retreat to the top of those stairs and hope the armor can't climb."

Aisling Mason wasn't listening. Emboldened by her newfound skill, she was hammering at the angel. The statue seemed to be losing more and more steam with each glancing blow she struck upon it. Bits of stone and golden flecks lay scattered about them. A moment later, she disarmed it, hacking off its remaining arm and rendering it mostly harmless. It bent down to strike at her with its remaining wing and she took the opportunity to bring her sword down upon its exposed neck. The angel's head fell to the ground and a moment later it crumbled to bits at her feet, its enchantment finally broken.

When Aisling turned back to her companions, she saw that Gilda was once again conscious. Her lip was bleeding slightly and a bruise was blossoming on her chin, but she seemed all right. Hans and Hoegabbler stood beside her, facing the rapidly splintering door.

"Come on, that armchair isn't going to hold them," said Gilda.

The four of them ran up the stairs and once they had reached the first landing, saw that it split into two other smaller staircases, each leading up into the tower before them.

"Left or right?" asked Hoegabbler.

"Right," said Aisling, moving to the front of the group.

For the second time, Aisling found herself surprised by her sudden burst of impetus.

Somehow she knew that they had to go right, that something was directing them that way. At the top of the spiral staircase was a single door. It reminded Aisling of the tower room in a story she had heard as a child.

The door in the story held a princess, who was being held prisoner by her wicked husband; an ogre in disguise. Perhaps here, in this enchanted palace, something similar sat waiting behind the door. As she moved to grab hold of the handle, she heard the distinct sound of twin bowstrings tensing behind her.

"Ready?" she asked aloud.

"Ready," replied the twins in unison.

Aisling pushed open the door into a small, squarish room. Burgundy curtains hung over two tall windows on either side of the room, drawn back to let in the dim afternoon light. A ragged-looking, long-haired man sat at a writing desk a few feet away. The quill in his hand stopped moving abruptly. He lifted it off the page and a droplet of ink fell at the end of his sentence.

"Don't shoot," he said.

"Who the devil are you?" asked Gilda, catching her breath.

"Lord DuMonde...at your service. Not to be rude, but I might ask you the same question.

This is my castle, after all," said the man.

He smiled then and got to his feet. He closed the book he had been writing in and replaced his pen. Then, after smoothing himself out slightly, he bowed low to the two young ladies. Hans and Gilda kept their bows trained upon him.

Even through his shabby appearance, Aisling could see that this was a very handsome man. His dirty blonde hair was long, sleek, but mostly unkempt. He wore a pair of tattered trousers and what remained of a silken shirt, but that was about it.

Lord DuMonde's skin was pale and scarred. The lingering memories of various cuts, scrapes, bites, and bruises seemed to be tattooed upon him in every place they could see.

"What is going on here?" asked Lord DuMonde, in a very thick French accent. "We've come to break the curse, my lord. We have a cure. We just have to find Lady

Isabelle to give it to her," Gilda replied.

"That much is easy, she'll be in the library, of course. Though I'm afraid that even armed as you are, you'll find she is more than a match for the four of you."

"Five of us, right? You will help us...won't you?" asked Aisling.

Lord DuMonde's ready smile faltered. Whereas before he had looked brave and handsome, he now looked terrified, pitiable even.

"I...that would be a mistake...Lady Isabelle has already made it clear that she does not wish to see me," he muttered, gesturing to the scars on his arms.

"Are you joking?" said Gilda, bewildered. "This is the only chance we have. Do you have any idea what your people have suffered because of her these past few years? Our friends are dying out there trying to keep her beasts from moving towards the castle so we can administer the cure. Do you really mean to sit here and do nothing?"

Lord DuMonde shrugged. He looked more diminished than he had when they had first arrived.

"There is nothing more I can do for her," he said. "I've tried everything to reach her.

With each day that passes she becomes less and less of who she was and more of the beast...more of the beast than I ever was. She wouldn't even be this way if it weren't for me. If I go with you, I'm liable to make things worse."

"This isn't about you, this is about the realm," replied Gilda, angrily. "What do you mean by 'more of a beast than I ever was'?" asked Aisling.

"It's my fault she's like this. When I met the Lady Isabelle, it was I who was the beast. She loved me, despite the monster. She showed me kindness and understanding. She reached deep within me to help me remember who I was.

We had barely a year of blissful happiness together when the curse struck again. This time it took her. She was different than I had been, she wasn't always the beast. She just transformed at night, at first. I tried to keep her confined, but I failed. Once she started attacking villagers and palace servants...things just kept getting worse. She attacked me and I fled," he explained.

"Wait, she attacked you and you haven't transformed?" asked Hoegabbler.

Lord DuMonde, jumped back at the utterance. It seemed he was not used to being addressed by a purple cat.

"Don't mind him. What he means is, you've been injured by her and you haven't transformed?" asked Hans.

DuMonde shook his head.

"He must be immune to the curse because he already had it," said Aisling.

She remembered when a strange, but mild form of the pox ran rampant through her little town a year beforehand and how the traveling dentist had told them that those who had already contracted the sickness couldn't be infected again.

"It doesn't matter," shouted Gilda. "None of that matters. What matters is finding her so that we can end this. Will you help us do that at least?"

DuMonde considered the request. Then, picking up a lighted candelabrum from his desk, he walked purposefully toward the door.

"Very well, I shall take you to her. Follow me."

Lord DuMonde led them back down the stairs to the landing.

"We should warn you," began Hans. "We disturbed some of your, um, enchanted suits of armor? Point is, they are likely waiting for us to come back down to finish us off."

"They will not harm me," said Lord DuMonde. "The Snarling Manor knows its master." "Was it always so…" Aisling searched for the word.

"Terrifying?" replied the lord, "in a way. My great grandparents were fond of sculptures, especially gargoyles. They believed that they warded off unfriendly magic. As they built up the castle, they added more and more of them. With each generation, the new lords would add their own personal favorites to the gallery. It wasn't until the curse hit me the first time that the damn things started to come to life. I suppose my ancestors were wrong, their presence did nothing to stop the witch's dark magic from coming in."

When they reached the landing, they could see a dozen or so suits of armor standing at attention on the stairs beneath, blocking their way.

"Let us through," commanded Lord DuMonde.

The suits obeyed, moving to the sides of the staircase and allowing the lord and his companions to pass unimpeded.

"This is creepy," said Horgabbler.

DuMonde continued to lead them through the castle. They walked past the ruined angel and down the now empty hall of armors. Though no other sculpted guardians rose to bar their way, Aisling noted that each statuary, tapestry, and portrait seemed to shift slightly at their passing. With each step they took, the Snarling Manor was watching them. He led them off the main hall, up some stairs and past a balustrade to the largest part of the keep. When they reached the large, ebony doors, he stopped.

"The library is just inside those doors, as I suspect is Lady Isabelle..." he said nervously and attempting to give a conciliatory bow.

Gilda glared at him impatiently as if she were waiting

for him to change his mind. When he made no attempt to move, she turned to face the others.

"If she is anything like what the villagers have described, we'll be in for the fight of our lives trying to get her to take the antidote. The best thing we can do is incapacitate her first and hope that once she's knocked out, we can get her to swallow the potion.

Aisling, that sword of yours made short work of the angel. It seems to cut through enchantments pretty handily. I want you to be on point for this one. If she's as animalistic as I think she might be, then she'll sense the power in the sword. We can capitalize on that fear and corner her. Hans, we'll back her up. Hoegabbler? Try and distract her as best you can, too."

With that, they pushed the doors open.

Chapter Twenty

The Beast Within

isling had never learned to read. It was not unusual, especially among her people.

Peasants just didn't have any need to read. Only nobles were allowed to learn to read and even amongst their kind, a girl who could read was very unusual indeed.

It wasn't as if they had a lot of books available or anything. Most houses, if they had any, only had the Bible, and that was a fairly recent development in England. Frankly, if they wished to read the Bible, they could have a priest read it to them during Sunday mass.

Still, it wasn't as though Aisling didn't want to learn to read. She did very much. There was just no one around to teach her and even if there was, she dared not speak of it aloud. She loved seeing books though, and even as a little child would light up whenever she saw someone reading one. She knew of the knowledge they contained. As someone who had loved hearing and telling stories all her life, she loved the prospect that a book might contain a story she had never heard before.

As she stared up at the remarkable room before her, Aisling could not believe her eyes. Before her was an entire room of books, scores and scores of them; books beyond counting. The walls of the room were made of polished dark green marble and set into each and every one of them were shelves and shelves of books. Two gilded spiral staircases stood at opposite ends of the room leading up to a second level that contained even more shelves of books.

A number of books had been removed from their shelves and lay scattered in piles around the grand room amidst comfortable sofas and armchairs, which looked as though they had been ripped near to shreds by some sort of animal.

Three giant mullein windows, larger even than those in the Gardener's Tower, stood upon the opposite wall. Aisling could see gray light peeking out from beneath the parting rain clouds. Even on such a cloudy day, the light illuminated the whole room. The Lady of Beasts crouched in front of the windows, staring out at the battle and flicking her tail reflexively.

Gilda slid her foot forward and it squeaked across the marble. The Lady's ears pricked up and she spun around, snarling.

The Lady of Beasts was indeed the chimera that the rumormongers had described her to be. She was female, that much was apparent, but her curvaceousness was where any indicators of her true gender stopped.

Auburn hair covered nearly every inch of her. Her hands and feet were little more than inhuman claws. A long, lionlike tail swished across the ground behind her. She had a bear-like, feral snout filled with rows of sharp teeth. Her ears, pointed like a wolf's, were flat back against her head, and two long curved horns jutted back from her forehead.

Aisling could see strong, sinewy muscles flex beneath her auburn fur. She began to prowl back and forth before them like a caged animal. She looked nervous, hungry, and ready to pounce at any moment.

"Lady Isabelle?" asked Gilda.

As if in reply, the Lady let out a terrible roar. It sounded like a woman's shriek and a wolf's howl all at once.

"Please, milady…we've come to break the curse. We have a cure," Gilda continued, swallowing hard.

"Gilda, stop! Don't get any closer. I don't think she can understand you," warned her brother, and she stopped moving forward.

Aisling drew her sword and held it in front of her. It gleamed in the brightening twilight.

The Lady of Beasts took one look at the sword and recoiled, hissing defensively. She looked afraid.

"Give me the remedy, Gilda. I think the sword is keeping her at bay. I might be able to get close enough," said the girl.

Gilda walked over to Aisling and slipped the potion vial into her free hand. She picked up her bow and crossed to the other side of the room, making sure to be as equidistant from her brother as she possibly could.

With her sword held aloft and the cure in her hand, Aisling inched closer to the Lady of Beasts. When she got close enough, Aisling beheld one detail that she had been sorely hoping to find. Regardless of how she otherwise looked on the outside, Lady Isabelle still seemed to possess at least one feature of her former self: her gray eyes. Unlike the bestial, inhuman eyes of the transformed villagers, the Lady of Beasts' eyes were human and darted back and forth frantically as the girl closed in.

Aisling felt confident with the sword in her hand, confident enough even to continue to walk forward towards the Lady of Beasts.

"I know you're scared," she whispered. "I promise we just want to help, we won't hurt you…"

"My love!" shouted a voice by the doors.

Aisling turned to see Lord DuMonde standing triumphantly by the doors. Her moment of distraction was all the beast needed to make her escape. She ran past Aisling, careful to avoid her sword entirely, and ducked behind a nearby armchair.

"Damn it, man! Now's the time you pick to find your courage?" cursed Hans.

But DuMonde wasn't listening, he was moving towards the Lady of Beasts, who was snarling more violently than she had when Aisling had her at the point of a sword. Aisling followed close.

"My lord, please. I appreciate you wanting to help, but I don't think this is the way," she implored.

"Please, Isabelle…it is I, your beloved. Surely, you remember me. Even like this, you must."

The Lady of Beasts leapt up onto the armchair. She stood hunched over, claws extended, and fangs bared. Gilda ran up to them with her bow drawn and nudged Aisling with her free elbow. The Lady of Beasts was going to strike, that much was clear. Yet despite all indications of this, Lord DuMonde kept walking.

"I don't know what he's playing at, but if he wants to be bait then I'm willing to oblige him. Better him than us, anyway. Be ready," whispered Gilda.

The Lady of Beasts sprang, too quickly for Aisling to see. Before he even knew what was happening, she was upon DuMonde, clawing at his chest and rearing up to bite down on his face. Without thinking, Gilda fired an arrow at her. It struck her in the shoulder, stopping her just as she was about to clamp down upon him. It was a warning shot and Aisling knew it. Gilda was close enough to shave the wings off a fly with that shot, she could have ended everything then and there, but she had held back. She didn't want to do things Chasseur's way.

The Lady of Beasts snarled and looked at the arrow in her arm. Fresh blood pooled round the snarls of her filthy fur. She bared her fangs again and hissed at Gilda. Below her, Lord DuMonde was unconscious. Blood trickled down the sides of his chest. She hadn't cut deep.

Hans had moved up to them now, flanked by a cowering Hoegabbler, who seemed as unsure of what to do next as Aisling was.

Without warning, the Lady of Beasts lunged at Gilda, slashing across her middle with ebony claws as long as hunting knives. She was fast, faster than any of them had anticipated. Even the keen eyes of the twins had not seen the attack coming. Gilda dropped her bow and doubled over in pain, clutching her bleeding midsection.

"No!" yelled Hans.

Aisling moved to strike the Lady of Beasts, but she was too slow. The beast dodged the blow as swiftly as she had struck Gilda. She spun around quickly, knocking Aisling out of the way. The girl fell, holding tight to the sword, but allowing the Lady of Beasts time to dash towards the other side of the room. She was stopped, by Hoegabbler.

Hoegabbler had transformed. He was no longer the striped and handsome purple cat, nor a rabbit, nor even his normal pudgy self. No, he had somehow transformed himself into an almost identical clone of the Lady of Beasts. None of them had seen it happen, probably because they were too busy staring at the now bleeding Gilda, but they knew it was him.

He possessed her horns, her tail, her claws, even her fangs. The only noticeable differences between the two of them were his eyes, which had remained bulging and yellow, and his fur, which was sleek and purple. He stood before her, this strange pseudo-mirror image of herself, baring his fangs. The Lady of Beasts was taken aback for a moment, confused by what she was looking at, and Hoegabbler took his chance. He slashed at her with claws he had never used and as they dug into her flesh, he pulled back.

She roared in pain and pushed into him, knocking the changeling onto the floor. They hit the ground with a loud thud and began to roll around, biting and clawing at one another.

"No, no!" shouted a panicked Hans, who was kneeling next to his sister, doing his best to staunch the blood with his cloak. The cuts were deep.

"It's all right. It's ok, Hans. Aisling, go after her. Help Hoegabbler. We need to e-end this," Gilda stammered.

Aisling turned around to see Hoegabbler curled in a ball and whimpering. His sleek purple fur was interlaced with dozens of tiny bleeding cuts and bite marks. Meanwhile, the Lady of Beasts had made it all the way to the opposite side of the room and clamored up the spiral staircase like a monkey. She stared at them from the secondary level of the library, growling triumphantly.

With the sword in one hand and the cure in the other, Aisling made her way towards the staircase. As she stepped onto the ornate metal grating, she could feel that it was more rickety than it had looked from a distance. She continued to climb, never taking her eye off of the beast, who paced back and forth atop the second floor balcony, waiting for her. No sooner had Aisling stepped onto the balcony, than she stopped, her human eyes darting wildly between her armed assailant and their injured companions.

"That's enough!" shouted Aisling.

She realized that this was the exact phrase her mother used to use when she wanted she and her siblings to calm down and that, without realizing it, she had said it in the exact same tone as well.

"This has gone on long enough," she said angrily. "We're trying to help you, to save you and your people. Can you not see that?"

Aisling was angry, angrier than she could remember being in a very long time. She looked at the monster before her. Everything that had happened, all the families torn apart by the curse, all the people who had died as a result; it was all on her. It all stemmed from Isabelle. It was all her fault.

The sword in her hand burned. It wanted to be used to smite, to punish, and God help her, she wanted to use it in just those ways. She moved forward, raising the weapon and completely ignoring the vial in her other hand. Suddenly, she heard a twitter from behind her.

The nightingale was perched on the railing, tweeting and tilting her head at her. She didn't sing this time, merely looked at Aisling. It was an innocent look, the look of an animal that was trying to understand the situation and when Aisling saw it, she realized her mistake.

None of this was Isabelle's fault, not really. It wasn't even Lord DuMonde's. Everything that had happened to Stonewall had been because of the curse; Maledicta's curse. Everyone had a dark side to them, even Aisling. Some people, like Chasseur, let it come out and used it, albeit misguidedly, for good. Some people weren't strong enough to control it. They allowed it to take over them, to reduce them to their basest, most primal natures.

That was how the curse took hold. It took the most primal, uncontrollable parts of a person and brought them to the surface. The way to cure it wasn't to force the afflicted to drink a magic potion or end their lives, it was to help them remember who they truly were. Aisling dropped her sword arm and put the vial into her pocket. Then, reaching into her satchel, she gently took out the rose that Lady Roselyn had given her.

As soon as the Lady of Beasts saw it, she stopped growling. The hair on the back of her neck smoothed over and she calmed. She looked like a dog that had just recognized that the person she had been barking at was a person she had seen a thousand times before. Cautiously, she began to move towards Aisling. She stretched out her paw as she neared the rose and in the light of the setting sun, Aisling could see that it was beginning to resemble less of a claw and more of a hand. Without warning, an arrow whirred past her face, striking the Lady of Beasts in the chest. She roared.

Aisling looked over to see Chasseur standing by the library doors with his bow in hand.

He knocked another arrow.

"Find cover, girl! I've got her now!" he shouted across the cavernous room.

"No, Chasseur!" yelled Gilda, who was still on the floor, cradling the bleeding wound in her side.

"Are you mad? She's cut you, you'll become like her unless I end this now." "Aisling was about to end it, you fool! Leave her be!" said Hans.

He had staunched as much of his sister's bleeding as he could and was helping the wounded Hoegabbler to his feet. He looked as if he was going to move towards his fellow rider, to stop him from making things even worse, but Aisling knew there was no way he would get there in time.

It was too late, Chasseur was covered in fresh blood, his eyes filled with rage and terrible purpose. He loosed another arrow and it struck the Lady of Beasts in her right shoulder. She howled in pain, roaring and hissing in Chasseur's direction.

"Please, my lady...you must..."

But Aisling never got to finish her statement. A moment later and she was being tossed hard into a nearby bookshelf.

The blow knocked the wind out of her and she dropped the rose, which fell from the balcony to the marble floor below. It hit the ground soundlessly, dislodging a petal. The Lady of Beasts roared in fury and leapt from the balcony.

She ran across the floor, bounding over piles of fallen books, making her way towards Chasseur, who dropped his bow and in one fluid motion, drew the bastard sword from under his bloodstained cloak. He swung upwards at her approach and his blade slashed across her chest. The cut was shallow and she fell sideways next to him, crouching like a wounded animal and howling in pain.

"You're all mine now, princess," said Chasseur.

A moment later and the two were engaged in combat once more. Hans had his bow trained on Chasseur and Hoegabbler was on his feet again, but both of them looked unsure of what to do next, or even whom to attack.

Aisling ran down the stairs as quickly as possible. She scooped up the damaged rose and moved towards the battle. Chasseur and the Lady of Beasts attacked one another furiously. She slashed at him, her wicked claws catching on his leather armor, while he did his best to stab at her when he could. His sword, dulled by the day's battle, barely got through her thick hide and fur. Still, Aisling knew they would tear each other apart if she didn't try to stop it.

"Chasseur, stop!" shouted Gilda, but her plea was drowned out by the sounds of battle.

Suddenly, the Lady of Beasts was on top of Chasseur. She had gotten under his swing and clawed her way up his chest. She bit into his neck, but he ignored it. It didn't matter to him anymore if he contracted the curse. Ending her would end it for all of them. He was doing what needed to be done. Using all his strength, Chasseur hauled her off of him, throwing her to the ground. The Lady of Beasts hit the marble floor with a resounding CRACK, that told them all she had broken something.

In an instant, she was back upon him again. Bewildered by the speed and ferocity of her attack, Chasseur stumbled backwards and into a nearby bookshelf, dropping his bastard sword onto the floor. The Lady of Beasts lunged at him, her razor-sharp fangs making contact with his neck. She pulled her head back and pulled out his jugular along with it.

Blood gushed from the wound, falling like crimson rain upon the hunter's already heavily-stained cloak. Instinctively, Hans released his bow. His silver-tipped arrow struck her right below the left shoulder, penetrating deep.

Chasseur and the Lady of Beasts fell to the floor in a crumpled heap, cursed blood pooling around them both.

Chapter Twenty-One

A Good Book

ord DuMonde was sitting upright now, holding his throbbing head and cradling his bloodied face. He looked over to see the bloody pile that was once his beloved, slumped over the body of her would-be assassin.

"What happened? Isabelle…no…" he wept.

Aisling walked over to him and bent down. She couldn't see much of the damage from where she stood, but the slowly growing puddle of blood beneath the fighters was proof enough that the outcome wasn't good either way. She had seen Hans' arrow pierce the Lady's breast.

She knew where the heart was located. She worried that they didn't have much time. She had no idea what would happen if Isabelle died as the beast. It might indeed break the curse as Chasseur had believed, but then again, it might also condemn all the cursed citizens of Stonewall to a lifetime of misery; and that included Gilda, as well.

The beast stirred abruptly and pulled herself up to a kneeling position. She groaned in pain, whining like a wounded dog as she pulled herself painfully away from Chasseur's body. She inched away from the corpse, slipping on the blood as she did so and making her way to a darkened corner of the room. When she had arrived, she curled into a ball, her head facing the wall. She moved much slower than she had before and left a trail of fresh blood behind her.

Aisling knew that it was now or never.

"My lord," said Aisling, "you have to reach her. Give her this. Before it's too late."

She handed him the rose and helped him to his feet. DuMonde took the flower and moved towards the beast, tears still streaming down his handsome, though newly scarred face. He held it out in front of him as he approached her, warily.

"My love...look. It's a rose. Your favorite....remember my love, please. Remember who you are."

The beast continued to whine pitifully in reply.

"Isabelle,please look at me. I love you. It doesn't matter what you look like, darling...you should know that better than anyone. It's not who we are on the outside, but who we are on the inside that counts. You taught me that."

As soon as he said it, the rose began to glow. The Lady of Beasts turned to look at it and through its gentle pink luminescence, Aisling could see tears welling up in her human eyes. She reached out with her left arm, though it pained her, and touched a claw to the crimson petals. A blinding flash erupted between them and Aisling and her companions had to turn their heads away. When it subsided, the rose lay still, its petals blackened and dried as if the flower had been sitting in a vase for days.

The Lady of Beasts was still on the floor, but the blood that had stained her fur was gone.

She looked up and her gray eyes met Aisling's. Suddenly, the fur began to fall away from her body. Her feral features were shifting back to those of a human. Her curved horns slowly receded into her head and her claw-like paws slowly transformed back into feminine and entirely human hands and feet. Her muzzle shrank and so did her teeth.

By the time all of the fur and fangs melted away, Aisling saw that the Lady of Beasts had actually been quite beautiful. Lady Isabelle had long, sleek auburn hair that reminded Aisling of Eleanor's, though it was much longer. Her lips were full and pouty and she had a flat nose that upturned just slightly at the tip. She had ample, slightly freckled cheeks, not unlike Aisling's.

Now that she was human again, she was naked. Aisling rushed over to her and undid her red riding cloak. She threw it over the kneeling lady and offered her a hand.

Every one of Aisling's muscles pained her. She had a cut across her cheek and the shoulder that had hit the bookcase felt as if it had been pretty badly bruised, but it was worth it. After the initial shock of the transformation had ebbed away, she turned to take stock of her companions. She rushed over to where Gilda sat.

"Are you all right?" she asked. "Never better," said Gilda, smiling.

It was a sincere smile, something that Aisling hadn't really seen on Gilda's face before.

Gilda breathed a sigh of relief. She was still wounded, of course, the cuts stung and the blood they wept was still soaking into her brother's cloak, but she was happy. She was happier than she could remember being in years. They had fought and hunted for so long, hunted survivors and their own people, and now it was all over.

"We need to find a healer, Gilda," said Hans. There was relief and worry in his voice.

"We will. It's all right. Let's just stay here a moment longer," replied his sister.

Lady Isabelle and Lord DuMonde looked at one another and a moment later, embraced, crying tears of happiness. Hoegabbler who had turned back into his cat form limped slightly, but seemed none the worse for wear.

"That was damn impressive, Hoegabbler. I didn't know you had it in you," said Hans. "Neither did I," replied the changeling, and Aisling could have sworn she saw his purple fur turn pink for the briefest of moments. He was blushing. "I had to try, though. After she hit Gilda...I couldn't let the rest of you get hurt."

Aisling stroked him on the head and he closed his eyes, purring.

"I am sorry about that," said an unfamiliar female voice standing above them.

Isabelle and DuMonde were standing beside them now. His arm was around hers and she was making sure to keep the cloak completely closed.

"I'm sorry about everything," she continued, looking ruefully over at Chasseur's lifeless body, "I never meant for any of this to happen. I didn't want anyone to die...I just couldn't stop myself."

"We know, milady," replied Gilda. "It was the curse," said Aisling.

"If our castle and the people have returned to normal, there might be a healer of some kind out there somewhere who can help," added DuMonde, "I'll go and fetch them, you wait here, my love. I will take care of everything."

He kissed her gently on the lips and dashed out of the double doors. Lady Isabelle knelt down next to Gilda. She looked troubled. Every few seconds, her eyes would slide back to the inert body of Chasseur, who was lying face down in a pool of his own blood nearby. Gilda placed a hand on Isabelle's knee.

"He resigned himself to that fate long ago, milady," she said, consolingly.

"Yes," agreed her brother, "it wasn't as if he was the type who was going to live to a ripe old age. Chasseur died in battle. He died fighting for his life and for his people. He honestly couldn't have hoped for a better death."

Their words were scant comfort to Isabelle, but she smiled politely and nodded her head.

Aisling knew how she felt. She stared at Chasseur and his words rang in her head, "…I do what has to be done to protect those who are left…"

She had come dangerously close to doing just that, to "doing what had to be done." She hoped beyond hope that she wouldn't have to keep making choices like that, but deep in her heart, she knew that the Seven Realms was going to continue to test her in ways she couldn't yet imagine.

"What happens now?" she asked.

As soon as she had uttered the words, her pack began to

shake. Lady Isabelle nearly fell backward in an attempt to both shield herself from whatever was going on in the satchel, and keep her dignity.

"It's all right, milady," whispered Hans, "watch."

Aisling reached into her satchel and removed the now shuddering scroll. It unfurled and the voices of the Crones rang out into the library:

"The clock has struck, the night was done, and though she did, but try to run, illusion shattered by the time, her visage marred by midnight's chime. A crystal queen to be was glass, and froze, in time, the ball en masse. For they shall never leave that night, until she fin'ly gets it right."

The scroll fell silent, the echo of its cryptic words lingering in the air. "What was that?" asked Isabelle.

"Aisling is a hero, a real, honest-to-goodness hero. I didn't believe it myself at first, but since we've met her, I've seen her do incredible things. She is destined to help save the Seven Realms…"

Gilda's words were cut off by a loud caw and a fluttering of wings. Chasseur's raven, Poe, had flown through the open doors of the library and landed next to his former master. He tilted his head as he approached and cawed softly. The bird nudged Chasseur's head with his beak, as if he was trying to wake him.

"I almost feel bad for it, eerie as it is," said Hoegabbler.

Without provocation, the raven turned and cawed angrily at the assembled companions. Then, it drove its beak hard into Chasseur's face and plucked out one of his eyes. Once it had retrieved its spoils, Poe flew towards the ceiling, then out the half-opened transom above the library window and out into the gathering dusk.

"Ugh," groaned Hoegabbler. "I take that back."

Lord DuMonde came back in soon after, along with a healer and the two remaining Red Riders, Emmanuelle and Fenton. All of them looked a bit worse for wear. Fenton wore his right arm in a sling, and Emmanuelle had deep cuts in her shoulder and thigh, but they were alive.

They explained what had happened, how as soon as the curse broke, the beasts they were fighting fell to the ground and transformed back into their human selves. It seemed that besides Lady Isabelle, none of them had any idea what had happened during the years they had been transformed.

The healer patched Gilda up and told her that she was lucky. If the claw marks had been much deeper, they would have torn open her entrails. He warned her to take it easy for the next few months and to avoid riding for at least a week, if possible. Lord DuMonde and Lady Isabelle invited the twins, Aisling, and Hoegabbler to stay in the Snarling Manor while she convalesced. They happily obliged.

The following days were full of much rejoicing. The general feeling in the castle was much as it had been in Verdenwald. The servants and guards, now freed from the curse, were more than happy to help return the once stately manor to its former glory. This proved much easier for the Snarling Manor than it had been for the Gardener's Tower.

The once sentient armors replaced on their plinths. The angel statue, though hacked to pieces, was repaired and replaced on the soon-to-be refurbished bannister. Tapestries and carpets were dusted, unused kitchen utensils and stoves were once again put to good use. Lady Isabelle insisted on cleaning up and organizing the library herself.

Gilda and Hans stayed together mostly, talking with their newly freed people and helping to properly bury the dead. Aisling, despite Hoegabbler's company, found herself bored and feeling slightly out of place after only a few days in the castle. She offered to help Isabelle with the library and she graciously accepted.

They began to clean and after a few minutes of watching Aisling struggle to discern the book titles written on their spines, Lady Isabelle approached her.

"Aisling, do you know how to read?" she asked kindly. Aisling blushed and shook her head.

"There's no shame in it, you know. I didn't know how to read either when I was younger and neither of my sisters ever learned to read. It took practice and a willing teacher."

"You have sisters?" asked the girl.

"I did, and three brothers, but I'm afraid a fever took all of them soon after I had come to live at the manor with Lord DuMonde. They weren't the kindest people in the world, my sisters. They were cruel, vain, and petty, but they were family. Even after my father lost all of his wealth and we were forced into penury, they still believed that the world owed them everything. I learned to read because my eldest brother believed that it might give me a leg up in the world if I ever escaped that life. So, he taught me," said Isabelle.

She paused and wiped a tear from her eye.

"I miss them all terribly. Though I am glad they did not live to see my folly, my weakness."

Aisling had never imagined that she could have had so much in common with Lady Isabelle. It seemed that she too had been a peasant, had many siblings, and had loved and lost those siblings to disease. Like Aisling, Isabelle's life had been full of circumstances beyond her control and yet, when faced with choices, even one so small as learning to read, she took those chances. Isabelle took control of her fate as best she could and had come out of it better than she could have expected.

Yet, Aisling couldn't help but also think about what had happened when Lady Isabelle lost control, when she allowed herself a moment of complacence. Sure, the blame for the curse still lay with Maledicta, but there had to be a moment where Isabelle allowed it in. With Roselyn, the curse had come from the spinning wheel. She knew she shouldn't touch it and she did it anyway, she couldn't fight it. What had Isabelle done to initiate the dormant curse?

"They say you're a hero, then?" Isabelle asked, breaking the silence.

"Oh, well. Yes, I suppose. To be honest, I don't know yet if I'm even qualified to say that. All I've done is follow what that bloody scroll told me."

She hadn't meant to curse, but the words had just come out of her. She clapped a hand to her mouth.

"I'm sorry, Milady…my apologies. Goodness, I…"

"It's all right," replied Isabelle with a warm smile, "we've both been through the bloody wringer."

The two girls laughed.

"Where did you get the scroll?" asked the lady.

"When I first arrived here, someone took me to meet three old women who called themselves the Crones. They told me that it was fated that I should come here, to the Seven Realms, and that I was destined to free all of you from Maledicta's curses. They also implied that this was essentially my only way home."

"Where are you from, if not from the Seven Realms?" asked Isabelle.

"Far, far away. Across the veil to another world, one that's…" she thought for a second, "…only slightly different from this one. Later on, I found out that last part at least was true. The only way I can go home is if all the curses are broken and if the true king and queen are put back on the throne. Frankly though, I still don't really know how someone like me is going to save the Seven Realms."

"Well," said Isabelle thoughtfully, "if what your friends tell me is true, then you've already helped save two out of seven. That's more than all the Seven Knights have done in a decade. I'd say that is enough to prove the Crones at least partially right. Don't you think?"

Aisling considered this for a moment. Lady Isabelle wasn't wrong. Regardless of her own lack of self-confidence, Aisling had indeed helped to save two realms and all their people from magical curses. Perhaps fate was right, after all. She decided that even if she was stuck doing its bidding, she was going to take a note from Isabelle's book and make the choices she could, when she could.

"Lady Isabelle…can you teach me how to read?" asked Aisling.

Isabelle gave a wide, toothy smile that crinkled her eyes at the corners and displayed her ample cheeks.

"It would be my pleasure. We have plenty of time to give you the basics. The healers tell me Gilda needs at least a few more days to rest up."

"Why would she need to rest up?" asked Aisling, sincerely.

"Because she and I are going with you when you leave here, of course," said a familiar voice behind them.

Hans was standing there holding Hoegabbler in his arms and absentmindedly stroking his fur.

"You can't mean it?" said Aisling, fighting back tears.

"Of course I do," replied Hans, "we had a deal, remember? My sister and I promised that if you helped us break the curse upon Stonewall, we would get you to the witch's palace at Caerleon. I guess the joke is on us though, 'cause it seems the only way to get you to Caerleon is to first help you break the curses on the other five realms"

Aisling ran over and threw her arms around him, hugging him, and by association Hoegabbler, tightly to her.

"And you know I'll be there," said the slightly squished cat.

"I can't tell you how much this means to me, Hans," said Aisling.

"It's the least we can do. Besides, with Lady Isabelle and Lord DuMonde reinstated, the Red Riders no longer have to keep the peace on their own. Fenton and Emmanuelle can help them out, of course, but I think Gilda and my talents would be much better suited helping you. Don't you agree, Lady Isabelle?"

Isabelle nodded happily.

"Now, I'm going to go and start making preparations. As for you, if you're going to learn to read, you should start. Gilda and I can help tutor you on the road."

Aisling wiped her eyes and grinned. Then, turning back to Lady Isabelle, the two sat down in one of the few undamaged armchairs and opened up a good book.

Chapter Twenty-Two

The Road Ahead

o….end..ded…the…fourth gr-gr-great agey…"

"Age," Isabelle corrected.

"Oh, yes. Age," said Aisling.

Despite the occasional hiccup, Aisling had made amazing progress in just the few days they had been in the Snarling Manor. It had been slow at first, as Isabelle had tried starting Aisling on simple books, books with letters and numbers and simple words. It wasn't until she discovered Aisling's penchant for storytelling that she decided to try her out on a history book. Once she learned that history books were essentially just well-recorded stories, Aisling began to excel.

In the past week, Aisling had learned much about the Seven Realms. She had learned about the ancient lines of kings and queens, how they had warred with other kingdoms, and how there had once been more than seven of them. There were apparently dozens of books on those ancient realms. Oddly enough, there were very few books written about the true king and queen and the hundreds of years that existed between their rise to power and Maledicta's. If there had been any books written on those golden times or even the tumultuous ones after, then even Isabelle's vast library was bereft of them.

She had asked Isabelle about them, of course, but even she did not seem to know where those volumes had disappeared to.

"I suspect it has to do with Maledicta's curse. She likely doesn't want anyone to remember anything before she came to power," said Gilda, who was sitting on a nearby armchair, placidly thumbing through a bestiary.

By then, Gilda was up and walking around the castle and had begun sitting in on their sessions as well. Now that Aisling's lesson was done for the day, Gilda decided that the four companions should begin to plan the next stage of their journey.

"I suppose so. I just assumed that if we knew anything about the king and queen, or their rule, we might be able to shortcut all this and take Maledicta out first," said Aisling.

"Don't think it works that way," said Hans, walking through the door with Hoegabbler perched on his shoulder.

Aisling huffed. She knew he was right, but that didn't mean she liked hearing it. "Aisling, could you recite the prophecy again?" asked Gilda.

Aisling did so. When she was done, Gilda frowned.

"I'm just not sure what the prophecy refers to," she said, ruefully.

"I might have an idea," interrupted Isabelle, who had

just finished shelving *The Age of Squalid Kings*, "it happened a few years ago, soon after I was married. Even though I was fairly new to the courtly lifestyle, I was invited to a number of balls and get-togethers with the other lords and ladies.

It's hard to remember every noble I encountered, but I remember meeting one girl who stuck out like even more of a sore thumb than I did. When I approached her, she introduced herself as Ella and let it slip that she had been a commoner before she had met her own husband. She was rather awkward and sweet about it, actually.

Adam, that is to say, Lord DuMonde, told me later that she was the Lady of the Isle of Glass, in the southernmost part of the Western Sea. Crystal, see? Glass? Maybe she's the next one you have to free from the witch's curse?"

"Why do they call it the Isle of Glass?" asked Aisling.

"According to *The Realms: In and Of Themselves*, it's because the island the nation sits on is made mostly of sand. Glass is their main export. That's what they call it in the common tongue, anyway. Its name in their language is...the name is...hold on," replied Lady Isabelle.

She rushed over to a bookshelf across the room and began running her hands along the bindings. A moment later and she pulled out a rather thick book, bound in well-worn brown leather. She opened it and scanned through the pages with her finger.

"Ah, here it is! The locals call it Sabbiaterra."

"That's a long way off," said Hans, who was gazing at a large map laid out on one of the newly installed tables in the room. "We would have to go through Gideon to get there and then we'd have to cross the Western Sea; that's where the Drowned Lady rules."

"That all makes sense, though. Aisling was told to help Lady Isabelle, but to do that she had to find us, the Remedy Bloom, and break Lady Roselyn's curse first. If our end goal is the Isle of Glass, then I'm sure there's a reason we have to go through Gideon and cross the sea before that," noted Gilda.

Aisling was feeling slightly overwhelmed. She poured over the map of the Seven Realms.

Hans was right, the road that led out of the woodland realms and through the large patch of flat earth called Gideon looked to be very long indeed. Nevertheless, the fact that all of her friends were here helping her and planning the way with her felt nice. Being prepared was always better than simply trying to fly by the whims of fate. Mapping out their journey also made her feel as if she had a hand in her own fate for once. She looked up from the map to find them all staring expectantly in her direction.

"What?" she asked, feeling awkward.

"How does that sound to you?" asked Gilda. "We'll head out in two days, make our way past the Stone Wall and on to the Golden Road to Gideon. Then, we'll see where the prophet deigns to lead us next. What do you say?"

Aisling had been so lost in her own thoughts that she hadn't even heard them mention the plan earlier, but her friends were plainly looking to her for approval. It felt odd to be suddenly thrust into the role as leader again, especially in such a relaxed, non-threatening situation. She didn't think she liked it much.

"Yes. That sounds good," she acquiesced.

Their plans decided, the companions prepared for the next stage of their journey together. Two days later, Aisling found herself walking out of the great wooden doors of the Snarling Manor and into a refurbished garden courtyard. Lady Isabelle and Lord DuMonde had come down with her to see them off. Hoegabbler, who was his purple rabbity self, came bounding up the steps towards them.

"Aisling! Aisling! I've got a surprise for you!" he shouted, excitedly. "Oh, yes?"

"Come, come!" said the changeling, and he led her down the steps to the gravely drive where Gilda, Hans, and their two horses awaited them.

Hoegabbler made sure everyone was looking and transformed. His rabbit's paws shot upwards, his ears shrank, his back enlarged, and his button nose elongated. Long hair seemed to pour out of his new and much thicker neck and a tufted tail replaced his tiny cotton one. Within a few seconds, Aisling found herself staring at an oddly shaped, though very familiar, purple horse.

"You found another shape!" she cried.

"I did!" whinnied Hoegabbler. Everyone applauded.

"My wife and I cannot ever thank you enough for what you've done for us and for our people," said Lord DuMonde, addressing the twins.

"It was our pleasure, my lord," said Hans and Gilda, bowing in unison. "Aisling," began Isabelle. "I have something for your trip."

She handed Aisling the two books she was holding. The first one, bound in green leather, was titled *Legends and*

Histories of the Seven Realms. The second, which was bound in black leather, lacked a title.

"Thank you, milady,but this one has no title," said Aisling, confused.

She opened it up and looked through a dozen or so pages, but found all of them to be blank.

"…and no words?"

"You'll also need this," added Isabelle, and she handed Aisling a bottle full of black ink and a bluish black feather that looked as though it had come from a raven.

"The green book is so that you can continue to learn to read the things that you enjoy.

Even in a place like the Seven Realms, there are still legends, and you have a lot to learn if you're going to be living here. Gilda, Hans, and Hoegabbler are worldly, but even they don't know everything. As for the black book, that is a journal for you to keep. You can learn to write in it with the quill and ink."

"I don't know how to write either, though…"

"Just copy letters and words at first, you'll learn how they should look and you'll be able to string them together the right way in no time at all. You're a bright girl, Aisling. I have no doubt that you'll pick it up quickly," Isabelle replied, and she smiled.

"Thank you again for your kind hospitality, my lord, milady," said Hans. He and Gilda bowed again graciously.

"No, my friends, thank you. You have done more for your realm than we can ever repay. I hope the rations we provided will be enough to get you past the wall," replied Lord DuMonde.

"We will be fine, I'm sure," said Gilda.

"And thank you for teaching me, Lady Isabelle," said Aisling.

Isabelle reached over and pulled Aisling into a warm hug. Her embrace felt so much like Eleanor's that for a moment, Aisling thought she might break down. She fought back her tears and leaned further into the hug.

"Good luck, Aisling."

As they rode, all four of them thought about the deeds they had done and the happy people they had left behind. They mused over the friends and allies they had lost, and the uncertainty of the adventure ahead of them. They were a few minutes past the now rebuilt village of Racine when the companions decided to begin speaking aloud.

"I wonder what became of Chasseur's raven?" asked Hoegabbler, who was bearing Aisling's subtle weight much better now than he had been at first.

"I guess once he had what he wanted and flew off, he just headed out into the wilderness.

Without his master, I suppose he's free to do as he wishes now," replied Gilda. "A pity the same can't be said for us," added Aisling.

Gilda smiled at her.

"You're not alone in this, Aisling. We're with you to the end. We'll help you see it through," she said.

Aisling flashed a weak smile. Knowing that they were with her was a comfort, of course, but the immensity of the quest that lay before her was still daunting. Beneath her, Hoegabbler pawed nervously at the ground with a violet hoof.

"Ready, Hoegabbler?" she asked, patting him on the

back of his neck. "Ready as I'll ever be," neighed the changeling.

"So, now that you're a full-fledged hero, have you thought up a name for that sword of yours?" Hans asked.

Aisling had indeed gone over that very thing for the past week. She had thought of a number of names: Curse Killer, Silver Slice, Witchbane. None of them sounded right when she said them aloud. They all seemed somewhat self-indulgent. She had only just come to terms with her newfound destiny, she didn't need to be all haughty about it. It finally came to her that morning, just as she was packing up to leave. She hadn't told anyone yet.

"Aye, I have. Don't laugh, all right? I think I'm going to call it Fortune," she replied, blushing.

"That's a great name. I love it," replied Hans, grinning his chubby-cheeked grin. "Me too," added Gilda.

"Fortune," whispered Aisling, tasting the name on her tongue again.

The nightingale who sat on Aisling's shoulder twittered in assent. The companions rode towards the Stone Wall. According to the twins, the wall was the barrier that separated the woodland realms and those across the western steppes. Beyond that was the sea and in the middle of that, the Crystal Keep from her prophecy. It seemed very far indeed.

Since her arrival in the Seven Realms, Aisling had fought trolls, wolf men, ghost trees, and corrupted princesses. She wondered what other challenges still lay before her. Yet, as they stepped out onto the road, she felt a sense of excitement well up inside her. The nightingale on her shoulder began to sing.

As always, her song was sad and beautiful, full of longing and an unspoken, familiar feeling. It crossed Aisling's heart half in hope and half in despair. This time though, the song had a different effect as well. The melody took her burgeoning sense of adventure and somehow bolstered it. Emboldened by the nightingale's song and her new friends beside her, Aisling rode on.

The raven named Poe had flown for days to reach the Black Hall and he was exhausted. He spotted her standing on a balcony just below the tallest of the castle's turrets. Clad in a thick fur cloak, the Pale Lady was shielded from the wintry winds slowly creeping in from the high north. She extended her arm at Poe's approach and the bird alighted upon it, relieved that his long journey was over.

The Pale Lady held out her snow-white hand and the bird dropped Chasseur's slightly desiccated eye into her open palm. It cawed feebly and she nodded her head in understanding.

"Two of her Majesty's agents thwarted by that wretched girl," she said, her voice soft and gentle as the quiet on a winter's day. "No matter. She will soon find that the Golden Road is not quite as smooth as it's painted in the songs."

Poe let out another caw and flew off into the darkening sky. Without a falconer's glove, the raven's sharp talons had dug into the Pale Lady's skin and crimson blood dripped onto the few snowflakes that had fallen upon the castle flagstones. The Pale Lady turned to walk back into the tower, leaving blood and icy snow in her wake.

To Be Continued....